RAGE OF DESIRE

How dare the Earl of Hampton act as if he had a hold on her, Juliana raged.

How dare he demand an explanation of what she was doing with a strange man in the scandalous Vauxhall pleasure gardens.

How dare he accuse her of adultery and worse.

And above all, how dare he hold her in his arms with a strength she found almost as alarming as the response that flared through her very core.

All she could do was fight both him and herself with every fiber of being. All she could do was snarl at him, "No! You men! You are all alike!" as her nails raked his cheek.

If only that were the truth. If only Hampton were like all other men, instead of being so dangerously different. . .

The Earl's Season

by

Emma Lange

A SIGNET BOOK

SIGNET
Published by the Penguin Group
Penguin Books USA Inc., 375 Hudson Street,
New York, New York 10014, U.S.A.
Penguin Books Ltd, 27 Wrights Lane,
London W8 5TZ, England
Penguin Books Australia Ltd, Ringwood,
Victoria, Australia
Penguin Books Canada Ltd, 10 Alcorn Avenue,
Toronto, Ontario, Canada M4V 3B2
Penguin Books (N.Z.) Ltd, 182–190 Wairau Road,
Auckland 10, New Zealand

Penguin Books Ltd, Registered Offices:
Harmondsworth, Middlesex, England

First published by Signet, an imprint of Dutton Signet,
a division of Penguin Books USA Inc.

First Printing, May, 1997
10 9 8 7 6 5 4 3 2 1

Chapter 1

"Marriage?" Juliana heard the harshness in her voice and looked out the window of the carriage, avoiding her friend's cheerful scrutiny. "No, Fanny. As I wrote you, I've no intention of marrying again. I plan," she went on after half a moment, her tone light again, "to be a very merry widow."

For the merest second, Fanny looked taken aback. Juliana might even have said she looked guilty, but when, in the next moment, her friend laughed, Juliana dismissed the notion. Gratefully. Had she thought there was reason to explain her near revulsion at the idea of marrying again, she'd have had to discuss her experience of marriage, and even had she and Fanny been as close as they had been at school, those long eight years before, Juliana would not have confided in her. The mere thought of the pity she would arouse stung her, and she had had enough of pain.

"Lud, these streets are crowded!" she said, turning her attention to the far more attractive present. "Do you know, I never imagined how many people there would be in London? I cannot see how your coachman negotiates among them all." Fanny laughed. She'd a gurgling, endearing laugh, and Juliana turned to smile at her. "I must seem the veriest country bumpkin to you, Fanny."

"And I adore it!" Fanny exclaimed, her pretty blue eyes twinkling brightly. "Not in years have I given a thought to the number of people in London. Yet now, looking through your eyes, Juliana, the somewhat stale scene out the win-

dow is fresh again, and I am amazed myself at the number
of conveyances and people. Oh, I know we shall have such
fun this Season!" She clasped her friend's hand, squeezing
it affectionately.

Juliana returned the touch with feeling. "I am so grateful
that you invited me to spend the Season with you, Fanny. I
can scarcely believe I am here."

"You are grateful to me?" Fanny shook her head, setting
her ostrich plumes waving. "No, no, 'tis I am grateful to
you, Juliana. I should have been all alone without you! I
vow that I felt quite put-upon when Charley informed me
he would miss the Season because the powers that be at
Whitehall thought he ought to travel out to Egypt for
heaven knows what reason. Honestly, one would think that
with Boney defeated and a peace agreed upon, diplomats'
wives could count on having their husbands with them!"

Juliana stifled a smile at Fanny's unique approach to
diplomacy. "Have you heard from Lord Charles, Fanny?
Has he reached Egypt safely?"

"Yes, yes! I received a letter from my dearest Charley
earlier this week. He said his trip was relatively uneventful,
but he was nonetheless tired. The poor dear! But what of
you, Juliana?" she asked, suddenly anxious. "Are you quite
certain you are not dreadfully tired? You only reached town
this afternoon, and yet I would insist upon dragging you off
to Gussie's dinner party forthwith!"

"You did not insist at all, Fanny. You asked, and I answered that I would be delighted to attend your sister's affair." Juliana smiled. She had half forgotten what a flighty
chatterbox Fanny could be, and had completely forgotten
how pleasant it was to worry over nothing. "And I must
warn you that if you remark again about overtiring me, I
shall have to believe that I look quite hagged."

"Hagged! No! Lud, no! You look ravishing! Egad, you
are more beautiful now than you were at seventeen, a trick
women the world over would give their eye teeth to learn! I
am certain Gussie will scold me for inviting you to town

the very Season she is bringing Sarah out. You will turn the head of every eligible male. You . . ."

Juliana burst into laughter. "Enough, Fanny! I shall not say another word about looking hagged, though you have generously overlooked all the indelible lines I did not even know to fear having at seventeen. I thank you, and I assure you again that I am not the least fatigued. I'd more than enough time to rest while my coach's axle was being repaired in Lower Menton. The village can be traversed in less than ten minutes on foot! Truly, I am very glad to be going out this evening."

And she was. Juliana felt buoyant enough to float, she was so glad to be going to a dinner party that evening. But then, in truth, her period of enforced seclusion had lasted far longer than the one day and night in the village of Lower Menton.

"Tell me about Gussie," Juliana said, dismissing all thought of her married life, "or Lady Danley, as I should call her, never having met her but through your stories, Fanny. She is older than you, is she not?"

"Lud, yes!" Fanny pulled such a ludicrous face, Juliana chuckled. It seemed to her that she had laughed more in the half day since she had arrived in London than she had in all the eight years before, but she did not dwell on the thought, only laughed again, half defiantly perhaps. "Gussie is the eldest of the three of us," Fanny said, "and since Mama's death has taken it upon herself to direct Alex and me—for our own good, you understand—though, I must admit that since I married, she has turned most of her managing tendencies upon Alex."

"And your broth . . ."

"Of course," Fanny continued, speaking hurriedly, almost as if she regretted mentioning her brother, "Gussie will be unusually diverted this Season with Sarah making her come-out. You will adore Sarah, Juliana. As she is my niece, I do recognize that I may be prejudiced, but I vow she is as lovely in spirit as in her person, and besides she has the wisdom to manage her dragon of a mother, for which talent I have the greatest admiration, never having learned it myself!"

Another carriage passed them, its way lit by two link boys who ran ahead in the street, each holding a flaming torch high. The bobbing lights briefly illuminated Juliana's face, revealing a smile that was not so full as it had been.

"I recall that you like to tease about your sister, Fanny, but in truth, you make her sound a trifle formidable. I cannot but wonder if she truly wishes to receive me tonight. And what of the others in your circle, Fanny? Will I be accepted by society? After all, I married a tradesman. Yes, he was a vastly wealthy tradesman, but still . . ."

Fanny interrupted firmly. "My dear, I adore teasing about Gussie because otherwise I would have to admit what a superlative person she is. You are not to worry a moment about tonight. Gussie longs to meet you. Lud, she has heard me sing your praises for years now. And as to the rest of society, I would not have invited you to town, had I thought you would be snubbed. There will be some gossip, of course. Sir Arthur was not only in trade but over forty years your senior, after all, but with Gussie and me behind you, the gossip will amount to nothing." Fanny giggled at herself. "How very top-lofty, I sound, do I not! Still, it is true, that we do have influence, and it is equally true that after we present you and everyone sees how beautiful and charming you are, you will be accepted—or perhaps I should say embraced—quite on your own merits! La, I can scarcely wait to see what a stir you will cause!"

"What I think I shall do is enjoy myself thoroughly," Juliana said, believing Fanny's sentiments merely a friend's prejudice. "I am in alt at the prospect of doing all the things you have written of, from riding in the Park, to attending Astley's and Vauxhall, to merely strolling down Bond Street."

"Oh, my dear Juliana, I can scarcely wait myself to do it

all with you! Lud, I cannot conceive why your husband could not bring you to town even once!"

"Sir Arthur preferred the country." Juliana tried for a negligent tone, then waited tensely to see if Fanny would press her on the subject of Sir Arthur Whitfield and his presumed love of the country, but her friend was diverted.

"Look, Juliana, we have all but arrived!" Fanny leaned forward to point out Juliana's window. "Shelbourne House is the one on the corner. It is very grand, is it not? When Gussie learned ice had damaged her own roof so badly she and Danley would not be able to inhabit their town house this Season, she was in alt. It is the truth, I promise you! Shelbourne House is far grander, you see, and being Gussie, she simply ordered Alex out of his own house. No, that is not quite true! She grandly allowed that Alex might share his home with her and her brood, which as you know includes not only Sarah, but three quite active boys." Fanny rolled her eyes playfully. "Is she not clever? She knew very well Alex would turn tail at the mere thought of living, not with her children, but her! And he did, giving over his entire house to her."

Once more, Juliana began to ask after the Earl of Hampton, Fanny's brother, but this time it was a footman opening the door that diverted her. Fanny's coachman had driven them under a portico so that they might step from the carriage directly onto the steps leading to Shelbourne House, thus sparing their delicate evening slippers the muck of the street. Two footmen in elegant livery waited to hand them up the steps, while at the top, before the ornate door, a dignified butler waited to show them inside. Through the open door, Juliana could see the light of many candles, and when she cocked her head, she fancied she could hear the hum of conversation. It was her first dinner party in years. And she was so eager for the company, for the conversation, for the simple joy of noise, that she forgot everything but the excited racing of her heart.

Chapter 2

Somewhere between the entryway and Lady Danley's drawing room, Juliana's stomach tightened into a knot. It was the murmur of those voices. She had only fancied she heard them at the entryway, but when the hum became unmistakable, Juliana's anxiety about her impending reception returned full-blown.

Fanny walked a little ahead of her, giving Juliana a running commentary on the palatial house that had been built by Fanny's grandfather, the eighth Duke of Shelbourne. Intricately worked plaster decorated the ceilings, Axminster rugs covered the floor where marble had not been used, and enormous crystal chandeliers lit their way. Here, Fanny had fallen as a child and broken a priceless Ming vase. Here, she had hidden to watch her brother coax a kiss out of a pretty, blushing maid.

Juliana smiled, but vaguely, her mind fixed upon the increasing volume of noise only a very large group of people could create. In panic, she wondered whatever had possessed her to come to London. What had she to say to these complete strangers? She had attended dinner parties in her youth, before her mother's death, but she had been so young she'd been expected to say nothing, only listen politely and keep her eyes demurely downcast. Now she was a grown woman with no practice at all in the light, easy social conversation that is expected at a dinner party, and knowing no one, she could not even look for a sympathetic face. She would look a fool, a tongue-tied, provincial, graceless fool.

She should never have come, she thought, her step slowing. Despite Fanny's assurances about the reception she would receive, Juliana felt suddenly, paralyzingly certain that every person in the room would shun her for being a grasping mercenary who had crassly sold herself to the highest bidder, an old cit they'd not have invited into their carriages were it pouring rain, while she . . . she had taken him into her bed.

But they had reached the drawing room already. Fanny had even walked into the light spilling out of the door. Juliana stood only a step away. She could not run. She truly would look a fool then, and cowardly besides, which she was not. She had survived Whitfield, and she had done it with her dignity intact. At once, Juliana straightened her shoulders, composing herself. Her demeanor, at least, would be serene and confident when the footman at the door announced her.

It was as well she prepared herself, for the man had scarcely finished gravely intoning "Lady Whitfield" when a strong, well-modulated female voice rang out.

"Here you are at last, Fanny! And Lady Whitfield! Do, do come in, please! I vow I feel I know you like a sister. Fanny has told me so much about you!"

Lady Danley stood taller than Fanny and she had a heavier build, with a broad bosom and matronly hips, but in the face she bore a distinct resemblance to her sister. Their eyes, particularly, were the same dark blue, sparkling with interest and warmth. The muscles of Juliana's stomach unclenched ever so slightly as Lady Danley seized both her hands and beamed delightedly.

"It is my pleasure to meet you, Lady Danley." Juliana felt her stiff mouth form a smile, seemingly of its own accord. "I am very grateful that you would extend an invitation to me tonight."

"Grateful?" Lady Danley laughed gustily. "My dear, I

see you are refreshingly modest! You will be the talk of the town tomorrow, for Fanny has not exaggerated a whit—for once. You are the most beautiful creature I have beheld in a very long while. Jove! I should send you out into the night forthwith, for you are certain to steal some of my Sarah's thunder, but there you are! Sarah's loss shall be my gain, for there is nothing so delicious as being the first hostess to present the latest sensation! Ah, my! Just look how everyone is staring at you in rapt wonder, my dear Juliana—I may call you by your name, I hope? You must call me Gussie, of course. La, la, and Adele Canning thought her soiree would be the most discussed entertainment of the evening. The poor dear!"

It was clearly impossible to resist Lady Danley. She was as overbearing as Fanny had suggested, but in such a good-humored, utterly outrageous way that Juliana found herself laughing half helplessly as she was swept headlong into the room, though Lady Danley had spoken no less than the truth. It did seem that all thirty of her guests had turned as one to inspect the new arrival in town. Juliana felt her breath catch in her throat again, though her anxiety was nothing to what it had been before Lady Danley had descended upon her and shamelessly assured her that she, a widow of twenty-and-five, would be the center of attention that Season. Of course, she would not be, but perhaps she would make friends. She longed for friends, for conversation with them, for shared activities, for so little as laughter.

"Where is Alex, Fanny?" Despite her nerves, and all the pairs of eyes studying her, Juliana quite clearly heard the question Lady Danley hissed sotto voce in Fanny's direction. "He was to escort you, and I trusted that you could see to him."

From Juliana's right, Fanny leaned forward to defend herself in a vigorous whisper. "You know very well no one, not even Father, has ever controlled Alex! He told me he would try to keep the night open, but when I had not heard from him by this morning, I sent you a note warning he was not likely to make an appearance. Has the wretch thrown off your numbers terribly?"

"No," Lady Danley admitted grudgingly. "Hetty Meechaum asked if she could bring an escort and having received your note, I told her she was quite welcome to bring her latest beau. Lud"—Lady Danley rolled her eyes, evidently sharing with Fanny the ability to take up a new subject as readily as she drew breath—"will Hetty ever realize she is decades past the age of falling in love with every gentleman who flatters her while he eyes her tidy inheritance?"

Fanny giggled under her breath. "And who is the flattering fortune hunter this Season?"

"Lord Blakely. He is there by—"

"Blakely?" Fanny repeated in a tone that prompted Lady Danley to give her a sharp look.

"Do you know him, Fanny?"

"Know him? No! I mean, that is, of course I know him . . . of him that is! He's such an unsavory reputation, I was only surprised Hetty would accept his attentions. That is all."

To Juliana's surprise, and some amusement, Lady Danley gave a worldly shrug. "Hetty is of an age to do anything she pleases, foolish or not, but in truth I have noticed that while she does fall in love at the wink of a practiced eyelid, she rather easily resists the temptation to open her tidy purse to said love."

Given the exchange, Juliana took especial note when she was presented to Lord Blakely later in the evening. He was an elegant-looking man, his dark eyes making a striking contrast with the silver hair at his temples, but she disliked him immediately. Attractive though he undoubtedly was, his eyes were cold and calculating, and when he bowed over her hand, he gave the diamonds at her throat such close scrutiny she did not doubt but that he could have estimated the necklace's worth as accurately as any professional appraiser. Worse was the wolfish, glittering smile he gave her afterward. He looked as if he'd have married her on spot, and feeling nearly suffocated by the thought of marrying any man at all, much less such an unsavory one, Juliana departed the viscount's company as soon as she could.

Juliana found most of the other gentlemen present considerably more enjoyable. Lady Danley had invited a goodly number of bachelors. She had her daughter to think of, after all, and the one or two other girls who were Sarah's friends, but some of the gentlemen were well into their thirties, and Fanny, giggling, said it was obvious her sister could not resist playing matchmaker. Juliana took Lady Danley's efforts in good part. She did want to meet people, and it helped that the gentlemen were quite gracious and welcoming. They were flattering, too, but though Juliana had little experience of unattached men, the compliments she received, from the stammered to the silky, affected her relatively little. She thought it likely that any new face, particularly an exceedingly wealthy one, would hold appeal.

Precisely because she was so self-composed and collected in the face of considerable male attention, most of the ladies present that evening accepted Juliana as well. Only a few of the elder ladies gave her rather cool and assessing looks when she was presented to them. Juliana did not fault them. They did not seem determined to disapprove of her, only cautious and wanting to observe her a bit, before they accorded her full approval. Mrs. Desmond, however, was a different matter. The mother of a girl Sarah's age, Mrs. Desmond's manner was plainly hostile. Giving Juliana a narrow-eyed inspection, she nodded only enough to be civil in greeting, and after dinner, when she sought Juliana out, it was to ask after another.

"I wonder," she asked without preamble, "what you know of the earl's absence tonight, Lady Whitfield? Given his promise to his father, I had thought he would be present."

Diverted by the clear hostility in Mrs. Desmond's manner and by the sense that she was being accused of something, Juliana could not think for a moment who the earl was.

"Pamela is deeply disappointed," Mrs. Desmond continued, her tone quite fierce. "We went to great pains to see her turned out well for this evening, and I think she has never looked better!"

Juliana had met Pamela Desmond before dinner. The girl was plain and rather shy, but Juliana could agree quite sincerely that she was dressed becomingly, and having finally deduced that Mrs. Desmond referred to the Earl of Hampton, Lady Fanny's brother, she was also able to add that having never met him, she knew nothing of his whereabouts.

She did not confide that his sisters seemed to know as little as she. Juliana would not have gossiped so with a stranger, but Mrs. Desmond's manner underwent such a chameleonlike change, Juliana was completely diverted. "Oh!" Mrs. Desmond cried, her hostility having become in the twinkling of an eye a rueful, rather guilty smile. "I, ah, thought you likely had met the earl."

And had suspected that Juliana had somehow prevented the man from attending his sister's dinner and meeting Miss Desmond when the girl had taken such pains with her appearance. Juliana might have clucked disapprovingly at Mrs. Desmond's overactive maternal instincts, but she gave the woman an engaging smile instead, for if Mrs. Desmond's instincts had led her astray, at least her instincts were engaged on behalf of her daughter, something which did not apply, as Juliana knew too well, to all parents.

The next morning Juliana rose early. She was too eager to see London to sleep late, though she and Fanny had not returned to Grosvenor Square before one o'clock the night before.

In response to her tug on the bell rope, her maid Randall came with hot chocolate.

Juliana frowned at the sight of her. "I did not mean to rouse you, Rand!" she exclaimed, throwing back the bed linens and slipping from the high bed. "If I continue to rise early despite the late hours these Londoners keep, then I wish you to arrange for one of the younger maids on Lady Charles's staff to attend to me in the early morning. I do not wish to abuse you."

"You are very kind, my lady."

"And I am quite serious, Randall. I have no intention of wearing you to a frazzle simply because I wish fully, really fully, to savor a London Season."

"I understand, my lady."

"But you will do precisely as you see fit," Juliana observed, wryly regarding Randall over the rim of her cup. "Your sense of duty is all very well, but I fear that you will fall ill from lack of rest. Promise me you will nap, at least."

The dresser's thin, angular features softened. "I will take what rest I need, my lady. I promise you that. And may I say how glad I am that you enjoyed Lady Danley's dinner party last evening?"

"How did you guess?"

"You look very happy, my lady."

The words "for a change" hovered in the air between them. Juliana's eyes met those of the servant, who had been with her since the day her father had taken her to Westerleigh Park in Lancashire to wed Sir Arthur Whitfield, but when she spoke, Juliana referred only to Lady Danley's dinner.

"Most everyone accepted me without so much as a raised eyebrow, Randall."

"And why should they not?" the dresser demanded, her mouth pursing now.

Juliana shrugged. "I thought there was the possibility they would not care to associate with the woman who married Sir Arthur Whitfield in his dotage. But most were very kind. You would have approved of Lord Soames, a wid-ower, in particular. He was my dinner partner, and a more well-mannered gentleman I could not have encountered." Juliana made a face. "Not all the gentlemen were as gen-uine and upright as Lord Soames. A few fawned over me, I suppose on account of my wealth, but as to the rest . . . oh, Randall, there was conversation, much of it ordinary to them, but to me, denied it so long . . ." She broke off abruptly and rose. Randall held her riding habit. Juliana stepped into it without word. The room had blurred before her, but Juliana blinked back the sudden tears unable to fathom why they would beset her now, when they had not for all those years. Perhaps, she thought, biting her lip, she cried from joy. She was free, quite free. She really was.

"Your riding crop is there on the table, my lady."

Juliana nodded. "Thank you, Randall." She crossed to the table, silently thanking Randall for rallying her. The sudden tears pricked her no longer, and once again she looked forward, not backward, to her first full day in Lon-don. "Well, I'm off, then." She lifted the riding crop to the brim of her stylish riding hat, playfully saluting Randall. "I shall tell you all about the Park when I return."

Fanny's butler Haskins awaited Juliana in the entry hall. She had advised him the day before that she wished to ride early, and after bidding her good morning, he told her that a mare had been brought around for her. "Lily is the mare Lord Charles prefers to ride. If she does not suit you, how-ever, my lady, you have only to say so and Jared will choose another mount for you. He's a good lad and will ac-company you to the Park this morning."

"Thank you, Haskins. I am certain Lord Charles's fa-vorite mare will suit me very well, and I do appreciate your seeing to her and to a groom for me." From outside, sounds could be heard. Thinking the groom was coming to fetch her, Juliana turned her smile from Haskins to the door, which just then swung open.

Had the man who appeared in the doorway been dressed

in rags, Juliana would still have known he could not be a groom. But he was not dressed in rags. He was dressed in evening clothes, or half dressed. Even in that first startled moment, she saw that he was not wearing his neckcloth but carried it negligently in his hand.

Her smile faltered. His, on the other hand, grew. Or rather, a part of it did, for his smile was decidedly lopsided. And thoroughly appreciative. Some undefinable feeling coursed through Juliana. She had never thought of herself as wearing armor, but perhaps she had been, for she felt as if the stranger's crooked smile pierced her, making her blood race strangely.

Who was he? Surely not Lord Charles. Fanny had said her husband was not tall, yet the top of Juliana's head did not quite reach this man's chin, and his shoulders were broad enough to block her view beyond the door.

Evidently he was as mystified as she, though much more pleasantly. "As not even the most powerful magician could rouse my sister before ten," he drawled as lazily as he grinned, "I know you cannot be Fanny, transformed for the very much better . . ."

"Lady Whitfield," Haskins intervened gravely, "allow me to present to you Lord Hampton, Lady Charles's brother. My lord, Lady Whitfield from Lancashire."

He knew of her, whether or not he had known she was to visit. His smiled changed, cooling subtly. As did his eyes. Taking in her first, perforce hazy impression of him, Juliana had not looked particularly at his eyes. Now she saw that they were almost the same golden brown color as his hair. And she realized there had been a gleam lighting them. She knew it by its absence, her name having extinguished it.

"Lady Whitfield." Lord Hampton bowed. He moved with natural grace, but Juliana knew from the bows she'd received the night before that Lord Hampton did not bow as deeply as he ought to have done. "Welcome to London. Though I am always the last to know Fanny's plans, I am certain you will enjoy playing Fanny's companion for the Season."

He did not approve of her or want her playing Fanny's companion. The new gleam in his eye, a distinctly mocking one, matched his ironic tone. Juliana's face heated. He might as well have said straight out that he thought she would enjoy riding Fanny's coattails through the Season, and there was just enough truth in the thought to bite.

He judged her. As she had feared Lady Danley's guests would, he judged her for marrying Sir Arthur in the first place, and now for using his sister's enormous cachet to get herself into the highest circles in London. But who was he to judge her so? She knew from reading between the lines of Fanny's letters that he was a rake. And for herself, Juliana could see he was a useless idler who stayed out until after dawn. A rake and a ne'er-do-well, he was—no matter that he was a duke's son.

Her chin lifted loftily. "Thank you, my lord," she said, her voice cool but calm. If she resented that she must once again mask her true feelings from a man, she was not sorry that she had learned long since how to do so. "Now if you will excuse me, my mount was brought around some time ago."

Without another word, Juliana walked by the earl, obliging him to step aside, but she neither thanked him nor acknowledged him in any way again. She saw no reason she should treat more civilly a man who had judged her before he had ever met her.

"Will you be taking nuncheon in today, my lord?" she heard Haskins say behind her.

"No, not today, Haskins," replied his lordship. Juliana could hear his voice clearly, as if he spoke while he watched her descend the steps. She knew he could not be admiring someone he had judged as poorly as he had judged her, but she was diverted from speculating on how much distaste he displayed by his subsequent remark. "I imagine I shall sleep well past noon today."

Juliana did not even think to fault the earl for his idleness. Sleeping past noon was something she had not done in all her life, but she was too shocked by where he meant to sleep to think of anything else. Why would he be discussing nuncheon and his sleeping habits with Haskins, if he were not residing at Fanny's?

Chapter 3

Juliana had returned to Grosvenor Square, had assured Haskins both that her ride had been most enjoyable and that Jared had acquitted himself in an exemplary fashion, and was climbing the stairs, keeping a wary eye out for the temporary master of the house when she recalled the remark that Mrs. Desmond had made about Lord Hampton the night before. *Given his promise to his father, I had thought he would be present.* Why should a promise the earl had made to his father cause Mrs. Desmond to take particular pains with her daughter's dress? Juliana had never claimed an exaggerated degree of intelligence, but she could answer the question easily enough, and her jaw tightened militantly. Her dear friend Fanny had had more in mind than the simple pleasure of seeing an old friend when she had invited Juliana to town.

Fanny often took chocolate in her room in the mornings with her two children. The night before she had invited Juliana to join them after she had ridden and had helped herself to whatever breakfast she desired downstairs in the breakfast room. Juliana had been looking forward to the event, small though it was, for when she had met Fanny's children, Sophie, aged six, and Harry, four, she had found them a surprisingly engaging pair.

When Juliana entered Fanny's boudoir, Harry crowed a greeting from his mother's lap, waving the sticky bun stuck in his hand, while Sophie, Franny's spitting image, slid from her chair and tripped across the room to take Juliana's hand. Juliana greeted the children warmly. She could not have done otherwise, but over Sophie's head she gave Fanny such an accusing look that her hostess colored.

The children wanted to know all about her ride: what horse she had ridden; which groom had accompanied her; what she had seen in the Park, and on the way Juliana answered them as playfully as she could manage, and she must have been amusing, though she could never afterward recall quite what she had said, for they giggled a good deal and asked for more. Carefully keeping her gaze from sliding again to Fanny, Juliana complied.

When the children's nurse came to fetch them for their morning lessons, they embraced their mother first, kissing her cheek, and then, to her surprise, both of them kissed Juliana farewell, too. In the deafening silence that fell upon the room after their departure, she realized that some of her anger had evaporated under the sun of the children's sweetness. But only some.

Before Fanny could speak, Juliana looked up from the fingers she held tightly laced together. "I met Lord Hampton as I was going out to ride this morning, Fanny. I gathered from his dress, or the lack thereof, that he is living here, while Lady Danley inhabits his house."

Fanny's guilty color deepened. "Alex is staying here," she admitted reluctantly, before rushing to add, "I would have told you, Juliana, but I was afraid you might not come! You had written how you wished to keep men at a distance, and though Alex's presence needn't signify . . . he leads his own life, I thought . . ."

Even before Fanny's voice trailed off, Juliana said in an unforgiving voice, "He has also made some sort of promise to your father about finding a bride, and no doubt setting up a nursery, has he not?"

Fanny gasped, her hand going to her throat. "But how . . . how did you know?"

"From a remark Mrs. Desmond made last night. I did not

know what she meant then, but I fit the pieces together after I realized he was staying here. Fanny, I must tell you that I feel as if you have betrayed me."

"Oh, Juliana! No! No! I wanted your company! I have not seen you in so many years, and with Charley away I felt so lonely."

"You have any number of friends you could have invited to stay the Season with you, Fanny," Juliana returned, unmoved by Fanny's beseeching look. "You hoped to matchmake. I suppose you thought that Lord Hampton might take an interest in me, because I have a little more conversation than Miss Desmond, who is too shy to raise her eyes even to meet mine." Juliana rose swiftly, as if she could not contain herself suddenly. At the window, she turned abruptly. "You decided that I should remarry, did you not, Fanny? Despite my avowal that I do not wish to put myself under any man's thumb again?"

"I thought . . . oh, my, Juliana!" Fanny broke off with a despairing wail. "You are so young, my dear. And beautiful and charming, and you've no children. I did think remarriage to a man of your choosing would be the best thing for you, yes. Yes, I did!"

"The best thing for me." Juliana repeated the words in a low, taut voice Fanny scarcely recognized. "Oh, God, to hear those words again! Whenever I have been told that what was being done to me was 'the best thing for me,' I have been pitched straight into hell. I trusted you, Fanny."

Fanny cried out at that and rose from her chair, but Juliana shook her head sharply.

"No," she said, forestalling the embrace Fanny wished to give her. "I know you did not do this maliciously, Fanny, and I know, too, that you cannot understand the depth of my feeling. Still . . . I had thought you would listen. I thought . . ." Juliana broke off before her voice could break and shook her head again. "What I thought does not matter. But I cannot stay in London. I really cannot under these circumstances."

"But, Juliana! Please! I meant no harm. I shall have Alex move to a friend's home."

"No, Fanny. He has more right than I to be here, and you and your children need a man in the house while your husband is away. I shall be gone by this afternoon."

After Juliana had left, Fanny sagged back in her seat and stared blankly before her for a long time. Juliana had stated in more than one letter that she did not wish to remarry. She had even asked for the assurance that Fanny did not mean to matchmake. Fanny had sent the assurance by the next post, blithely lying. She'd not even thought to invite her old friend to town for the Season until her father had written to report that he had secured, at last, Alex's promise to look seriously for a wife.

The Duke of Shelbourne had been ill with influenza at the time, and if not at death's door, he had been ill enough that they had all been reminded of his mortality. When he had felt at his lowest, feverish and aching and coughing painfully, he had called Lord Hampton to his bedside and begged his son to promise to look to the succession of their line. The earl would have said anything to soothe him then and could not recant his promise now that his grace was hale again. Too, they knew another bout of influenza this next winter could take him.

In alt that Alex must at least consider marriage, a state she had been strenuously urging upon him for years, Gussie had determined to parade before her brother every girl making her come-out that year. Fanny, however, had thought of Juliana. She had not seen her friend since Juliana had left the Rutherford Academy for Young Ladies on account of her mother's death. She had had over a year to go before she graduated, but she had not returned. Instead, half a year later, when she had been seventeen, she had written to announce she was already wed to Sir Arthur Whitfield. Fanny had heard of him, of course. Everyone knew of Whitfield. Despite murky origins and an even murkier history, he had become one of the richest men in the land, but he was leagues beneath Juliana in class and decades older, besides. Shocked to her toes, Fanny had wanted to press for details, to learn how the two had met, for example, but for once she had controlled her impulses. Even when they had been schoolgirls, Juliana had not cared to be harried for information she did not give of her own accord.

Upon Sir Arthur's death, Fanny had all but dismissed him and his marriage to Juliana from her mind. With Alex to think of, she had wondered only if Juliana had changed a great deal, but in the end she had decided that even the passage of eight years could not diminish the beauty of a girl who had been striking in a coltish way when she had first entered the Rutherford Academy at a mere thirteen. Juliana had lost that gawky, undeveloped look in the time Fanny had known her, adding feminine curves to the potent combination of dark chocolate hair, porcelain fair skin, and those somewhat mysterious, slightly tilted, deep violet eyes.

And she was rich as Croesus. Fanny clapped a hand over her mouth, appalled at herself, but she had been that crude in her thinking, though Alex did not lack for wealth. To the contrary, he would inherit one of the largest estates in the country, but still, no harm could come from more wealth. And so she had lured her old friend to town.

When a knock sounded at the door, Fanny startled. "Yes?" she called out, anxious and hopeful at once. But it was her brother who stalked through her door, fashionably clad in tight buckskins and a bottle green coat. There was nothing fashionably languid about his stride, however. He had unpleasant business to conduct, and he meant to have that business concluded to his satisfaction.

"You do not appear overjoyed to see me, Fanny," Lord Hampton observed, eyeing his sister's drawn expression with little sympathy. More than one woman had poetically compared the earl's eyes to warm honey and perhaps they were even then that same tawny amber color that so appealed to women, but to Fanny his eyes looked hard as amber agates.

Her lips trembled. Alex almost never got angry with her. Yet he was angry now and for much the same reason Juliana was. Lud, but she had made a muddle of her attempt to interest them in one another. She started to say something, she scarcely knew what, to stave off the confrontation his stormy expression promised, but he never allowed her to begin.

"You promised me a refuge, Fanny," Lord Hampton began grimly. "I distinctly recall your precise words, yet even as you offered me sanctuary from Gussie and her endless parade of candidates, you were inviting your widow to live here for the Season. Great God, Fanny! Am I not to have even a moment's rest from the marriage mart? Must I have my promise to take a wife thrust in my face even over breakfast?"

Fanny might have assured Alex that he would not be faced with Juliana at all, but she did not think so clearly. It was the second time in the space of only a few hours that she'd been taken to task. Frustrated, and guilty, too, she took advantage of a sister's prerogative: she lashed out on a tangent.

"I do not think you want a wife at all!" she accused, though more pettishly than furiously. "You neglected to make an appearance at Gussie's as you had promised to do."

"Devil it!" Lord Hampton muttered the oath low, but he rubbed his forehead hard with his knuckle. Fanny watched, mercilessly pleased. "I entirely forgot Gussie's affair," he admitted to her further satisfaction.

"Were you too distracted by your latest high flyer, Alex?" she asked sweetly.

Fanny ought to have known to quit while ahead. Failing to do so had gotten her into trouble before, and now Alex's at least somewhat remorseful expression vanished as completely as if it had never been. "Gentlemen do not discuss high flyers with ladies, Fanny, even ladies who are their sisters. But they do discuss wives and the getting of same. Endlessly, it seems. And, to answer your first observation, no, I do not want a wife. I have been marvelously happy free of leg shackles, but I made my promise to Father, and no one knows better than I why I made it."

Fanny found it impossible to hold her brother's pointed gaze. It was Alex who had gone down to Chatsworth Hall the moment he had been informed of their father's illness and then stayed nearly two months until the duke had been pronounced completely well.

"I only thought . . ."

"You knew," Lord Hampton interrupted ruthlessly, "that I would object, and so you did not even see fit to warn me of Lady Whitfield's advent, if she is a lady."

"Juliana is every inch a lady!" Fanny cried, seizing on the only point she could dispute. "What do you mean that she is not a lady?"

"By birth she may be a lady but she is not one by her actions, and you know it as well as I, Fanny." Lord Hampton's mouth quirked unpleasantly. "No true lady would invite a man of sixty or more, who had not an ounce of breeding or culture in him, to lay his hands on her body in order that she might, in her turn, get her hands on his admittedly considerable wealth. It is the behavior of a lightskirt, and I have used the most gentle term I can think of out of deference to you."

"Alex!" Fanny stared up at her brother in dismay. If she had expected some initial objection to Juliana's presence in the house, she had never considered that he would object to Juliana herself. "You do not know her! She is nothing like that!"

"Nor do you know her," Lord Hampton countered flatly. "You were an impressionable child when you were at school with her, and you have not so much as laid eyes on her since. You have no idea who she was or who she's become in the near decade since you parted."

"Perhaps I was young at school, but I kept company with Juliana day after day for much of three years. In that time, even I could not help but learn something of her character!" With complete conviction, Fanny continued, "She never gossiped or indulged in backbiting as most of the girls did, nor did she seem the least aware that she was a beauty of unusual degree. Any other girl who looked like her would have lorded it over the rest of us, but Juliana did not. She was intelligent and excellent good company—a bit more self-contained than the rest of us, perhaps, but still able to laugh and enjoy herself. Now I have seen her again, I would say she is much the same, but that she is a degree or so more reserved."

Alex veered restlessly off toward the window. He could not deny that the widow Whitfield was unusually reserved. When women met him, they fluttered their lashes, or they smiled, or they simpered, or they blushed, or in some way or other betrayed an interest in him. Alex did not make the observation to puff himself up. He was so accustomed to having an effect upon women, he scarcely noticed it any longer. He only noticed the opposite: Lady Whitfield had looked straight at him with no sign of a smile but for the fading one she had evidently given Haskins.

Her lack of response was all the more remarkable, for his decided one. Expecting to see only grave-faced Haskins at the door, he had been entranced to find a stunning beauty with exotically tilted, thickly lashed violet eyes and a mouth made for his. He'd smiled in blithe anticipation. Of course, he had thought her one of the diplomat's wives Fanny sometimes put up for a night or two when they had to make a trip to town and had nowhere to stay. Fair and easy game, in other words. Not for a second had it occurred to him she might not be married, not a woman with her looks. Jove and then to find she was Sir Arthur Whitfield's widow. A half-wit could have guessed why Fanny had invited her to town. Having all his wits, Hampton had been furious. And contemptuous.

Whatever maggot had gotten into Fanny's brain, the woman was decidedly not a candidate to become the Countess of Hampton, eventually the Duchess of Shelbourne. Alex thought of his mother, a woman of elegance and grace. Her father had been a squire. She had married up, as the saying went, when she married the Duke of Shelbourne, but his father had been attractive, intelligent, and cultured. He thought his mother had loved his father, but at the very least she had respected and liked him. Certainly she had not married merely in anticipation of her husband's death.

He had made no effort to hide either his displeasure or his distaste upon meeting Lady Whitfield. It had been too early in the day for polite masks . . . or perhaps his disappointment had been a bit too great to control. In his mind, at least, he'd already had her in his bed. And that though he had just left Antoinette's. Lord Hampton's eyes narrowed slightly. He did not usually want a woman so soon after a night with his mistress—immediately after, actually, but there had been the unexpectedness of it all and her unusual beauty besides. The earl shrugged off any unease he might have felt about his sharp response to the widow Whitfield and turned his thoughts, instead, to the reaction she had betrayed in regards to him, just at the end, after Haskins had made her identity known, and she had read his less-than-flattering expression. She was self-contained. Fanny was right there, too. She'd lifted her chin haughtily and addressed him in a voice as cool and unmoved as the depths of the sea. Contemptuously, Hampton wondered if she had learned that regal manner at her husband's knee. He had been old enough to dandle her there.

Abruptly he turned away from the window to fix his sister with a determined eye. He had spent an inordinate amount of time musing on Lady Whitfield, when in truth

his disagreement with Fanny was not limited to the unsuit-
ability of the one woman.

"I will find my own wife, Fanny, in my own time. Do
you understand me?"

She took the sharply put question badly. "Indeed, I do,
Alex! I understand that you mean to find a bidable, unexceptional creature, who will not interfere with your mistresses!"

If Fanny had thought to rebuke her brother, she failed entirely. A distinctly amused gleam lit his amber eyes. "How
astute you are becoming, Fanny, if no less improper in your
musings. Though I did promise Father to look for an acceptable wife, I did not promise that I would change my
way of life, nor that I would live differently from every
man in my class, your good Charley excepted. I am thirty
years of age. I manage vast holdings effectively and without the least interference, and will do the same with my
life. You may trust me to keep my word, Fanny, or you
may become Gussie."

"No! I have never been so managing as . . . oh, devil it,
what am I saying? I have been even worse than Gussie!"
Fanny bowed her head, plainly experiencing a fit of remorse, but Lord Hampton realized it was not the time to
tease her when she lifted her head and he saw the distress in
her eyes. "Alex, I may not have forewarned you of my invitation to Juliana, but you see, that is the least of my sins. I
lied outright to her, and she says I have betrayed her! She is
no more eager for marriage than you, you see."

Women with designs on marriage said many things.
Alex's lifted brow conveyed a mocking skepticism. "I com-
mend her for the sentiment, if she speaks the truth. However, crying betrayal smacks rather heavily of a Cheltenham tragedy do you not think?"

"You are too harsh! You do not know how completely I
lied. I swore to her, in writing, that I would not thrust a
gentleman upon her, yet that was my principal purpose in
inviting her to town. I did betray her trust. I simply did not

accept how adamantly set against marriage she is. Oh, Alex, I think her marriage to Whitfield must have been quite dreadful!"

Alex all but laughed aloud. "Fanny, now you are the one creating a Cheltenham tragedy. She is a striking beauty. The old dotard would have doted on her from the moment he set eyes on her."

But it was as if his sister had not heard him. "She was so happy last evening," Fanny murmured. "She was so excited to be in town, to see London at last. Lud, she was even delighted simply to be looking out the carriage window at the crowds."

The widow Whitfield happy and excited, her violet eyes sparkling with light. Alex looked down upon his sister, forcing himself to concentrate upon her, and after a few moments he succeeded only to realize with a sinking sensation that her face had crumpled.

"Fanny, Fanny." He fished in his pocket for a handkerchief. "Here, dry your eyes, pet. Good Lord, I did not mean to reduce you to tears."

"Oh, Alex, it is not you. It is Juliana. She is leaving."

"Leaving London?" Lord Hampton repeated. "But why in the name of heaven did you not tell me? I'd have spared you a browbeating and these tears."

Mopping her tears, Fanny disregarded his logical question in favor of her own query. "Do you accept now that she is deadly serious about not having a man pushed at her? If only I had known! If only she had not been so happy last night. Truly, Alex, she reminded me of a poor man's child looking in the window at a rich child's toys. She was that eager for the sights and entertainments of London. She wanted to attend the theater, to see Astley's and the Park, and . . ."

"Say another word, Fanny," Hampton warned dryly, "and you shall reduce me to tears, too."

Fanny sniffed unhappily. "Men do not cry."

"Perhaps," the earl agreed with a resigned sigh, "but

speaking for this man, at least, we are loath to see women do so. Hush now, Fanny. If she truly is set on remaining a widow, there should be no difficulty. I shall patch it up with her for you . . . if you will cease crying," he repeated warningly, for Fanny's tears were running freely down her rosy cheeks.

Fanny made no attempt to stem the streaming flow, but they only made her wobbly smile all the more appealing. "Will you try, Alex? Oh, will you truly? What will you say?"

He shrugged. "The truth, I suppose, which is that I've as little desire to marry her as she has to marry me. If that does not persuade her to stay, then she's beyond reason."

Chapter 4

Lord Hampton had not gone to her room with the intent to spy. Twice he had sent a maid to request she attend him in the library. She had refused each request, leaving him, if he were not to disappoint Fanny, little choice but to come to her room himself. She was the one who had left her door ajar, and catching sight of her before he knocked, he decided she owed him a little for making him play the beggar.

She stood at the window that looked over the small garden at the back of the house. Since her ride, she had changed into a morning dress, usually a plain garment for wear in the house, when there was no one to see. Hers was not plain, however. It was made of the thinnest cambric, a linen almost as costly as silk, and trimmed with three, not one or two, rows of Belgian lace. Her old husband had indulged her in another way as well. He had not, evidently, insisted she wear a dowager's cap. At least she was not wearing one now, though she had made some concession to her widow's status. She wore her dark hair up, twisted into a chignon at the nape of her neck. In the dim entry hall, Alex had thought her hair black. Now with the light from the window shining upon it, he could see its rich sable tones were warmer than pure black could ever be. Despite himself, he wondered, his hooded eyes on her, if her hair would feel as warm slipping through his fingers as it looked.

Whitfield had gotten his money's worth. Alex's gaze slid

downward. She was sweetly curved, but slender nonetheless. Eventually, almost reluctantly, he took in how still she stood. He'd half expected her to be tearing about the room, shrewishly supervising some downtrodden maid hard at work packing. There was no one in the room with her, though, and she was hardly acting the virago he had expected. The large window dwarfed her, making her appear small and somehow lonely, and because she'd clasped her arms about her waist, her shoulders appeared slumped. His eyes narrowing suddenly, Hampton flicked a look at the windows, but she was not trying to play on his sympathies. He could not see his image reflected there.

He propped an arm against the door, studying her a bit more intently. Perhaps it was only illusion. Perhaps she was not sad at all, but if she was unhappy about leaving London, why did she not simply depart Fanny's and set up her own establishment? She had the wherewithal, certainly. Whitfield had left her one of the richest women in England, but Alex had the answer. To be accepted by society, she needed Fanny. A calculating woman, she would realize that while the hangers-on and the fortune hunters would accept her with open arms, those in the upper circles of society, those with wealth and lineage, would not stoop to receive the woman who had wed Arthur Whitfield, unless they saw she was accepted by one of their own.

Little wonder she hugged herself. She must feel the greatest fool for the drama she'd enacted with Fanny. Certainly, she had no one to blame but herself for dashing her hopes of making a grand splash in society. But what of this business about not remarrying? Alex studied her hard, as if her straight, slender back would yield him answers, and in a sense it did, for the luxurious material covering her back was surely the answer. She did not want to yield control of her immense estate to another.

It was possible she meant to proclaim a distaste for marriage until the man she eventually chose to take as a husband agreed to sign some sort of agreement voiding the law of the land and leaving her property in her hands alone. It had been done before. Or perhaps she really did not intend to marry, only to have a discreet succession of affairs. Given her looks, she'd not lack for offers. Far from it.

The earl stared a moment longer at Lady Juliana Whitfield's back, brooding now. Why should he not take her as his mistress? The answer, that he could not care even in that way for such a calculating woman, made his mouth curve. Antoinette likely knew the size of his purse to the last coin. But Antoinette had never pretended she was not for sale. She did not call herself lady nor think to inveigle her way into Almack's. And God above, she'd never stooped to taking a sixty-year-old man into her bed as this one, this mercenary sham Fanny called friend had done.

He should turn on his heel and leave. And have Fanny pine the Season away. She would, too. She could be that foolish, whereas if the woman stayed, Fanny would take her measure eventually. His jaw set, Hampton acted before he could think better of it. Straightening, he rapped on the open door.

"Come in, Rand. But not a word more, I beg you. I could not go another round this morning even with a flea."

Only then did Lord Hampton feel as if he trespassed. She had revealed little to him while she stood silent, but speaking, she betrayed herself. And he'd have wagered a very great deal on the suspicion that she would not care for him to know she felt unable to go another round with a flea.

"I am afraid, Lady Whitfield, it is neither a flea nor your maid at your door."

The earl won his imaginary wager. The still, drooping figure he had observed for some moments vanished so utterly and so quickly that he might have doubted his own observation, had he not half expected the change.

Lady Whitfield whirled about, her spine stiffening, while her chin shot into the air. "What are you doing here, Lord Hampton? This is my room!"

So. If he had not found the tempestuous virago he had

expected, he had found the regal witch Whitfield had created. Lud, but she could have been a queen the way she called him to account.

Hampton had not been often called to account by anyone, and, particularly not by women. And he found he did not much care for the feel of it, even though the eyes of the woman demanding the account flashed with such heat and emotion they were a sight to behold.

The earl returned her a deliberately dispassionate, contrastingly cool look. "I courteously requested you to meet me on neutral ground, Lady Whitfield, but when you refused me the right of a hearing, you left me no recourse except to intrude upon your privacy."

"We are not in a court of law!" she shot back, undaunted by his too-even tone. "There are no rights to be honored here, but even if there were the matter you wish to discuss is a disagreement between your sister and me. I wish you to go at once."

She walked toward him so forcefully, the thin cambric of her morning dress snapped about her ankles. If she had appeared drained of vitality earlier, his appearance at her door seemed to have restored it with interest. Hampton did not move, he only watched with narrowed eyes as she marched on him.

"Go, my lord! You have no right to intrude so!" She caught hold of the door, as if she meant to slam it in his face, though she scarcely came to his chin and seemed not to have a bone in her body that was not so fine and light he could not snap it with one hand. Lord Hampton might have admired the spirit she displayed, might particularly have admired the consequent heaving of her round, high breasts, but she did, in fact, attempt to shut the door upon him.

The earl simply held up his arm, countering her effort with his weight. "I will go," he said. They were not a foot apart. He could see the storm in her eyes, the heat in her cheeks, the tension drawing her full mouth tight; and he could smell, too, the gentle scent of the rosewater she had dabbed on the smooth, creamy skin so close to him.

"You are right to say I have no business being here," he snapped, damning her in his mind, for her passion only ignited his, though his passion had naught to do with anger. His tone could not have reassured her, but it seemed his words did, for though she kept her thick-lashed, tilted eyes trained on him, she did relax her grip on the door. "However," Hampton went on, his tone a degree more moderate, "you are not right to say I have no reason to wish to speak with you. It is in large part on my account that you have had your disagreement with Fanny."

"I do not . . ."

He cut off her protest peremptorily. "Hear me out, if you please. You have everything to gain from doing so, Lady Whitfield, for I believe you looked forward to a stay in London. However, if after we have talked, you should still feel you must leave, then of course you must know you may. You cannot fear I would restrain you physically."

He said it quietly, but he said it to mock her melodramatic storming of the door, and he expected she would flush with embarrassment. He did not expect she would duck her head completely, so he could see nothing but her sleek dark hair smoothed back to the thick coil at her neck.

He shoved his hands down into the pockets of his breeches, balling them into fists for the pleasure of it. She clearly was a witch, with her jewel-like hair and eyes. He wanted to take her in his arms. He wanted to look into her face to see why she hid from him.

"Come to the library with me, Lady Whitfield." Hampton regretted the sharpness of his tone, for he had meant to request not to order, but she had worn away what little patience he had. It passed all understanding, or at least his, that he should feel a surge of protectiveness toward a woman who at a mere seventeen had possessed enough steely will to get herself married to a money bags forty years and more her elder. "Or, if you prefer, we could meet in the gardens. I ask, you understand, on Fanny's behalf. She is truly distraught."

It was no less than the truth, but Hampton wished to learn if Fanny's distress concerned her as to inform her of what she must know. He was thwarted in his intentions, however. The sound of footsteps made him look around to see a spare, middle-aged lady's maid approaching. If she did look to him, she did it so swiftly, he did not see. It was her mistress's eyes she met. But not in the expressionless way of a normal servant. The two exchanged a look, and in the maid's at least there was sympathy, but it was astonishingly, a sympathy not unmixed with a degree of chiding.

Diverted by the maid—or the thought that she, a servant, might chide the regal, overspirited, not always so reserved Lady Whitfield—Hampton only heard Lady Whitfield draw a deep breath. He thought it did not sound like a vastly happy breath, and he found when he looked to her again that her violet eyes were darker than usual. "Very well, my lord." She sounded stiff, regally so, he thought. "I shall come to the gardens in a few moments."

With that she turned away from the door, dismissing Hampton as completely as if he were the maid. His eyes hardened. He had never, he was quite certain, been sent on his way quite so summarily by anyone, man or woman. It was not, however, an opportune moment to teach this woman manners to match her beauty. Giving her stiff back a lazily ironical bow, Lord Hampton left her to her maid.

You cannot fear I would restrain you physically.

Juliana turned from the door with her hands fisted in the folds of her dress. He'd mocked her. Mocked her, when he knew nothing! What could he know, he who prejudged her from his lofty, pampered heights? Everything had been given to him on a sterling plate! Oh, but she'd have liked to lash out at him, to fling in his face how little he knew.

Devil take him! And not least because he had spoken no less than the truth. He would not restrain a woman physically. God knew how she could be so certain of it. Clearly not from her own experience of men, yet Juliana would have wagered all she had on the intuition that Hampton would never strike a woman to bend her to his will.

He would not have the need, she thought rather sourly in the next moment. And he knew it as well as she. He had stood in her door supremely confident of his ability to persuade her to his desires. Lud, he must have persuaded scores of women to his ends by now. If he had had to persuade them; if they had not simply fallen into his arms, beguiled by those honey gold eyes. It was impossible to look into them and not—at least fleetingly—imagine them softening.

When Rand opened the wardrobe, the walnut door creaked slightly, startling Juliana, and she bit her lip. But what if she had imagined his eyes softening? Did not everyone want approval? And besides, she was no fool yearning uselessly. She knew very well that the only way she would ever see approval in his eyes was by imagining it. The desire had affected her a moment only.

Rand turned away from the wardrobe, a question in her eyes. Juliana shook her head in response, though she could not have said, had she been pressed, whether she meant, "No, do not pack," or "No, do not pack yet."

Rand, however, nodded as if she understood and went to the dressing table to tidy the comb and brush and the few bottles there. Juliana abruptly left the room. There was no point in stewing. She knew Hampton disapproved of her, but she did not know the extent of his dislike. If he was rude or mocking or otherwise offensive in the gardens, she would have her answer and know she could not stay.

As to Fanny . . . Juliana winced, thinking of the dramatics she had inflicted upon poor Fanny. Her old friend had had no idea what emotions her scheme would trigger. True, she had lied outright, but she had meant no harm. Juliana did believe that, and oh God she did not want to scuttle back to Westerleigh. Not yet, not after seven and one half years there! Not defeated!

"May I be of help, Lady Whitfield?"

"Oh, Haskins!" Juliana looked up with a start. "I did not see you, but yes, will you show me to the gardens, please?"

"Yes, my lady. You may use the library."

The butler led Juliana along a carpeted corridor to the library. There, a set of French doors opened onto a terrace that ran the length of the small but well-appointed house.

Even before Haskins murmured that his lordship awaited her by the pond, Juliana saw the earl. He was impossible to miss. He was too tall, and his golden brown hair gleamed in the sun.

Sophie and Harry were there, too, Sophie drawing with their nurse Mrs. Jones, and Harry suddenly grinned. He was handsome whether he smiled or not, but when he smiled a startling warmth lit his features, and Juliana was not the least surprised that Harry should shriek for joy over his uncle's response.

Seeing Juliana first, Sophie hurried to show off a drawing she had made of the house and a tree in the garden. It was fine sketch for a six-year-old, and Juliana complimented her.

Sophie grinned, delighted. "But you must also see Harry's . . ."

"Don't tell Lady Whitfield!" Harry shouted, trotting forward, the jar in his hand. "Let her see first, Sophie! You will like him, Lady Whitfield. Look!"

The little boy thrust the jar toward her expectantly. He had blue eyes, not amber, but something about the shape of his features and the way he smiled reminded her of his uncle. Harry would be persuasive, too, one day. Juliana glanced at the earl. She had seen that he followed his nephew, but she had not acknowledged his presence. Nor did she greet him then. He was not smiling outright, but he was amused, his mouth slanting up at one corner and his eyes glinting as he waited for her to refuse the questionable treat of surveying whatever crawling creature Harry had captured.

But Juliana was not so missish. Or would not be with Hampton there, expecting missishness. She took the jar and peered as interestedly as possible into its muddy depths. For a moment she feared she would have to disappoint Harry and tell him his prize had escaped, but just as she was giving up, something moved, and Juliana finally distinguished a fat, undulating worm. She did not know what monster she had expected, but a worm was so manageable she laughed. "He is a very nice, fat worm, Harry."

The little boy jumped up and down. "I knew you would like him, Lady Whitfield. I mean to keep him, too!" He looked belligerently at their nurse.

A placid countrywoman who had raised eight children of her own, Mrs. Jones looked entirely unruffled. "You may keep him for today Master Harry, but I know you would not wish to keep your prize overlong from his mother and father. For now, however, it is time we go inside, children. Harry, you may bring your worm. We shall have to name him after we find him food in the kitchen."

The protest that Harry had opened his mouth to blurt out died unspoken. Without further ado, he ran off toward a door that led to the kitchens while Sophie hastened to gather up her colored pencils.

"Good-bye, Uncle Alex. Good-bye, Lady Whitfield." Skipping after Mrs. Jones's comfortable bulk, Sophie waved to the two she left behind. "We shall tell you what he eats."

"I shall hold you to the promise," Lord Hampton called back.

Juliana merely waved, but she'd rather have liked to go with the children. As had happened earlier in Fanny's room, they had broken through her guard. Perhaps with Fanny it had not mattered so much that she was more vulnerable, but with Lord Hampton it did.

"Do you have any brothers and sisters, Lady Whitfield?"

Juliana glanced at him. It was the sunlight, of course, but his eyes seemed a softer honey gold than before. She sought out the children's retreating backs, again. "Yes, my lord. I have a half sister and a half brother, both older."

"Ah, I thought they might have been younger and had enjoyed visiting a married sister, who did not object to collections of crawling fauna."

He was commending her a little and smiling. Juliana could hear the warmth in his voice, and knew he expected she would make some equally light and amiable response, but the subject of her family inspired little lightness.

"What was it you wished to say, my lord, when you asked to speak to me?"

There was a pause. Juliana sensed the earl was studying her, wondering perhaps at her failure to prattle on about her family. She simply outwaited him, gazing steadily into the clear waters of a small, ornamental pool.

"I wished to remark that just as Fanny did not inform you of my presence in Grosvenor Square, Lady Whitfield, so she failed to forewarn me that you were coming. And like you, I was not pleased to learn of her omission."

Juliana glanced up briefly at that, but his face betrayed quite as little emotion as his voice. Whether he had been furious or merely mildly put out, she could not tell, though she did not doubt that he had taken the news of her residence at Fanny's poorly. After all, it had been only hours since she had watched his expression cool the moment he learned her identity. He thought her cold and mercenary. Had he fretted that he might not be able to withstand her if she took an interest in him? The thought was absurd, of course, but it bolstered her somehow to have made a joke at his expense even if only in her mind. He was so detestably formidable.

"Fanny had out and out promised me a place of refuge from the marriage mart, you see." Now there was a very dry note in his voice, and it, as much as what he said, pierced through some of the resentment that had built again in Juliana. He had prejudged her, but it was true as well that Fanny had played the same trick on the two of them. Juliana found herself meeting his eyes before she could think better of it. Just in their depths, she could see a glint of amusement that made her want to smile back. She did not, but he seemed to sense her weakening. Holding her gaze with his, he said reasonably, "We share a grievance, Lady Whitfield. But I think we share as well an affection for Fanny, even with her faults. She is not like Gussie." His mouth quirked in a wry expression of which Juliana doubted he was even aware. "Fanny, you see, understands the word 'no' and now we have each read her a deserved lecture, she desires more than anything in the world to repent and be forgiven. Fanny would never insist that you change your mind on marriage."

Of course Fanny would not. She was too sweet-natured, and besides, she had no legal right to do so. Only a father could legally insist his daughter wed as he willed.

"You are right to remind me of Fanny's good nature, my lord," Juliana said, abruptly cutting off the unpleasant train of her thoughts. "I ought not to have forgotten that she would heed my wishes in the end, and I find that I hope she will be kind enough to forgive me the scene I enacted earlier. I do want to enjoy a London Season." She saw Lord Hampton's eyebrow arch in an ever-so slightly cynical way and guessed he felt superior for having deduced her wishes. Accordingly, looking him directly in the eye, Juliana made herself admit, "You were entirely right there."

But he did not gloat. His gaze unreadable, he inclined his head a little. "Fanny was my source of inspiration, though it would not be any great difficulty to guess that a woman would look forward to London during the Season."

A woman. What of a lady? Juliana lifted her chin at the Earl of Hampton. "Then we are agreed, my lord?" she asked coolly. "I shall promise to honor your wish for a refuge from the marriage mart and make no overtures toward you concerning marriage, if you will promise to honor my desire for quite the same thing."

He had not been outright rude or insulting. She could abide him enough to stay in London, but she wished to pay him back a little for that "woman." And it seemed she had succeeded. He did not answer her at once, but studied her enigmatically before he remarked, equally coolly, "It would seem we have made a bargain, then, though in truth you were safe all along. I have never cared for the chase, you see. Enjoy your Season, Lady Whitfield. I am certain you will, actually, with Fanny to ease your way."

And so he had the last word, or sting. There was quite enough truth in his remark to make Juliana flush, and worse, she knew he had seen her reaction, though he inclined his head and turned on his heel at once, leaving her there wishing she could snatch back every reasonable word she had said and leave Grosvenor Square on the instant. Lud, but she hoped they would be able to avoid each other.

Chapter 5

"Oh, Juliana, I cannot tell you how glad I am that you have forgiven me for thinking to matchmake between you and Alex. I did not mean to disregard your wishes. Truly, I did not! It is only that I thought to introduce him to a lady I knew to be not only beautiful but more interesting than the young girls . . ."

Juliana turned away from the cheval glass before her, leaving the errant tendril she'd been repinning to wave in the air. It was perhaps the hundredth apology Fanny had made her in the last two days, but this was the first time outside the confines of Fanny's house. They were attending a ball, Juliana's first. Fanny having torn the hem of her dress, they had retreated to a retiring room for repairs.

Mindful of the maid sewing by candlelight on the far side of the room, Juliana kept her voice low as she took Fanny's hands in hers. "It is I who owe the apologies, Fanny. I reacted out of all proportion . . . I cannot explain but that I am sensitive . . ."

She took a deep breath, clearly reluctant to continue, and Fanny leapt to her rescue. "You have no need to explain anything, my dear! I lied to you, Juliana!"

Fanny would have gone on, but now it was Juliana who interrupted, holding tight to her friends hands. "You did, but for no evil intent, Fanny. I shudder to recall my melodramatics now. And I am so glad to be here. Fanny, you are very good to allow me to ride your coattails into society."

"Ride my coattails?" Fanny laughed merrily enough that the maid looked up to smile with her. "Perhaps I may take credit for presenting you, my dear, but you have done the rest. Or do you think my house is as full of flowers as any florist's shop on my account? Why I did not receive half so many tributes when I made my come-out! Society has embraced you, fallen over you, delighted in you, Juliana, and on your own account, for you are beautiful, charming, amusing . . . !"

"Stop, Fanny! Please. You begin to sound like Lord Dalyrimple."

Juliana rolled her eyes, but Fanny smiled smugly. "Dear Dalyrimple adores you, as does everyone else, and on your own merits."

"I rather think my purse may have something to do with Lord Dalyrimple's enthusiasm. Nay, Fanny! No more on my charms, please. But let us do agree on another subject. Let us have done with our apologies. May we?"

Fanny nodded solemnly. "Indeed, yes. I shall not even whisper another apology, so long as you know I am mortified by what I did."

"As am I." Juliana gave her a smile. "We are agreed just in time, for your hem is repaired." She nodded toward the maid, who came to slip the dress over Fanny's head again. While the maid worked, Juliana straightened Fanny's turban then stood back to judge the results. "Yes, I do believe we have you looking once more the prettiest wife at the ball."

"Then we are a perfectly matched pair!" Fanny giggled, taking Juliana's arm as they left the room. "For you are certainly the most stunning widow!"

"I am grateful for your kind eyes, ma'am." Juliana laughed in her turn. "And while we are about it, why do we not pronounce Sarah the loveliest of girls making a come-out? She is in my opinion."

"In mine, too! Still, there are some very pretty, very nice

girls here tonight, and I think it very bad of Alex to be so late."

Fanny paused to greet two ladies on their way to the retiring room, presenting them to Juliana and exclaiming over the "crush" of guests honoring their hostess, Lady Bute. When they were on their way down the stairs again, Juliana hesitated, but in the end could not keep herself from asking casually, "Do you believe Lord Hampton will come tonight?"

It was certainly not the first time the question had been voiced. Almost since the moment they had arrived a little over an hour before, a veritable stream of ladies, most mothers but a few not, had asked Fanny what she knew of her brother's plans, and Lady Danley had fretted over the question in the carriage on the way to Lord and Lady Bute's, for she had stopped in Grosvenor Square to take Fanny and Juliana up with her and Sarah.

Still, Juliana knew, if Fanny could not, that she did not ask out of entirely idle curiosity. She had thought of Lord Hampton rather a good bit in the week since they had made their bargain in the gardens and he had left her after that parting shot about Fanny. Most of her thoughts had been less than friendly, but once or twice she had found herself wondering where he was and what he did, for he was so seldom at Grosvenor Square that she had not seen him, only heard from Fanny or Rand that he had come but left again, or that he had not returned for the night at all.

"One can never say with any authority what Alex will do, my dear," Fanny admitted with no little frustration. "Ah yes, you may smile! You think me the complete sister, do you not? But I tell you it is true. Alex does as he pleases with this exception: he keeps his word. Which means that he must make an appearance at some time or other this Season. He might prefer to have the perfect wife fall into his lap and thus spare him the tiresome task of meeting each of this Season's crop of hopefuls, but even Alex's luck is not that good."

In the ballroom again, they made their way to the corner where Fanny and her friends had comfortably ensconced

themselves. With each dance, there were new people coming to sit and chat or to ask for a dance. To Juliana the ball
seemed something like a kaleidoscope, always changing,
always interesting, always new. If she found one person un-
likable, she could be certain a nicer or more entertaining
person would soon follow.

Already, she felt a fondness for one gentleman in particular. Lady Danley had whispered in her ear that though Mr.
George Porter was one of the best-connected gentlemen in
the room, he was also, in Lady Danley's blunt words, a bit
of a slow top. And Juliana had found it true that Mr. Porter
did lack the quick wit of a gentleman like Lord Houghton,
who could make her laugh with a single, dry observation,
but Juliana sensed in Mr. Porter a sweetness that she liked
as much as Lord Houghton's laconic humor.

Mr. Porter had come to ask if he might have the honor of
leading her out for a quadrille when a stir by the door
caught Juliana's attention. Lord Hampton was being announced. It had been nearly a week since she had seen him
and in the interim she seemed to have forgotten, if not his
looks, then the degree of self-assurance he possessed. There
were other handsome men at Lady Bute's ball; some as tall,
some with shoulders as nicely made, and some as elegantly
turned-out in black evening dress, but no other man possessed anything close to Hampton's effortless presence. It
seemed as if half the room turned to remark his arrival.

Lady Bute hastened to greet him with the kind of glee a
hunter might display upon bagging a rare tiger. Bearing
down on him as well, with rather more purpose in her expression, was his elder sister. Yet, despite the frown Lady
Danley wore, Juliana saw soon enough that Lord Hampton
needed no one to defend him. He cut off whatever lecture
Lady Danley may have thought to read him for his tardi-
ness by the very simple expedient of laying his finger
lightly on her lips. He said something as well, and it took
no wit at all to guess that he warned his sister he would
leave the Earl and Countess of Bute's ball the very moment

Lady Danley said one more tiresome word to him. Of course, he smiled charmingly all the while he gave his warning, bending low to his sister, a light dancing in his eyes. She, it really was no surprise to see, responded to his charm with a smile of her own, an affectionate, entirely indulgent smile, though she had been railing about him for the last hour and more.

For a second, Juliana felt such envy she knew it was wrong. But life seemed so easy for him! His sisters adored him; his father never thought to force him to marry, only asked him to take serious stock of the marriage prospects making their bows that Season; and the girls themselves . . . Juliana's mood suddenly began to lighten. Mrs. Desmond, she saw, was not wasting a moment. The woman was all but dragging her daughter to meet the earl, and Lady Danley, facing toward Mrs. Desmond while Hampton did not, held him in place for the capture with some doubtless fond, ever-so-sisterly repartee.

"I say, Lady Whitfield, you are good to dance with me. Most of the ladies scatter when I approach 'em. Can't seem to keep my feet off theirs, if you know what I mean. I do try, but 'tis as if my feet have a mind all their own."

Juliana gave Mr. Porter a grateful smile. She did not want to gloat over Lord Hampton's immediate fate at the hands of Mrs. Desmond and Lady Danley, at least openly. "Well then, Mr. Porter, your feet have taken it upon themselves to avoid mine, for I have not felt their touch even once."

"More like, it is your feet that have done the avoiding, Lady Whitfield." Mr. Porter sighed morosely. "I've not got a shred of grace about me. Not like Hampton, there. I see he's come, though this affair is a tame 'un. Has to marry, don't you know. Poor chap. Promised his father or some such. And they'll all be after him, all the mamas and their daughters, like hounds after a fox. Not that Hampton'll be caught unless he wants to be. He's too canny by half, but Lud, they'll run him, see if they don't."

It was too much, particularly as Mrs. Desmond had just

pushed her shy chick forward, all but thrusting the girl into his arms, while the earl, evidently aware that his sister had played some part in the meeting, shot Lady Danley a deadly look.

Juliana laughed aloud, and Lord Hampton lifted his head. She looked away before he found her, if he did. She'd no wish for him to know he held any interest for her, and indeed to prove to herself that he did not, she put him from her thoughts.

"You make the finding of a wife seem a rather trying task, Mr. Porter," she observed a bit later when the dance had ended and he escorted her to the refreshment table. "I wonder that you dare to come to London yourself."

"But I ain't on the marriage mart!" Mr. Porter blurted, looking startled. "Hope you ain't lookin' for a husband yourself? Hampton would be the man for you. All the ladies want him."

He did not want her, however. It surprised Juliana that the thought should sting, and she took great care to speak mildly. "I am not looking for a husband at all, I assure you, Mr. Porter. As far as I am concerned Lord Hampton is simply Lady Charles's brother. But may I ask why you are not, ah, on the marriage mart, as you say? You are not married are you?"

"No, 'tisn't like that. I'm betrothed. Have been since she was six or so. Nina's father owns the estate next to my father's, you see."

"Yes, of course. But is Miss . . . ah . . ."

"Stuttles. She's Iphigenina Stuttles, but I call her Nina. Iphy wouldn't do. Sounds . . . foolish, don't you think?"

"Yes, I quite agree." Juliana determinedly swallowed a smile. Mr. Porter looked very earnest. "But is Miss Stuttles here somewhere in this amazing crush of people?"

"Nina? No, no. She's only sixteen, you see. She's a good girl, comfortable, you know, and no great wit. We'll suit, like you and Hampton would, if you'd a mind to be inter-

ested in him. You've both of you got bottom, and assurance, too, and the kind of looks to make heads turn."

Juliana had only met Mr. Porter twice before. She did not
know on what basis he had come to the conclusion that she
had spirit or assurance. And as to his conclusion that she
and Hampton would suit, it was so laughable that she simply ignored it. "You are very kind Mr. Porter. I thank you
for your compliments, but I should prefer not to hear any
more on the subject of my looks. I would like us to be
friends, you see, and I do not think friends pay a great deal
of attention to appearance."

"Friends?" Mr. Porter turned pink with pleasure. "I say,
Lady Whitfield! You do me an honor! You must have le-
gions of friends, but I've only a few, really."

"Then we have something in common, Mr. Porter. For
you are wrong. I have very few friends. But come, as a
friend who knows a great deal about town, tell me a bit
about the other guests. For example, who is that very erect
and formidable lady who seems to be holding court there
by the potted palm?"

The august woman was Mrs. Drummond-Burrell, one of
the patronesses of Almack's. Mr. Porter knew her well,
being cousin to her husband, and after they had finished
their punch he presented Juliana to her. Juliana found the
woman cool and rather haughty, but not, in all, disapprov-
ing. Indeed, Fanny later told Juliana excitedly that Mrs.
Drummond-Burrell reported having been rather taken with
her, evidently a compliment of the highest order.

Juliana danced often that evening. Lord Houghton led
her out for a country dance and made her laugh so with his
running, sotto voce commentary on the other dancers that
she could scarcely recall the steps. A Lord Kettering also
paid her attention. Fanny told her that he was considered
one of the most eligible bachelors in town, as he was of an
old, exceedingly wealthy family, but Juliana did not care
for him. He not only regarded her rather as if he were un-
dressing her, he had no conversation about anything or any-

one other than himself. Lord Soames was a pleasant relief. As she had when she had met him at Lady Danley's, Juliana found the viscount impeccably mannered and mercifully restrained in his admiration of her. He did tell her she looked well, but he did not go on and compare her eyes to gems or her hair to the night or her skin to satin. And when she commended him for his calm, he had the wit to amuse her by saying he had seen her grimace at a fellow who had been waxing poetic too long and too effusively.

Toward the end of the evening, Mr. Porter asked her to dance again, and she accepted. He had not danced with anyone else, and though he had seemed quite happy talking with whomever joined their loose group, she did not wish him to feel rejected.

As they approached the dance floor, Mr. Porter stopped suddenly and exclaimed happily, "Hampton, by Jove! I thought you'd be too busy inspecting all the young misses to have a word for old friends. You know Lady Whitfield, of course. She does me great honor, saying we are friends. She's not got many, you know."

Lord Hampton glanced to Juliana, his look unreadable. "No, I did not know." She sensed he did not believe she had told Mr. Porter the truth, and her chin went up, though she told herself she should be pleased that disbelieving her, he would not question why she had few friends. "Good evening, Lady Whitfield." He gave her that slight, lazy bow before he looked to Mr. Porter again. "George, it is interesting that you should mention the subject of friends, for I have come in the hopes that you will stand my friend just now." Hampton could not have taken Juliana more by surprise, but he never looked to see her eyes flare wide. "I wish you to allow me the honor of leading Lady Whitfield onto the floor. If you do not, I shall be snared by Gussie, who's a silly bird-headed chit with her this time. They are, I might add, only seconds away."

Flicking a curious glance behind Lord Hampton, Juliana saw that Lady Danley was, indeed, sailing toward them, playing frigate to a small, bobbing tug of a girl. Short and rather squat, the girl had unwisely chosen to give herself height by piling her curls atop her head and adorning the resulting strange cone shape with three silvery ornamental birds, one of which had unfortunately slipped during the evening so that it appeared to be pecking her ear.

"Miss Wycherly." Mr. Porter nodded wisely. "Poor chit's got a mama determined to rig her out in the latest craze. You're best away from her, Hampton. She's not an ounce of conversation either, and I vow Lady Whitfield would prefer to dance with you, anyway. I can't keep my feet straight, you know."

"That is not in the least true, Mr. Porter!" Juliana thought it time she spoke for herself, as neither of the gentlemen seemed inclined to consult her wishes. "You are a very pleasant dance partner, and Lord Hampton may. . . ."

"Alex!" Lady Danley trilled her brother's name sweetly. "I have Miss Wycherly with me as you can see. She has just confided how dearly she wishes to dance, and I told her you would be happy to oblige her."

Lord Hampton's handsome face fell into an expression of perfect chagrin. "Alas, Miss Wycherly, I would, indeed, be happy to oblige, but Lady Whitfield has just consented to be my partner for this dance. Mr. Porter is free, however. You do know one another?"

Miss Wycherly, her eyes fluttering distractingly, allowed in a high, squeaky voice that she and Mr. Porter had met the year before. Whereupon, before Lady Danley could speak, before Mr. Porter could even so much as nod, or Juliana could protest again, Lord Hampton possessed himself of Juliana's hand and all but dragged her onto the dance floor.

"That was very bad of you, my lord!" As they were joining a set, she had perforce to keep her voice down, but the look she gave him was not quiet.

Lord Hampton's expression was not so easily read, but he gave a rather careless shrug. "George will manage better than I. Gussie will allow him to escape, while she'd have forced the girl on me, and I could not abide looking at those birds for an entire dance much less listening to her voice."

"You could have asked Miss Desmond to dance then." Juliana looked around in frustration, wondering why the music did not start, but couples were still coming onto the floor. She wished they would get on with it. She did not want to stand longer than necessary with a man who only danced with her to avoid dancing with a disaster of a girl.

But Miss Wycherly was not the only reason Hampton had condescended to dance with Juliana, as she soon learned.

"I have danced already with Miss Desmond," he said, drawing her attention from the dawdlers. "To dance twice with a partner is to indicate a particular interest in that person. You would not have me raise Miss Desmond's hopes unreasonably, would you, Lady Whitfield? But perhaps that is not the custom so far north as Lancashire. You were about to dance a second time with Mr. Porter."

Juliana did not remark that Lord Hampton had, evidently, taken some notice of her earlier in the evening. She was trying to think if she had ever been warned against dancing twice with the same gentleman, but if she had, she had been told so long before, she had forgotten it. The only dances she'd ever attended had been informal affairs with neighborhood families, when she had been very young.

She would not confide that to Lord Hampton however. She would sound too pitiful, and besides, she doubted that the earl had advised her of the rule merely to be helpful. His expression might be bland, but she had heard an accusatory edge to his voice.

"Are you acting my chaperon, Lord Hampton?"

He subjected her to a long, considering look. "It is possible customs are not quite the same so far from London." She made him no answer and only waited to hear what he really thought. "Or perhaps you mean to attach George Porter to you?"

Why did he care, she wondered, but she warned herself

against asking. The look in his eye did not bode well, yet, only a moment later, she heard herself say, "What can it matter to you?"

His expression hardened, just as she had warned herself it would. "I have known George Porter since our school days and have an especial fondness for him."

And would keep the poor, sweet man from a calculating witch like her. Having known very well what he thought of her, Juliana could scarcely credit that her heart would seem to drop. "I like Mr. Porter," she said through stiff lips. "We have become friends."

"Because you have not any?" He mocked her.

"Look about you, Lord Hampton," she snapped. "Shall we count those I can call friend here?"

He did not address whether she could count him a friend. There was no need. "George is exceedingly well connected."

"So he is." Juliana felt again that odd ache that seemed to weigh down her heart. Why should Hampton distrust her so? Was it her fate that men always would do so? He had had a smile for everyone else that evening, but he regarded her as if she were little better than a thief. "And, as perhaps you observed, he kindly presented me to Mrs. Drummond-Burrell earlier in the evening. So, I have, indeed, benefited from my association with Mr. Porter. If you object to my being friendly with him, however, you will have to speak to him. He has been kind to me, Lord Hampton, and I mean to be equally kind to him, whatever dark suspicions you may have. Now, I fear I have lost all interest in dancing this dance. You will excuse me? And forgive me for not thanking you for hauling me onto the dance floor to save Mr. Porter from my clutches? In future, I feel confident, you will refrain from asking me to dance, but should you feel the need to save another, be warned, my lord, I will refuse you."

Juliana spun about, but Lord Hampton did not allow her to leave him standing alone in the set. He left with her, placing his hand lightly on the small of her back. She

would have liked to wrench away from even so little con-
tact with him, but she was aware that their abrupt departure
from the dance had caused heads to turn. When Hampton
would have steered her back to Fanny's group, however,
Juliana did resist. Without a word, she walked straight out
of the ballroom, making for the retiring room, where mercifully she had a few minutes alone to compose herself.

In the ballroom, Fanny hurried up to her brother. "Did
Juliana take ill, Alex? You left the set so suddenly."

"No, she is not ill." Before he could be questioned further, he asked abruptly, "Fanny, do you think Lady Whitfield knows that to dance twice with a man signifies a high
degree of interest in him?"

"Well," Fanny considered briefly. "I suppose she must. I
mean, one would have to be a recluse or a slow top not to
know. But why do you ask?"

"Nothing really, just some idle remark she made. Ah,
look, here comes Gussie advancing upon me with another
chit."

"Where?" Fanny craned to look through the crowd. "I do
not see her, Alex."

"I know her plumes, Fanny. They are the gray ones waving alongside Dalyrimple now, and as to the chit, she's had
one by her all evening."

Fanny chuckled at his tone. "Have they all been so unap-
pealing?"

"One must go about the task of choosing a wife carefully, Fanny," Lord Hampton replied diplomatically.
"Which is why I shall take my leave of Lord and Lady Bute
now, for if I meet one more chit tonight, they will all blend
together, you see, and I will have accomplished nothing."

"Oh, I see very well, Alex," Fanny replied, laughing.
"But do not forget that you have given me your word that
you will attend Almack's Wednesday next."

The earl made a face, but he did nod before he escaped
with a last wave.

Chapter 6

The candles had burned deep in their sockets at White's.
Two footmen moved quietly about the shadowy periphery
of the famous club's gaming room, removing the brandy
and claret glasses left behind after hours of play, yet taking
great care not to disturb the single tables of players that remained despite the late hour.

Lord Hampton slouched carelessly in his deep, comfortable chair. He'd long since removed his cravat, absently
tossing the starched linen onto a nearby table. The eyes he
lifted to study the man across from him were half closed,
giving the impression that he had either drunk too much or
was nearly asleep or both. The men seated on either side of
him disregarded his appearance, knowing it to be deceptive,
for they had played often with the earl over the years. But
the gentleman he scrutinized did not belong to White's.
Lord Blakely had come to the club as a guest of Lord
Mitchell, who was now sound asleep and snoring lightly,
his knee touching Hampton's discarded cravat.

"Very well, Blakely, I shall play awhile longer." Alex
shrugged negligently. "But only awhile. I mean to be off
when the candle there burns out."

"Will White's not replace the candles more than once?"
Lord Blakely smiled thinly, his gaze shifting briefly to the
candles. "How surprisingly frugal you Tories are. Or is it
that you wish to be off to the famous Duvenay's arms,
Hampton? I cannot say that I blame you. Nor even if the

arms you seek are those of your sister's guest, the excep-
tionally wealthy and attractive widow Whitfield."

"Here now! I'll not hear Lady Whitfield spoken of in the
same breath with an Impure." Mr. George Porter struggled
up from the comfortable depths of his chair. He'd been half
asleep, staying on from inertia as much as anything, for he
was not playing. "She's not one of Hampton's fancy
pieces."

"And how would you know, Porter?" Lord Blakely
asked with silky insinuation. "Are you so close to the
lady?"

"Here now! She is a friend, no more no less. She's not
got . . ."

Hampton sighed loudly, interrupting Mr. Porter. "We are
playing cards here, gentlemen. Or, making the attempt.
You've not forgotten how to deal, Blakely?"

The viscount was not pleased to be prodded. He stiffened, and a distinct flash could be seen in his black eyes.
But when Lord Hampton met his look, appearing exactly as
indolent and rather bored as before, Lord Blakely shrugged
off his pique. "I thought you were the one had lost his taste
for cards, Hampton, as your legendary luck seems to have
deserted you tonight. But I am pleased you will continue to
put Lady Luck's favor to the test, and it would be my pleasure to deal."

Five men sat at the table: Blakely, Hampton, Lord
Robert Mannering, Hampton's closest friend, and the Honorable Mr. Thomas Godolphin, an elderly eccentric, who
was rarely to be found outside White's well-appointed
rooms. George Porter, roused by his unpleasant exchange
with Blakely, watched.

Lord Mannering won the first hand; Blakely the next
two; Mr. Godolphin the next; then Blakely again won, this
time three hands in a row. As the viscount raked in his winnings, Mr. Godolphin gave Hampton an ironic look. "It
would seem Blakely's still in favor with the gods or Lady,

or whomever is in charge of luck, for you've even less now and the hour's nearly gone."

Lord Hampton merely inclined his head in casual agreement, but Lord Blakely gave a braying laugh that echoed about the quiet, nearly empty room. "I can always feel when my luck is strong! Jove but I think I could even impress Lady Whitfield favorably tonight and that would be a piece of luck, given her purse."

"I have heard a good deal about Lady Whitfield," Mr. Godolphin observed, adding unnecessarily, as he never went anywhere but to White's, "though of course I have not seen her. Is she worthy of all the comment she has raised?"

Lord Hampton studied his cards, seeming uninterested in the question, and so it was Lord Mannering who said simply, "Lady Whitfield is a diamond."

"Of a certainty, she's as bankable as a diamond," Lord Blakely added, the faintest trace of bitterness edging his voice now.

Godolphin shot him a shrewd glance. "Do you find it hard to stomach, Blakely, that a scrap heap owner, such as Whitfield was in the beginning, should have amassed a fortune to equal a prince's?"

"Whitfield was not even so grand as a scrap heap owner in the beginning." Blakely sneered dismissively. "He began his life as no better than a rag boy, collecting refuse—garbage—off the streets to sell."

"He collected cleverly then," Lord Mannering observed, "for he grew rich."

"He grew rich, because he was a bloodsucking moneylender," Lord Blakely shot back, such loathing in his voice he found himself scrutinized curiously by the others. Twin spots of color rising on his sharp cheeks, he explained stiffly, "I had dealings with Whitfield once. He had a coarse peasant's mien and a bully's temper. His widow paid for her riches, I warrant." He looked to Mr. Godolphin then, some personal grievance clearly pricking him. "I'd add that she's adopted deuce unwarranted airs, Godolphin.

Her father was only some petty baron too pinched to bring her to town for a proper come-out, and when she married the rag picker, she sold herself as plainly as a . . ."

"Careful, Blakely." Lord Hampton's voice sounded so soft and gentle it raised the hairs on George Porter's stout neck. "I would not care to hear my sister's guest slandered."

Blakely tensed, flushing. It was not the sort of mistake he normally made, but it was late, and he had drunk as deeply as anyone, and she had treated him like an underling. Jove, it had galled him, that cool, scarcely civil manner! He wanted to fling in Hampton's face that his sister consorted with no better than a whore. How satisfying that would be. But though Lord Blakely knew himself to be a good shot, he knew Lord Hampton to be deadly.

"I did not intend slander, Hampton," he said, his thin lips scarcely moving. "It is only that I find the advances of those in the lower orders galling. Whitfield was made a baronet for God's sake. And why? Because he gave the crown a pretty penny!"

"It has ever been so. That titles are bought, I mean," Goldolphin observed, but distractedly, for he was studying his cards. Lord Mannering had thrown out a note for one hundred pounds. "I'll see you, Mannering."

Lord Hampton sat out the round, but Lord Blakely, joining in the play, won with three aces after the betting had gone to five hundred pounds. His thin lips curled in something closer to a smirk than a smile as he leaned forward to rake in his winnings. "Jove, but I cannot think when Lady Luck has been half so good to me," he murmured loudly enough for all to hear, then added, casting a sly look at the candles, "This will be our last hand, Hampton. You've deuced little time to regain your favor with Lady Luck."

It would have been impossible to guess from the idle way Hampton sprawled in his chair that he had lost the price of a middling estate that night. He seemed neither to have a care in the world, nor the slightest inkling that

Blakely was needling him. Still, Mr. Porter, slanting him a quick glance, thought Lord Blakely rather foolish to gloat so openly. Lord Hampton's expression appeared to him a little too bland.

"One hand, eh?" The earl threw an idle glance at the candles. "Well, you are right, Blakely. Doubly so, for I agree the Lady is rarely wooed in so short a time."

It was Lord Blakely's deal. He accepted the cards from Lord Mannering with his braying laugh. "I should say never is she wooed in so short a time, Hampton, but I cannot, for fear you might not play."

"You are a wise man, Blakely." The viscount shuffled the cards, and Hampton watched him a moment, his expression growing thoughtful. "But are you a game man, Blakely?"

The viscount looked up, uncertain. "I say, what?"

"Are you game?" Hampton repeated, drawling lazily. "Game to make the night memorable. God knows it has been a bore thus far. Why do we not bet five thousand apiece on this next hand?"

Blakely stared, seeming uncertain whether or not Alex joked. Mr. Godolphin was not so bemused. He chuckled deeply. " 'Tis too rich a wager for my blood, but I'd take pleasure in watching the outcome. What of you, Mannering?"

" 'Tis a rich wager, but I could use some excitement. I'll play."

The earl gave his old friend a sweet smile. "Good for you, Robin. But what of you, Blakely?"

"Well . . . 'tis rich, yes. Yes, it is, but I've had Lady Luck on my side. I should like to pl—"

Before Blakely could finish, Hampton interrupted but offhandedly, as if he said nothing of import. "Of course, I would call for a new deck of cards."

"A new deck?" Lord Blakely bristled instantly. "What are you implying, Hampton?"

"Why, that Lady Luck would dismiss my suit out of

hand if I came to her with old cards. Will you play with a new deck, Blakely, for five thousand pounds, or would you prefer to pronounce the night ended now?"

Blakely licked his lips. If he rose, he would keep vouchers totaling a little over one thousand pounds. If he stayed, he could lose all he'd won and so much more. He alone at the table knew how he had won so consistently the night long, and he alone knew he'd not have the opportunity to mark a fresh deck in so little time. Still . . . he had, in truth, been dealt good cards through no effort of his own. Lady Luck really had been with him. He'd only aided her a little. Surely, Hampton's fortunes could not reverse themselves so completely in just one hand.

"I shall play," he said, his voice revealing none of his calculations.

Lord Hampton called for one of the footmen to bring them a new deck and with a nod of his tawny head indicated the deck should go to Lord Blakely. The viscount dealt briskly, seemingly unaware that the quiet in the room had changed subtly. Where it had been lazy, now it was pregnant. Everyone but Hampton sat a little straighter in their chairs.

Idly, Lord Hampton examined the cards the viscount had dealt him and then called for two new ones. Lord Mannering took three cards, the limit, while Blakely helped himself to two.

Seated to Lord Blakely's right, Lord Mannering would have begun the wagering, but with the wager established, he showed his hand, instead. "A pair of fives," he announced, glumly revealing the less-than-scintillating cards he held.

Only Lord Blakely betrayed emotion, and that no more than an indrawn breath. Looking to him, though, Mr. Porter's heart sank. The viscount's eyes were glittering, as if they could literally see victory.

Still, the viscount could not claim the two notes totaling ten thousand pounds lying so temptingly in the center of the table until Hampton had revealed his hand. Unlike his friend, the earl did not announce what he held. One by one, he laid down his cards. First he showed a ten of spades, then a jack of hearts, then a queen of clubs, then, slowly, a king of clubs. If his last card was an ace of any suit, he would have a flush. A royal flush and four of a kind would defeat him, but only those two combinations. The tension in the room had become such that even the footman carrying out a spittoon from the far side of the room stopped to watch as Lord Hampton tossed down his last card. It was the ace of spades.

The blood drained from Blakely's face. "You . . . you have won." He stared stupidly at the cards, as if he could not tear his gaze away. "I shall have to . . . to give you a note, Hampton."

It was a moment before Lord Hampton answered, long enough for his hesitation to penetrate Blakely's distraction. When he had the viscount's attention, Hampton finally nodded. "Very well, Blakely. I shall take your note, but you understand you will not play again until you pay it."

Lord Blakely lurched to his feet. His cheeks had turned a dull red. "What in the blazes do you mean by that?"

Hampton held his gaze as easily as if they were speaking of the weather. "It is common knowledge, Blakely, that you are run off your legs. No gentleman could in conscience play with a man who owes what you do."

"But . . . but it needn't get out that I owe five thousand pounds."

Lord Blakely cast a desperate glance around the table. None of the gentlemen present were gossips, but Hampton shook his head, unmoved. "You cannot play, Blakely, if you cannot pay. None of us here tonight could, in conscience, allow you to play with our friends and acquaintances, when we know you cannot make good your losses. We are gentlemen."

George Porter's breath caught in his throat. Hampton had not outright called Blakely less than a gentleman. He had not put any particular emphasis on "we" either, and his expression was bland as ever, but the implication of his remark was clear, for if gentlemen did not play when they could not pay, but Blakely, who could not pay, wished to play, then . . . Mr. Porter looked tensely to the viscount, waiting for him to call Hampton out.

"You'll regret that, Hampton. My father may not be the Duke of Shelbourne, but I know the behavior of a gentleman as well as any man here."

Blakely hissed the words through clenched teeth, but George Porter breathed a little easier. Had he meant to risk Hampton's abilities with a pistol to avenge his honor, Blakely would have issued a challenge, not that pale threat.

Lord Mannering rose from his seat, ending the scene. "Take Mitchell and go, Blakely. 'Tis past time." Lifting his hand, he signaled for a footman to come to carry Lord Mitchell from the room.

After Blakely stalked from the room, Mr. Godolphin sighed with almost voluptuous pleasure. "Jove, that was well done, Hampton! Exceedingly well done, indeed. The man could not resist such a wager."

"No," Hampton agreed simply. "Greed makes its own logic."

"Lud, yes!" Godolphin chuckled, his great middle jiggling like jelly. "His greed drove him to accept your wager even after you added the condition of a new deck. Damn but the man turned puce! I knew for certain he'd marked them then."

"Blakely marked the deck?" Mr. Porter looked at the earl in amazement. "But why did you not call him out, Hampton?"

The earl shrugged. "The truth is I cannot say for certain he did cheat as I could not find his mark on the cards, and unfortunately, my finer feelings would not allow me to put a bullet in him on suspicion alone."

Lord Mannering laughed. "I would not have objected. No man's luck is so good as Blakely's was tonight, but still, you took an enormous risk, Alex. He might have left here a nearly wealthy man."

"Perhaps, but with the two of us playing him, he'd only one chance in three of winning. I thought the greater risk was that he'd refuse my wager in the first place, yet in the end he played trout to my bait quite nicely."

"Quite nicely, indeed," Mr. Godolphin agreed. "But do be warned, Hampton. He's a wretch of a man. I should keep an eye out for him, if I were you."

Lord Hampton did not appear terribly concerned. Collecting his cravat, he murmured something about needing his bed more than vigilance. The two younger men followed him out of the club and found outside that a thick fog had rolled in during their play.

"Jove!" Lord Mannering surveyed the soupy murk in disgust. "Well, it is not the weather for a walk, Alex. I know you purposely sent your carriage on, but you'd lose your way at the first cross street. Shall I take you up in my carriage and deposit you safely in Half Moon Street with 'the Famous Duvenay'?"

Lord Hampton shook his head. "No. I shall take advantage of the offer George has not yet made and allow him to deposit me in Grosvenor Square at Fanny's instead. I've Almack's to attend tomorrow, you know, and I wish to be in fighting trim."

"The better to avoid being caught?" Lord Mannering laughed. "Damn, if I do not think I shall go along to Almack's as well just to watch the fun."

"Miserable wretch," Hampton said pleasantly. "But do come, please. I shall put Miss Wycherly on you. You deserve her."

With a negligent wave he was off to George Porter's carriage before Lord Mannering could inquire as to just what was amiss with Miss Wycherly.

"Thank you for allowing me to impose upon you, George," Hampton said when he and Mr. Porter were comfortably settled in the latter's carriage.

"No imposition at all! M'home's in Grosvenor Square, as well you know." Mr. Porter fell silent a moment then suddenly he rounded on the earl, blurting, "I'm that glad you wiped the floor with Blakely, Hampton. Even had not he cheated, I would be glad. He was wrong to slander Lady Whitfield."

The clip-clop of the horses' hooves striking the pavement of the street could plainly be heard in the quiet that followed. Then gently, almost as if he were loath to break the silence, Hampton said, "You have come to hold Lady Whitfield in high regard during this past fortnight she has been in town, have you not, George?"

Mr. Porter nodded, turning to look out the window. "She never makes me feel a fool, you see." It occurred to the earl then that matters might be worse than he had thought, and that he might do George Porter a favor by reminding him of his betrothed, but Mr. Porter spoke first. "I know I cannot have her," he said, still addressing the window. "Couldn't even if I were not betrothed. She is as far above my touch as the stars in the sky, but I'd not see her tarnished by such as Blakely." He turned abruptly and spoke in a rush, as if he did not wish to give himself time to reconsider his words. "Perhaps I haven't any right to ask this, but I would know if you mean to make her your mistress, Hampton. You've no need for another. You have Miss Duvenay."

George Porter, transformed in the twinkling of a pair of violet eyes into St. George. Hampton did not smile at the thought. "You are right, George, and I doubt, anyway, that Lady Whitfield would agree to play the part."

"But she don't want a husband," Mr. Porter returned with some force. "She told me so, and you have a way with women, Hampton. Everyone knows it."

The earl considered the exchanges he had had with Lady Juliana Whitfield, including the last, when she had advised him he need never ask her to dance again. If he did have a way with women in general, he appeared to have lost it with her in particular.

"I am looking for a wife, George," Hampton said, a shade too evenly. "Not a mistress."

Mr. Porter seemed to accept that, for he said nothing until they had nearly reached Grosvenor Square. As the carriage driver slowed to take a turn, he asked in a quiet voice, "Do you think she ever did feel the brunt of Whitfield's bullying temper?"

"How should I know, George? She has not confided in me."

Hearing his testy tone, Hampton took a long breath. George could not know he'd been considering that very question himself, nor of course that he was not well pleased to realize he had been thinking of her. Damn, but he thought about her more than he liked. He might be doing anything—anything, only to realize of a sudden that he'd been thinking of her for a while. He couldn't even be certain why he'd pushed Blakely so far tonight. True, he had suspected the viscount was cheating, but five thousand pounds was an impossible sum. Blakely would never be able to pay it. Nor, more to the point, had Hampton been thinking of exacting quite such a full measure of vengeance. Not until the wretch had all but called her a whore. And why should that have incensed him so? He'd done the same!

Devil take her, but had she suffered at Whitfield's hand? Why would the man beat her? Hampton would have liked to throttle her himself once or twice, but really to strike her? "No." He had not meant to speak aloud, and certainly not so forcefully, but when George turned a questioning look upon him, the earl gave up keeping the thought private. "No," he repeated. "I cannot imagine that a woman with her looks did not have a man as old as Whitfield eating from her hand."

Mr. Porter seemed to nod, yet he said rather quietly, "But there are shadows in her eyes, Hampton. Damn me, if there aren't."

His head propped against the soft plush of the carriage

seat, Lord Hampton closed his eyes. Clearly, he was growing old and sentimental. If he had had any doubt, he knew it now, for he had entertained the same fancy as George Porter—St. George—would-be guardian of Lady Whitfield, she, of the violet eyes that were too beautiful to have the least shadow darkening them. But he had thought of shadows, in a sense at least, that day he'd gone to her room to persuade her to stay in town. As she had stood before the window that dwarfed her so, her shoulders had seemed to droop with the load of some unseen weight.

Devil it! She had to be a witch. Here he was half convinced her husband had beaten her, yet his only information on Whitfield's temperament came from Blakely. Blakely, for God's sake! The man was almost certainly a cheat, and when he'd met Whitfield he had been, by his own admission, trying to weasel out of a debt he owed. Of course, Whitfield had bullied him. None of that had to do with her, however. If she did not want to remarry, it was because she wanted control of the money Whitfield had so successfully collected from Blakely and the others who had been foolish enough to have borrowed from him. There was nothing more to her decision. Nothing, and he would not allow George's romantic fantasies to persuade him otherwise.

Chapter 7

"You look very fine, my lady, if I may say so."

Though Randall looked quite satisfied, she did not exactly smile. Juliana did smile. "You certainly may flatter me, Rand, particularly as you're the one who has labored to produce the results. I am glad you suggested this dress. I had feared it might be too plain, but I see now it is quite nice."

The dress was velvet and cut simply, its lines flowing straight, without flounces or reams of material, from a high waist, caught just beneath her breasts. The straight neckline went off her shoulders, ending in gently puffed sleeves that were edged with a ribbon of satin worked with gold thread. The same ribbon edged her neckline and was repeated in a broader band at the hemline. What the dress lacked in gewgaws, however, it made up and more in color. As a widow, Juliana could wear bolder colors than a young girl, and the mantua maker had taken advantage of that allowance, using a velvet of crimson—not a bright red at all, but a deep one with a trace of purple. The color perfectly set off Juliana's eyes and contrasted strikingly with her cream pale skin and dark sable hair. In keeping with the simplicity of her dress, Juliana wore in the curls Rand had pinned atop her head only a single strand of pearls. At her throat, she wore a double strand and simple pearl drops in her ears.

Randall said, quite correctly, "You need no more, my lady."

"I need you, Rand," Juliana replied, looking the other woman in the eye. "Thank you. I feel well girded now for Almack's."

Neither woman said how unimaginable an evening at Almack's, indeed anywhere in London, had seemed not so long ago. Randall merely allowed herself a small smile. " 'Tis the others tonight who should gird themselves, I think, my lady."

Juliana laughed at that, but Fanny voiced a similar sentiment when Juliana entered the drawing room, where they were accustomed to meet before they went out in the evening.

"Oh, my dear Juliana! The gentlemen haven't a chance this evening!" she cried, clapping her hands together.

Fanny's glance strayed over her friend's shoulder, but Juliana was distracted, looking down at the velvet dress. "I am glad to hear you do not think this color too much. I would not want to embarrass you, Fanny."

"Embarrass me?" Fanny all but gaped, her attention firmly fixed now on Juliana. "You could not embarrass me if you went dressed in bilious puce. Lud, you'd likely bring the color into fashion! And I do wonder if you will tell me how it is, Juliana, that you can have such a slender waist? Oh, I know you will say something about not having had children, but my waist was not so willowy as yours when I was ten!"

Juliana chuckled despite herself. "You are trying to distract me, Fanny. And are doing, as usual, an excellent job of it, but I meant to tell you how grateful I am to you for this evening. I have heard of Almack's for so long, I am in alt to finally see the Assembly Rooms."

"You'll be disappointed." Fanny grinned cheerfully. "They are drab and the refreshments are no better, but I suppose the company is the best. However, you owe me no thanks at all. 'Twas you who charmed Clementina Drummond-Burrell."

"Her husband's cousin presented me to her. She could scarcely look down her nose at me." Juliana sent Fanny into peals of laughter, mimicking Mrs. Drummond-Burrell's haughtiest look, but she continued more soberly after a moment. "And you were the one, Fanny, who made it possible for me to meet Mr. Porter and all the others. I do thank you, you know."

"You have thanked me quite enough, Juliana! I would not have enjoyed myself half so much this past fortnight without you. Your pleasure has made mine. But come now, I shall grow maudlin if I say a word more, and Alex will make mock of me."

Juliana could not control her reaction. She jerked about. And there he was, leaning casually against the wall by the bay window, a glass of claret in his hand. Juliana knew her jaw had tightened, likely visibly, but she could not unclench her teeth. She resented fiercely that he had not made himself known, allowing her to rattle on unawares.

Lord Hampton straightened away from the window, and slowly inclining his head, swept her with a comprehensive glance.

"Fanny is right," was all he said.

Still, somehow he had taken the wind out of her sails. Juliana could not recall for the life of her what Fanny had said, but she could not doubt the gleam lighting his eyes. Her jaw loosened, almost despite her wishes.

"I am glad to know you value your sister's opinions, my lord." Juliana made no effort to fight the half smile that quirked her mouth. She'd made Fanny crow with glee, and that was why she smiled, not because Hampton had smiled, too. Then, because she knew she must, she did say simply, "Thank you."

She turned away at that, though it took a little effort to break free of the earl's gleaming gaze. It helped that Haskins entered with a glass of sherry for her, and that Fanny was rattling on excitedly about how prompt they must be— for Almack's hallowed doors were closed at precisely eleven—and how relieved, not to mention glad, she was that her brother had condescended to accompany them at the last moment, for she had not been certain that if left to himself he would manage to arrive in time.

At that, Lord Hampton arched an eyebrow at his sister. "Having just proclaimed you right, Fanny, I am tempted to take back my words."

"Well, you know you are always late, Alex! I think you were very wise to come with Juliana and me. Very wise and very good, too, for I should not only have been disappointed, but beside myself having to listen to Gussie go on and on about how I cannot manage you. Manage you! La, as if I could, but let us be off so that we may arrive in a timely fashion."

In the carriage, Juliana felt ill at ease. Intensely aware of Hampton across from her, she spent much of her time looking out the window, leaving the conversation to Fanny and her brother. But at Almack's, it was Fanny who half deserted Juliana. They met her good friend Mrs. Adrienne Daviess upon the stairs, and Fanny passed into the Assembly Rooms first, leaving Juliana to enter with Lord Hampton.

When they paused in the doorway, Juliana saw Fanny had been right. The famous rooms were plain, the better, she supposed, to show off the glittering company gathered in them. Everyone appeared turned out in the first stare of fashion. Diamonds gleamed in the candlelight, rubies shone deep red, and the whispering rustle of silk could be heard everywhere.

As could the rustle of whispers. In a brief glance about the room, Juliana saw half a dozen women whispering excitedly behind their fans and glancing to the door. She did not mistake that they were looking at her. Indeed, they were so obvious, she could almost hear them crying gleefully, *Hampton is here! After him, girls!*

Given her less-than-amicable relations with the earl, it was odd that Juliana would feel a measure of sympathy mixed with her undeniable amusement. He would manage the hue and cry after him easily enough, but were she in Hampton's position, she'd not have liked to feel as if she were about to be pounced upon by at least two dozen husband-hunting girls and their mamas.

Quietly Juliana murmured, her eyes on a mother dragging a shy daughter to her feet, "I think Mr. Porter was not wrong: the marriage mart does remind one of a hunt, where, in his words, you, my lord, are the fox."

She had taken him by surprise. But even as his brow lifted fleetingly, his amber eyes lit with a distinct, if lazy gleam in his eyes. "The comparison has occurred to me, Lady Whitfield, but I have tried to console myself with the thought that at least the marriage mart hunters want me alive."

He was charming then, amused by his situation and smiling with her. Charming the way brandy is, a heady taste shot through with a dangerous warmth. To experience it was to want more.

Juliana took alarm and reminded herself that he was a rake, a man who would put himself before any woman, and that he was a rake who on deuced little evidence had concluded the worst sorts of things about her.

Even as she did, though, he was saying quietly, the humor in his eyes fading, "You'd have received your voucher for Almack's without Fanny, you know. Perhaps not so soon, but eventually." Juliana stared, too surprised to respond, yet she could not say he regarded her with approval. On the contrary, he looked more guarded than not as he continued. "The patronesses would not risk losing half the men here to whatever entertainment you attended. Even Robin is mesmerized, and here come both Houghton and Porter now."

Juliana did not see Mr. Porter, but Lord Houghton's thin, lanky figure was unmistakable. She had confided in both men that she was a trifle anxious about her first appearance at Almack's and could not but be grateful that they would come to her side. As to Lord Hampton, if he had complimented her, it seemed he had done so grudgingly and only because he recognized that he had done her an injustice too great to overlook.

They were announced, and Fanny hurried to join them.
Without another word to Lord Hampton, Juliana turned
away to greet Lord Houghton. He wanted her to join the
next set with him, and she did, laughing at some light remark he made. Next, Juliana danced with Lord Soames and
then with Lord Mannering. She knew him to be the
"Robin" to whom Lord Hampton had referred earlier in the
evening, but though he was Lord Hampton's good friend,
Juliana enjoyed Lord Mannering's company. He was not so
clownish as Lord Houghton, but he was amusing. A steady
stream of gentlemen followed, so many, indeed, that after
dancing every dance for over two hours, Juliana took
refuge with Lady Danley and Mrs. Daviess.

Juliana had thought Lady Danley would be discussing
the several young men who had showered Sarah with attention that evening. At that moment Sarah danced with the
Earl of Melford, a splendid marriage prospect, but Lady
Danley scarcely gave the boy a second glance. Her interested gaze was riveted upon her brother. Hampton danced
with a girl the gentlemen termed a "pocket Venus," for she
was small but very pretty and so lushly formed despite her
diminutive stature that she was voluptuous.

"Do you think Alex is taken with her, Adrienne?" Lady
Danley demanded of Fanny's friend.

Now, Mrs. Daviess had her own candidate to present to
Lord Hampton, but her niece Miss Petersham had not arrived in town in time to receive vouchers to Almack's. Accordingly, she frowned slightly. "Miss Liddell has said
nothing to him, Augusta. I cannot see how Lord Hampton
could possibly find her diverting."

Lord Hampton did seem to find something appealing
about the girl, however. Juliana noted that he smiled appealingly enough as they danced. Lady Danley said as much and
Mrs. Daviess replied that he was simply too well mannered
not to look as if he were enjoying himself. Juliana, recalling
the guarded look he had given her at the door, thought
waspishly that manners had less to do with his charming

smile than the girl's low décolletage. Were Miss Liddell obliged by some unforeseen circumstance to bend at the waist, Juliana judged she would be in serious danger of exposing the entirety of her very full bosom to the company's gaze. Perhaps Hampton was anticipating the sight.

Juliana called herself churlish for the thought and was not sorry that Lord Soames came then. She did not dance with him. Fanny had echoed Lord Hampton's remarks on the significance of dancing more than once with the same partner, and though she had added that as a widow Juliana could behave with more latitude than a younger girl, Juliana did not want to do anything to encourage the gentlemen to think she had revised her attitude toward remarriage.

Still, she was happy to talk to Lord Soames. She liked and respected the viscount the more she knew him. He took his responsibilities in the House of Lords seriously, while Juliana had yet to hear Lord Hampton say he had even been near Parliament. Nor was Lord Soames a philanderer who kept a mistress even while he sought a wife. He was too upright. Indeed, the only fault Juliana could find with him was that he was a widower with two young girls. It did not take a powerful intellect to deduce that he was looking for a mother for his children, but he had not made Juliana uncomfortable on that score. When she had warned him that she did not mean to remarry, he had appeared to take her sentiment in stride, saying only and somewhat at a tangent, that losing a husband or wife was a difficult thing.

When Lord Soames seated himself, Juliana pulled her thoughts from Hampton and his delectably small, perfectly lush dance partner to ask the viscount if he had heard from the daughters he'd thought it best to leave behind with their governess in Surrey.

It was a happy choice of topic, as Lord Soames had received presents from his daughters that very day. "Mary sent me a pair of embroidered handkerchiefs. Their governess Miss Morton is particularly proud of Mary's prowess with a needle, and I've a good many beautifully embroidered items, but alas, if Mary sends something to me, then Beatrice, too, must produce something to send up to town to prove what a studious girl she has been."

Juliana began to smile. "And Beatrice is not so good with a needle?"

"She is not," Lord Soames admitted dryly. "She has, in fact, knit me a scarf that I am certain my poorest tenant would not wear, the stitches are so uneven. In her note, she remarked on the odd holes scattered throughout, but she said she thought I would like to have it anyway to keep off the chill, as she recalled that I have a tendency to take cold in the spring."

"Well, you are a most fortunate father then," Juliana remarked. "For though you may not have a perfect scarf, my lord, you do have a loving child. I think you've the best of the bargain."

"How wise you are, Lady Whitfield." Lord Soames gave her a warm smile. "Perhaps someday you will meet Bea, and you can tell me then whether you still think she's any redeeming qualities. I fear she is quite a hoyden."

"Every girl should be a hoyden at ten, I think."

Juliana thought of her own childhood. It had been a good time for her. Her mother had been alive to protect her for the most part from the ill will of her half brother and sister, though, in truth, as they had been, respectively, ten and eight years her elder, she had not seen a great deal of them. And she had been too young to understand the significance of her father's absences, or what those long bouts of drunken gaming and trysts with expensive mistresses would mean for her in the end. She had known nothing of financial carelessness, nor known to fear that the beauty more than a few commended her for even then would in time become a marketable commodity.

After a little, Lord Soames offered to fetch her a glass of lemonade. Happy, sitting quietly in her corner, resting her feet, Juliana accepted. While she waited, she glanced about to see that Mrs. Daviess and Lady Danley had taken themselves off as well. Wryly, Juliana wondered if they had gone to eavesdrop upon whatever conversation Lord Hampton would have with Miss Liddell at the end of their dance, but scanning the glittering, elegant crowd before her, she saw no sign of the pair.

And little wonder. Lord Hampton approached from her other side, taking her by surprise, when he paused before her and flicked an enigmatic look at the empty chair beside her. "I find it difficult to credit that the estimable Soames has abandoned you, Lady Whitfield. He appeared prepared to live in your pocket for the evening."

Juliana could not be delighted with such a greeting, if for no other reason than that, as usual, Hampton seemed to find fault with her. "Lord Soames sat by me for one dance, my lord. I cannot think that is sitting in my pocket. Or may I not converse with a man twice in one evening, as it would seem I ought not to dance twice with the same gentleman?"

Lord Hampton shrugged carelessly, as if the matter did not really interest him. "The more you speak with a gentleman, the more you convey that you enjoy his company. However, I did not come to discuss the inestimable Soames. Mrs. Daviess observed to me that she has never seen us dance together and asked me if there is ill will between us. However our relations might be characterized, I cannot think they are so bad as that. Nor can I want you to be hurt by purely idle speculation, and I assure you, if Adrienne Daviess has noticed that we keep a distance, then a good many others will have as well. Come, and do me the honor of this next dance. You'll not have to suffer my attentions much, only long enough to quiet the gossips."

He extended his hand, evidently expecting her to see reason, but Juliana knew the next dance was to be a waltz. When she did not immediately put her hand in Lord Hampton's, his eyes flashed with his displeasure. "I am well aware that you said you would refuse to dance with me should I ever presume to ask, but this is for your good."

Her eyes could flash as easily as his. "If you had given me a moment, I might have thanked you for looking out for me, my lord, but still refused. I cannot waltz, you see." She had not wanted to admit it and looked as put out as she felt.

He misunderstood. "You've not been approved? Jove! I thought Houghton would have asked for permission to lead you out, or Soames, or Kettering or Robin, even. Well, come along. I'll ask Sally Jersey. She's just there."

Lord Hampton nodded to his right, but Juliana scarcely followed the direction he indicated. He had reached down and taken her arm, and was half lifting her from her seat. Juliana stood. She did not want to look like a balky mule, but when she put her hand on his arm, she dug in her nails hard. Of course she did not hurt him. Her gloves and his coat sleeve were between them, but she communicated her urgency. He looked down at her, a tawny eyebrow lifted in question. Feeling put upon, for she did not care to proclaim her deficiencies so openly, Juliana said quietly but distinctly, "When I said I cannot waltz, I meant that I do not know how. Thank you, my lord, for thinking of me, but here comes Lord Soames now. He asked if he might bring me lemonade, you see, and I was thirsty."

She was babbling, but Lord Hampton was regarding her with as much surprise as she had expected. Not that he gaped at her. Of course he did not, but he did subject her to a penetrating look, as if he could not credit she would not know the dance that had been the rage for the last few years. Perhaps he was trying to decide whether to believe her.

Juliana lifted her chin. She was not about to argue the matter with him. If he did not believe her, so much the better. He would not wonder at her ignorance.

But she had held his gaze too long. He read the truth somehow. "That is a pity," he said slowly. "You would look especially graceful at the waltz."

Chapter 8

Fanny and Juliana were to go shopping in Bond Street the next morning, but the weather proved uncooperative. Looking out the drawing room window, Fanny sighed and shook her head. " 'Tis coming down in sheets, Juliana. I do not think I want new ribbons so much as to get a soaking for them. What of you, my dear? Would you not object to wet skirts and muddied slippers?"

Juliana wrinkled her nose. "I will be perfectly content indoors. Perhaps I can finish this little apron." She motioned to a piece of work in her lap. "I should, as Sophie's birthday is only a few days away."

"She will adore the clothes you have made for her doll, Juliana. Lud, she loves Mary. Mary!" Fanny shook her head. "Can you imagine a more prosaic name for a doll?"

As if their conversation had conjured the child, Sophie skipped into the morning room, preceding Haskins, who carried an arrangement of flowers in each hand. "Aunt Juliana, look! You have more flowers." Juliana had become Aunt Juliana the week before, when she had spent another rainy morning cutting out paper dolls with Sophie and making paper boats with Harry. "There are so many today!" The little girl went on, as proud for Juliana as if she had been her mother. "Jerym is bringing some and Maude, too."

When the maid and footman to whom Sophie referred brought in four floral arrangements apiece, and another

maid came with yet more, Fanny surveyed the results, looking as pleased as Sophie.

"Did I not say you would enjoy a great success, Juliana?
Just look at all of these flowers. Lord Soames has sent you
roses, and these orchids come from . . . Lord Kettering!"
She waved the note that had come with the flowers, having
shamelessly opened it. "Lud, he has spent a fortune on this
tribute to you."

"He grows orchids in his hothouse," Juliana said, cocking her head to study the blooms. "They are a lush flower."

"I like the roses!" Sophie swept up the bouquet and
placed it by the orchids. "They are the color of Aunt Juliana's lips."

"Lud!" Fanny laughed. "What a fancy you have, Sophie.
Let us see if Lord Soames has turned as fanciful." Once
again appropriating Juliana's mail, she read the note nestled
in the middle of the pink roses, then shook her head. "No,
you've not transformed the poor man entirely, Juliana, but
he is captivated. 'A simple tribute to the lady who took Almack's by storm last night. Sincerely, Lord Soames.' Very
nice, really."

"Smell one, Aunt Juliana!" Sophie plucked a rose from
the assortment, but was diverted when she saw the little
apron upon which Juliana had been working. "What is this,
Aunt Juliana? Are you going to have a baby?"

"No, Sophie. This is for a friend."

"Good! I am glad you are not going to have a baby!"

Understandably caught off stride, Juliana raised her
brow. "You are? And why is that, Sophie?"

"Because you play with Harry and me. Aunt Gussie
never does, nor any other lady who has her own children.
You will not have any, will you?"

Sophie looked so hopeful it was the time to smile and
lightly assure her of her dearest wish. But Juliana found the
smile and the lightness difficult to summon. Before coming
to London, she had rarely been in the company of children.
She had thought of them, of course. Had she learned she was

increasing, she'd have been spared Sir Arthur Whitfield's attentions at least for a time. But she had never considered the real joys a child could bring until she met Harry and Sophie.

Having children meant having a husband, however. Juliana sniffed the rose Sophie held half forgotten in her hand. "No, Sophie. I'll not have children. Hmm. The roses do smell sweet."

"Uncle Alex!"

Juliana looked up with a start. She had neither heard him stroll through the door, nor sensed Lord Hampton's presence. She wondered if he had heard her exchange with Sophie, but decided that even if he had, he'd not have been able to divine her regrets.

Sophie distracted him anyway, making a dramatic, sweeping gesture. "Look at all the flowers Aunt Juliana has received, Uncle Alex! She took Almack's by storm last night. And she is not going to have a baby."

Juliana could feel the heat in her cheeks quite plainly, and that was even before Lord Hampton's eyes met hers. "Well," he said, addressing Sophie, but regarding Juliana, "it is good to know that the latter does not necessarily follow the former."

Juliana did not want to laugh, to be companionable, to show amusement at his humor. She wanted to hold herself aloof from the Earl of Hampton. When he had out-and-out disapproved of her, their relations had been relatively simple. She had resented his disapproval, and they had avoided one another as best they could.

But the night before had left her unsettled. There had been the approval in his eyes when he had swept her with that look in the drawing room. She remembered it rather well, better than any other look she'd received the night long. Of course, it was the unexpectedness of receiving approval from him that had caused her to remark it, and had the one look been all, she'd not have felt so on her guard. But it had not been all. There had been that odd moment in the doorway at Almack's. She had teased with him, wanted, she could not but admit, to laugh with him.

And she wanted to laugh now, again, with him, despite the fact that he had not seemed pleased to tell her he thought she'd have been invited to Almack's even without Fanny's backing. And though he had asked her to dance only for appearance's sake. But he looked so handsome now in Fanny's drawing room, tall and well made with the crisp white of his neckcloth setting off the tawny color of his hair and eyes. As if he needed anything to set off his eyes, given that golden glint dancing in them.

She couldn't resist that light. Her mouth curved.

Fanny giggled. "Alex, you are a rogue! Though . . . well, I suppose we ought to have no more of that subject! Feast your eyes, instead, on Juliana's flowers."

"Did Aunt Juliana take Almack's by storm as Lord Soames said?"

The piping query came from Sophie. Juliana took the answer in hand before Lord Hampton could do so. "That is only a figure of speech, Sophie. Lord Soames was being kind."

"Lord Soames is playing a new part," Lord Hampton said to Sophie, taking up where Juliana would clearly have preferred to leave off. "He is playing the gallant, though in this case, he is also being quite accurate. Your au . . . ah, Lady Whitfield was, indeed, the toast of the evening."

Juliana felt rather as if her perceptions were being turned end over end. Again. Hampton's eyes gleamed more than ever with laughter, though she did not know whether he laughed at nearly referring to her as an aunt, or whether he teased her about being the toast at Almack's.

She knew there was nothing light about her own expression. Indeed, she suspected she looked mulish, but Fanny never gave her the opportunity to say she had scarcely been anything so grand as a toast.

"You were the toast of the evening, Juliana! You may not look impatient when we only tell the truth. But, Alex, you danced with a girl who received almost as much attention as Juliana. What did you think of Miss Liddell?"

Juliana occupied herself with returning her work to her sewing basket. It was a topic for a brother and sister to discuss alone. She did not want to hear what he thought of the pocket Venus.

"Miss Liddell is the sort to cling," he said. From the corner of her eye Juliana saw him idly trail a long finger along the edge of a large, showy purple orchid. "Are these from Kettering?"

She pretended she had not heard, though from the sound of his voice she thought he had addressed her. Fanny answered for her, anyway.

"Yes. Juliana says Kettering grows them in a hothouse. Are they not beautiful?"

"In the wild, perhaps." Juliana could almost see him shrug. "In a London drawing room, they seem a trifle much."

"Oh, Alex!" Fanny wailed. Juliana had to bite back a smile, the wail was so despairing. But then she, too, had thought the orchids overmuch. "You are the most difficult man to please. Everyone recognizes that orchids are beautiful, just as everyone found Miss Liddell delightful. A wife should cling at least a little."

"Yours perhaps, Fanny," Lord Hampton drawled wryly, "but not mine."

"But Mama cannot have a wife!"

Once again, despite herself, Juliana smiled. Sophie sounded so shocked.

Lord Hampton chuckled. "So she cannot, little cabbage. Ah, but it would seem Lady Whitfield can have more flowers."

Giving up any pretense of not listening, Juliana looked up. Haskins had come again, this time with a bouquet of camellias. Against the dark green leaves, the flowers were a velvety white.

"They are beautiful!" Sophie exclaimed.

"I have always adored camellias," her mother agreed. "They smell so sweet and look as soft as velvet. Who are they from, Juliana?"

Sophie had buried her nose in the flowers the moment Haskins set them on the table, and it took Juliana a moment to extract the accompanying note. She did not look at Hampton, but she sensed his attention and wished he were not there, though she could not have said quite why. With or without him, she'd have been equally embarrassed about the tributes. She did not want to be neglected, but she did not want to be treated like a girl making her come-out, either. She was not going to marry anyone ever again, no matter how many flowers a man sent, nor if he said in a note accompanying his camellias that they reminded him of her satiny soft skin.

"Lord Houghton," Juliana said to Fanny, only just resisting an impulse to crush the note. She enjoyed Lord Houghton very much as a friend, but she did not want him thinking about the texture of her skin.

"Houghton!" Fanny was crying, all delighted. "I did not know he had it in him to be so thoughtful."

Somehow Juliana's eyes met Lord Hampton's. The teasing glint was gone from his. Indeed, she could read little in his expression, though she could say without doubt that there was nothing sympathetic in his eyes. Of course there was not, she thought, looking away from him. He likely believed she said she did not want to marry simply to create interest in herself.

"Will you go with Lord Houghton to Sally Jersey's dinner party now?" Fanny asked.

"No." Juliana regretted her snappish tone the moment she spoke, and added more calmly, "I cannot, actually. That is the night Mrs. Daviess has invited us to Vauxhall."

"Why, you are right, Juliana. What a pity. But, Alex, do you mean to be as constant as Juliana? You did tell Adrienne last night that you would go to Vauxhall."

Lord Hampton had been inspecting the camellias with

Sophie. At the question he straightened and gave his sister one of what Juliana had come to think of as his "narrowed" looks.

"Did you know, Fanny, that Mrs. Daviess happens to have a niece who will be in attendance that night?" The wave of pink that rose in Fanny's cheeks spoke for her. Lord Hampton's expression hardened considerably. "I had quite forgotten she had a niece until Robin mentioned the chit. Lud, but I feel like a medieval Italian who must have a taster for all his food, only in my case, I must have Robin to point out the hidden dangers in every invitation."

"You do mean to go, though?" Fanny begged. "Adrienne would be disconsolate if you did not. And you needn't give the child a second glance, if you do not wish. Stephen— that is Adrienne's husband, Juliana—will be there and . . ."

"Yes, I shall go, Fanny, because I did promise, but henceforth, I ask that you at least wiggle an eyebrow if there is a chit involved in an invitation."

"Do you mean you want me to wink at you, Alex?" Having gotten her way, Fanny could laugh gaily, but she was not to get an answer, if she had expected one.

Harry came pelting through the door, shrieking excitedly. "Everything is ready, Uncle Alex!"

"What is ready?" Fanny wanted to know, and frowning at her son, added, "And you must not run everywhere, Harry. Gentlemen walk, stroll, amble, or otherwise carry themselves from place to place in a dignified manner."

"Yes, Mama. May we go now, Uncle Alex? May we?"

If Harry had even heard his mother, he obviously had not taken her words to heart. He was clearly prepared to dash out of the room at the same pace he'd entered. Lord Hampton took his hand. "We may go, Harry, when we have invited the ladies. The surprise is for one of them, after all. Sophie, is your birthday approaching?"

With the one question he made Sophie as excited as her brother. Squealing she raced to take her uncle's other hand, and soon enough they all found themselves in the music room. A large box stood in the middle of the room and odd sounds could be heard issuing from it.

Fanny looked wary at first, but she proved no better able to withstand the appeal of the spaniel puppy Sophie discovered within the box than her daughter was. Indeed, it was Fanny who held the puppy in her lap while Sophie went to fling herself at her uncle.

"As she is house-trained already, you may keep her in your room, Sophie, but Eakins here will help you to train the pup."

Eakins was the groom who had stayed with the box. He nodded, eyes twinkling, at Sophie, and when Harry suggested that they begin training right then, Eakins was agreeable.

There had been so much noise that when the children, the puppy, and the groom departed, the music room seemed in Fanny's words "silent as a tomb."

"I believe we should remedy that," Lord Hampton drawled unexpectedly. "I arranged to present Sophie her puppy here, because I had a notion as to how we might profitably spend this rainy morning."

Juliana looked at him in as much surprise and curiosity as Fanny, though she did not really think she would be included in his plans.

"Why whatever shall we do, Alex?" Fanny asked.

"Why," he replied, "we shall teach Lady Whitfield the waltz."

"The waltz?" Fanny echoed in bemusement. "You do not know how to waltz, Juliana?"

"No," Juliana admitted slowly. "I do not, but I hardly think anyone need waste time teaching me." She looked, reluctantly, to Lord Hampton. His eyes were warm again. And soft somehow. "That is . . ." she stumbled clumsily, "that is you are very kind to suggest it, my lord, but . . ."

"But," he interrupted, his mouth lifting in the lopsided smile that had affected her that first time she'd met him, "you haven't an excuse that will persuade either Fanny or me." When Juliana's brow lifted, his smile only deepened. "Overbearing, am I?"

"I was thinking arrogant, actually," she replied, fighting the urge to grin like a fool, "but overbearing will do. I do not wish to take up your time . . ."

This time it was Fanny who took charge. "Nonsense, Juliana! We've nothing to do this rainy morning but teach you the waltz. Everyone waltzes but the dowagers! You do not want to be thought a dowager, do you? Honestly, I cannot understand why Sir Arthur would wish you to sit out every waltz. I know that a great many people considered it improper, but Lud, that was years ago. Now," Fanny went on without a pause, "these are the steps."

Lifting her hem slightly so that Juliana could see her feet, Fanny demonstrated the basic steps of the waltz. Juliana watched, though it took her a moment to concentrate. Had the subject not been so painful, she'd have laughed at the breezy way Fanny assumed Sir Arthur had even allowed her to attend a ball.

"Now then, do them with me." Fanny took Juliana's hand, and side by side they went slowly through the box pattern of the dance. "Again," Fanny said some half-dozen times. Then, "Now I shall play while you practice with Alex. You will do very well, only remember to lead with the outside foot."

There was no way in the world that Juliana could have objected. She'd have seemed a missish fool. Lord Hampton stepped forward, and taking her right hand, placed his on her waist.

She had not, she realized, fully appreciated how tall he was, nor how well made until she settled her fingers upon his shoulder. He was nothing like Sir Arthur, and though no man had held her so closely since Whitfield's death, she scarcely thought of her husband. Certainly, she was not afraid.

No, she was not afraid, though she was a little overwhelmed with sensation. At the first note Fanny played, Juliana looked up at the earl. She could not read much in his expression except that he did not appear overwhelmed by their closeness. But of course he was not, she thought, steadying. He was merely teaching her a dance.

"I shall press your back with my hand, when I mean to lead you in a turn, but for the time being, we shall make the simple box Fanny taught you. Are you ready?"

When Juliana nodded, Hampton led her to the right. "One, two, three, and to your right again. And back. Left. Forward. And right. Good, now you've done it studying your feet, try looking up."

Juliana made a rueful face, looking up. "I feel clumsy as an ox."

After half a moment, he said, "Oxen are rarely clumsy, actually, and you were made for the waltz." Then, before she could consider what he might have meant, Hampton pressed her back as he'd said he would. "Now we are going to turn."

She tried to follow, but misstepped. "Lud, I stepped on your foot, my lord!"

"So you did, but I wore my oldest boots. Your hobnail slippers won't damage anything."

She laughed, as he had meant her to do. "My slippers may not permanently damage anything, but even they will put your man to the trouble of polishing your boots again."

"Hobbes would polish them if there were not even the suspicion of a scuff. He thrives on the activity, and you, meantime, have been too distracted to make one misstep."

Of course Juliana stumbled then, when he made her self-conscious again, but she shrugged off the mistake with a chuckle and forced herself to concentrate again. One, two, three. It was not so difficult. She only had to remember about the outside foot. Half absently, she thought again about the feel of the earl's shoulder beneath her hand. It was not so broad as a blacksmith's, of course. He was built more like one of the Greek statues of Lord Elgin's that she'd seen. Athletic but lean. He smelled good, too. The very stray thought threw Juliana off. She stumbled again, but Hampton danced on.

Following his lead, Juliana decided to be grateful for her last stumble. Her thoughts had gotten away from her. Hampton was a rake. Like her father had been. And by definition, rakes cared little for anyone but themselves. Certainly her father had not. He had made her mother cry, and he had . . . but Juliana did not want to think about what her father had done to her. He was dead now, and her marriage behind her.

One, two, three. Hampton led her effortlessly. She admitted he could dance the waltz. He seemed able to carry her. Or perhaps it was the music that made her feel so light, as if she were floating. One, two, three.

The music ended. Just in time. She was only almost disappointed.

Fanny clapped. "Bravo, Juliana! You waltzed as if you have waltzed all your life."

Juliana felt breathless, though she had not realized she was exerting herself so much. Her cheeks were warm, too. She smiled at Fanny. "How could I not do well with you to play for me, and Lord Hampton to lead me? Thank you both."

She ended by looking at Lord Hampton. He was not smiling. In fact, he looked a little grim. But he bowed as he ought. "The pleasure was mine, I assure you, Lady Whitfield." His voice was low, but she thought his tone as perfunctory as his words. Evidently he had put himself out only because he did not want Fanny's guest to seem backward. "You'll not have to sit out a waltz again," he added, seeming to confirm her thoughts. She did not know why she was disappointed. It was kind of him to care at all.

"No," she said. "Well, thank you again, Lord Hampton. Fanny."

Chapter 9

The pleasure gardens at Vauxhall were quite as charming as Fanny had promised. Strings of gay lanterns illuminated winding, elaborately planted walks that led slowly to an elegant rotunda. There, the patrons of the gardens enjoyed the shaved ham and arrack punch for which Vauxhall was famous, and after dinner danced on the floor of the rotunda to music provided by a small orchestra.

Juliana enjoyed the stroll her party took through the gardens before dinner, and she enjoyed the dinner itself, as well. It was only that she'd have enjoyed herself more had she not been so acutely aware of Lord Hampton. No other man affected her in quite the way he did. She did not always know where Lord Mannering was as the party made its way down one of the broader avenues, tall, stately trees arching over them. She did not keep an eye out for Mr. Porter or Mr. Daviess. But then none of those gentlemen disapproved of her, or seemed to waver, tantalizingly, in that disapproval.

Nor did it help that Hampton looked as well as he did. Juliana did not like to admit that she was influenced by mere looks, but she cared even less to lie to herself. That night, as he usually did in the evening, the earl wore black. Juliana could recall easily enough how he had looked in evening dress by morning's light that first time they had met at Fanny's door, the black setting off his tawny brown hair and the amber eyes that were such a close match. By candlelight, with the starched white of his cravat playing against his black coat as well, he looked not only more striking than any other man present, but more striking than any man had a right to be. It was impossible not to be aware of him.

And there was more still that made him attractive that evening. Lord Hampton had gone to school with Mr. Daviess, Lord Mannering, and Mr. Porter, and the four former schoolmates kept the party entertained with absurdly funny stories of their school days. As the dinner party was small and festive, everyone spoke out as they wished, addressing the table as a whole. Juliana was seated on the same side as Hampton, but she could see him well enough when he leaned forward, and so she was able to catch glimpses of him laughing, his expression open and warm and so compelling that everyone laughed with him.

Mrs. Daviess' niece, Miss Petersham, to whose presence Hampton had so objected to Fanny, sat beside the earl. Juliana commended him for sparing the girl any sign of his annoyance. It was not Miss Petersham's fault that Mrs. Daviess had given Hampton to believe the party would include only adults well off the marriage mart, and he was right to display the same charm and courtesy toward her that he did the other members of the party. The girl flowered as a result. Demure by nature as well as training and awed by the fashionable company around her, Miss Petersham had kept her very nice gray eyes downcast for much of the early part of the dinner. But with Lord Hampton smiling upon her, charming her between bouts of schoolboy reminisces, she found the courage to lift her head and in time even to meet the earl's golden brown eyes. She blushed, but happily, and from the stars dancing in her eyes it was obvious that she was half in love with the man on her right by the time the flaming cherries were served up for desert.

At Miss Petersham's age of nineteen, Juliana had been married already for two years. Now she felt a lifetime older than the fresh, young, starstruck girl, and so she was not sorry when the dancing began and she need not watch Miss Petersham gaze raptly up at Hampton any longer.

Dancing presented its own problems, however. Juliana knew she must dance with Lord Hampton, given that Mrs. Daviess had been the one to notice that they kept a distance from one another at entertainments. She told herself that she would manage calmly enough when the time came. Perhaps there had been a memorably dreamy quality to their waltz; perhaps she had been unusually aware of him even. But of course, she would have become aware of his scent! They had been so close together how could she have failed to notice the warmth of his body or the subtle hint of bay rum? And besides, she need not dance the waltz with him. She had already, displaying the kind of manipulative ability for which Hampton had once scorned her, prompted Mr. Porter to ask her to reserve that dance for him.

When the time came to waltz, Juliana was pleased with how well she remembered her lesson. Mr. Porter was astonished.

"Jove, you must have been funnin' me when you said you'd be dancing the waltz for the first time this evening, Lady Whitfield! You were made for it, you know. You're graceful as a reed, and you dance as if you've been waltzin' all your life."

"Thank you, Mr. Porter. I find I enjoy the dance."

Juliana could not but wonder if, when Hampton had said she was made for the waltz, he had meant she was graceful. Perhaps it was something all gentlemen said. It did not matter much, of course. She was not likely to dance the waltz with him again. He had asked her for the waltz that night, mouthing some nonsense about claiming the rights of an instructor, but he had settled readily enough on a quadrille when she had told him Mr. Porter had claimed the waltz. Of course, Hampton had only wanted to demonstrate to Mrs. Daviess and the others that they were on equable terms. Fanny and Lord Mannering had been in their set,

along with Mrs. Daviess and her husband. Juliana had paid
them as much attention as she had Hampton, and the
quadrille had passed quickly. Now, much later, she danced
the waltz with Mr. Porter. It did not seem quite the same
dance as the one she had danced with Lord Hampton in
Fanny's music room. She did not float once. Poor Mr.
Porter plodded, really, but he was a good soul and he was
trying to entertain her while they danced. Juliana upbraided
herself for allowing her thoughts to wander away from her
partner.

". . . with the result that the first time I drove a gig, I
overturned it," he was saying, looking chagrined.

"And what did you do, when you turned over, Mr.
Porter? I take it you did not sustain injury?"

"No, nor the horse either, and so I was quite free to curse
the beast who had run away with me at length and at great
volume, too, I can assure you."

Juliana chuckled. Perhaps Mr. Porter was a trifle slow,
but he was not without humor. "And did cursing help?"

"It did not right the gig, no," he admitted, a bit of a twinkle in his eyes, "but I felt a great deal better afterward. The
worst of it was that my cousin Larchmont was there. He is
older, don't you know?"

"Ah, and Larchmont was arrogant with age?"

Mr. Porter awarded Juliana a most approving look. "That
was it exactly. I have never heard anyone put it better, Lady
Whitfield. I'd the last laugh, though, for I went off to
school and met Hampton. He had me down to Chatsworth
one holiday and taught me to drive. You ought to have seen
the look on Larchmont's face the next time we raced. I
won, by Jove!"

Juliana cried bravo, pleasing Mr. Porter enormously. He
remarked how indebted he was to Hampton for the victory
over his arrogant cousin, and she could not but agree,
adding to herself at least, that it surprised her that the earl,
as a boy, should have befriended someone so much less fa-

vored by the gods than he. She could not but admire him
for it.

"I say . . ."

Looking up, Juliana saw Mr. Porter frown. "Is something
amiss, Mr. Porter?"

He shrugged rather bemusedly. "I vow my eyes must be
playin' tricks on me, but I could swear I saw Lady Charles
leave the rotunda with Lord Blakely."

Juliana turned her head in the direction he was looking,
but she could not see over the throng of people on the
dance floor. "You must have confused Lady Charles with
another, Mr. Porter, for in confidence I shall tell you that
she has said she does not care for Lord Blakely."

"Few do who've any sense to claim," Mr. Porter responded with more certainty than was his want. "He's a
thorough rotter. Why only a few nights ago I was present at
White's when he . . . well, I suppose I'm not to tell you
what he did. Hampton did not see enough to accuse him
outright, but I can and will say he served Blakely his comeuppance. He brought him down hard, but though Hampton
was right to do it, he made an enemy of Blakely. And
Blakely can be deuced ugly when angered. I wouldn't want
to see him around Lady Charles."

Her curiosity piqued, Juliana speculated upon what
might have happened. It seemed likely the unpleasantness
had involved cards, but she was wondering if it might not
have been a disagreement over a woman when Mr. Porter
turned her in the dance and by sheer chance, the crowd
parted so that she seemed to look down a long row. At the
end of it a couple danced, the man dressed in the dark-blue-
and-silver-braided uniform of the Thirteenth Light Dragoons, the woman dressed in something gaudy. Juliana
scarcely noticed the woman. Her gaze fixed upon the man.
As if he felt the weight of her stare, the lieutenant turned,
and Juliana found herself staring into a little loved, but very
familiar face.

In the next instant, couples danced between them again,

cutting off her view, yet she had no doubt that her half brother had recognized her. He was Hugh Delany, Lord Blackmore now that her father had died. She had thought Hugh's regiment safe away in India. But no, he was here at Vauxhall. The bottom of her stomach seemed to fall away. He had not merely gaped in recognition. His face had darkened with rage.

Juliana knew nothing but that she must escape the dance floor. Right then. Not for anything, not for all the gold in Sir Arthur's coffers, not even for the sake of her soul, would she have Hugh accost her before the others, and though she did refer to everyone in the Daviess' dinner party, the one face that came to her mind was Lord Hampton's.

No. She literally shuddered at the thought. Mr. Porter felt the response, and looked down at her, his eyes widening when he saw how pale she was. "Lady Whitfield?"

"I . . . I am not feeling quite the thing of a sudden, Mr. Porter." She made no attempt to smile. She felt ill, and he saw it.

"Come then," he said without further ado and to Juliana's everlasting gratitude. "We shall go and sit down." He led her to their box. Juliana saw no one. All her senses were attuned to the far side of the floor. She heard no roar of pursuit, but he would come. She knew better than to doubt it.

At the door of the box, Juliana found the presence of mind to send Mr. Porter away. She needed some cool water, she told him, and after she had assured him she could seat herself, he hurried away in pursuit of it. She had not acted a moment too soon. Mr. Porter had only just disappeared in search of a waiter, when Hugh came. Before her half brother could say a word, Juliana exited the box. A waiter hurried up. Mercifully Mr. Porter had missed him. Juliana bid the man tell Mr. Porter that she had met an acquaintance and gone into the gardens with him for some air. Then, jerking her head toward the entrance of the rotunda just behind them, she turned about and left her half brother to follow her into the night.

He walked a step behind her, his bulky shadow looming over her, large and menacing. For a half second, Juliana wavered. She could throw herself upon Lord Hampton; appeal to him for support against Hugh. She would have to explain a good deal. He thought her family more or less like the families of the others in his set. Miss Petersham would have been glad to see her brother, or half brother as the case was, but then Miss Petersham had never been beaten senseless by her brother; never kicked in the ribs like a dog.

No. Juliana could not bear for anyone to know the kind of family from which she came. She'd only her pride left after all that had been done to her. She would not lose even that now. She kept walking, determined to deal with Hugh herself, balling her hand into a fist in part to combat fear.

In a little, they came to a dark alcove in the hedge. Juliana took one step inside, then turned. As she had hoped, Hugh's momentum carried him by her. To be certain he would not corner her in the alcove, she stepped back so she stood in the opening of the hedge. If Hugh threatened her, she could run, and for a heartbeat she spared another thought as to how different she was from Miss Petersham and Fanny and the rest. But then, they had never felt the lash of a man's hand. Not like she had. Juliana bit her cheek lest she give way to fear. She had to face Hugh. For her own sake, she knew she had to face him.

"You look that pale, my Lady Whitfield." Hugh's florid, heavy face twisted in an ugly sneer as he looked her up and down, his beefy hands fisted on his hips. "Didn't you expect to see me in London when you came to kick up your heels with your rarefied friends? Thought I was safely stowed away in India, perhaps? Ha! I wouldn't give anything for the look on your face tonight."

Juliana would not have thought it, but she had forgotten just how repellent Hugh Delany could be. She'd remembered only his fondness for using his fists on those weaker than him, and forgotten details, like his coarse, belligerent face and his grating voice. Only with an effort could she make herself stay, and she kept her fist balled in the folds of her skirts.

"By contrast, you look very well Hugh, in your fine uniform," she said. "You must feel quite the thing in it. You ought to, of course, given what you did to me to get it."

Juliana's voice trembled with such bitterness, she had to pause for breath, and Hugh pounced with a roar. "Damn you to blazes, you little witch! I'll not listen to you whine! Everything always had to be the best for you. Your mother would not stand for less. And why? Because she was gentry, while Father found my mother when he was drunk in a tavern! Well, having a barmaid for a mother does not make me less than you. I deserve what's coming to me! The old goat died, leaving you rich as a princess, and what do you do? You cut my allowance in half! I'll not stand for it, do you hear me?"

"I hear you very well, Hugh. But I am no longer a child you can bully. I told you in my letter that I am giving the money to a home for foundling children. I hope it will accomplish some good there. As for you, you've enough to live well. I shall continue to give you half of the allowance Sir Arthur sent you, because there is some relation between us, but no more than that. I'll not allow you to profit out of all proportion because you beat me into submission. I wear the scars still."

"I took care not to mark you! And you deserved a beating, you whining witch. You defied your own father."

What use to say she wore the scars on her soul? Hugh likely did not believe in souls. He had followed her to her mother's sister's house where she had fled that wretched night her father had announced he'd betrothed her to a man of sixty. Hugh had overpowered the one doddering retainer at her aunt's door, and finding Juliana trapped in the library he'd beaten her so, he'd knocked her to the ground. For good measure, he'd kicked her then, when she lay defense-less on the floor. In her worst dreams, she relived the feel of the toe of his boot on her ribs. He was her elder brother, supposed to protect her, perhaps even from the father who had sold her for his women and his gaming and his ruinous rum. But Hugh had taken care only to avoid scarring her. Sir Arthur might have rejected her, and so her face had healed. But not her soul.

" 'Twas I who learned that filthy rich Whitfield was lookin' for a wife!" Hugh angrily thumped himself upon his thick chest. " 'Twas I who made you rich so that you could come to town and hobnob with the *ton*. 'Twas I, and by God, I'll not stand by and let you keep a farthing of what is mine by rights."

"Rights? Dear God, but you are a warped creature, Hugh Delany! You and father sold me to a man who kept me prisoner for six years, and you knew he would. You knew he was mad. You knew he killed off his second wife. Ann told me. Why do you think I ran that night?"

"That bitch of a sister!" Hugh swore so violently Juliana shrank back a step, though his anger was not directed at her then. "She was always jealous of you, jealous of your looks, of your blood, of that air you have, even! Ha, and then she was sick with jealousy when she realized the money you would have. She wanted to put you in the way of a beating, and she did; but she was quick enough to use the money Whitfield sent upon your marriage. Squire Aps-ley's wife she is now and proud of it, even if she is stuck up there in Yorkshire, looking after a harridan of a mother-in-law. Did you not think to cut her allowance? Well, blast it all, I don't care about Ann! Never did. It's my money I want. You'll give me back the full allowance Whitfield promised me."

Hugh half lunged, raising his fist. Juliana knew the feel of that fist, knew the pain it could inflict. The moment of truth had come. "Do it, Hugh," she said in a low voice that betrayed only a suspicion of a quaver, "and you'll not receive even a ha'penny in allowance."

He froze, suddenly uncertain. "You cannot do that!" he roared, and even in the dark of the alcove, Juliana could see how red he went.

"Whitfield made no mention of you in his will, Hugh," she said, a trifle quickly perhaps but nonetheless clearly. "Nor are you mentioned in the marriage settlements, not even as Father's heir. What you receive from me now need only be as much as I am moved to give you. That not-at-all-ungenerous sum you will continue to receive as you have the last two quarters so long as you never, ever approach me again. I am done with you, Hugh, and your bullying. Never come near me, not where I am staying in town, nor at Westerleigh, though I cannot think you would trouble yourself to travel all that way to Lancashire, when you did not once in the six years I was wed."

"Whitfield would not allow me to come!"

"No," Juliana said bitterly, "I suppose he'd no wish for you to see what you had wrought for me. But I know as well that you never asked. There is no mention of me in your letters to him, only appeals for more money. You spend quite freely, Hugh, but you will receive from me only what I have said, and nothing at all, if you ask for more. Now, as this will be our last meeting, I shall bid you farewell."

But Hugh knew only that she was physically weaker than he. "Now, see here, you witch!" He caught her arm as she turned to leave. Juliana tried to pull free, but he tightened his grip punishingly. "I'll not . . ."

"Lady Whitfield, is that you?"

Juliana froze. It was Lord Hampton. Dear God. He would find her brawling with her half brother in a public place. She could not bear even the thought, but she must answer, for he was coming.

"Yes, Lord Hampton," Juliana called out, amazed to hear that her voice sounded normal, or nearly.

She did not expect what happened next. Hugh released her arm, pushing her in frustration, but releasing her nonetheless. Juliana did not stop to question why. Later she would wonder if the Earl of Hampton was so well known that Hugh recognized his name and feared it. Just then all she wanted to do was escape. Still, she paused long enough to repeat her warning. "Never approach me again, Hugh. Never, or the consequences will be as I have stated."

That was all. She did not again wish him farewell. She spun around and hurried out of the shadowy recess onto the gravel path. Hampton was approaching, looking beyond her to the alcove. Juliana prayed Hugh would keep to the shadows. He sickened her, and she neither wanted to be associated with him, nor ever to think of him again.

She was trembling, or shivering, Juliana knew not which, knew only that she must compose herself for here was Hampton. He was staring hard at her. She could not guess what he saw. Lanterns lit the broad walk, but their light was scattered. Then she felt him shift his weight, as if he meant to pass her and enter the alcove. Juliana caught his arm, digging her fingers in, though she knew not that she did it.

"Please. I should like to return to the rotunda."

Juliana bit her lip. Her voice sounded frantic. Little wonder. She realized her heart was beating as if she had run for miles. None of that mattered though, only the thought that she must get herself and the earl away from Hugh. She could not be certain he would not come bellowing out of the alcove, that even still he might contrive some punishment. At the thought she began walking, and with her fingers tightly clasping Lord Hampton's arm he had little choice but to go with her.

In comparison to Hugh, Hampton seemed very tall and cleanly built, an elegant thoroughbred to Hugh's bull. But Juliana could feel the muscles in the arm beneath her fingers. He was strong. Lean but strong. And she had never felt smaller. Perhaps she had faced Hugh. Perhaps she had even dealt with him, but she feared him, still. She thought she always would, and quite suddenly Juliana wanted nothing in the world so much as to melt into Hampton's strong arms. She wanted him to hold her safe against his chest. Dear God, but it seemed to her that she had been alone forever.

"George feared some harm had been done to you." His voice was taut. He stopped abruptly, forcing Juliana to halt. They were closer to the rotunda where lanterns abounded. She could see his jaw looked hard as a rock and his pleasing mouth was drawn in a thin, threatening line. He was not her savior. How could she have thought so? She felt weary as death, suddenly. "George said you disappeared from the box after you complained of feeling ill, and yet I find you trysting in a dark alcove."

"I . . . I was not feeling well." It was so far from being a lie, Juliana just caught back a shaky, half-hysterical laugh, swallowing hard. "The, ah, box felt confining, you see, and I thought a breath of fresh air might help me. Then, I encountered . . . an acquaintance. We had a matter to discuss. I . . . I told the fellow at our box. I did not know I was gone so long. I am sorry to have worried Mr. Porter."

"Devil it!" Hampton swore, growling. "Have you sympathy only for George? What of Fanny and the rest? No one knew what to think. You have cast a blight over their evening for a moment's tryst!"

"No!" the denial conveyed more pleading than conviction. "I did not mean to worry anyone. I . . ."

She did not know what to say, could not seem to think with Hampton looking at her that way. He might as well have found her with her skirts around her waist, and she did not want him to think that ill of her. She wanted to sag against him, to beg for refuge. Instantly Juliana released her hold on his arm and took a step back. She felt as if she did not know herself, as if she might do something she would never consider but for the horrid confrontation with Hugh and the shadowy night.

"Who was this acquaintance?"

He bit out the question. As if he had the right to bark at her and to think the worst. Her chin went up. "I have said all I wish to say," she told him, gaining some strength from the feeling of being wronged. "I met an acquaintance and went with him for some air, and now I wish to go to the others."

Lord Hampton ignored her, making no move, only holding her gaze with his penetrating one. He seemed intent on reading her mind. She felt a bubble of panic. He was so tall and strong and assured . . . and she, she was spent. She could not seem to get it out of her mind that she wanted his touch.

"Lady Whitfield! Hampton!"

Juliana did sag then. She was saved from Hampton, saved from her own reckless, hysterical impulses. It was Mr. Porter and Fanny. Juliana moved quickly away and tried for the life of her to pin a smile on her face.

Chapter 10

"Good morning, Rand." Juliana spoke over her shoulder, avoiding Randall's gaze. "I did not feel up to riding this morning, and I would like you to bring a breakfast tray here, please. I have a headache this morning."

She had missed her ride a few mornings, when she and Fanny had returned very late from some entertainment the night before, but she had not taken a breakfast tray in her room before, and she had not suffered from a headache since Sir Arthur's death.

Juliana could feel Rand's eyes upon her. They were shrewd eyes, all in all, and would not have missed the dark circles Juliana sported. She had not been affected by those since Sir Arthur's death, either. Resigned, she turned, meeting Randall's gaze this time. "Perhaps you could bring me some of your headache powders with my chocolate, though I do not want you to say I feel ill, only tired. I do not wish to concern Lady Charles."

"Of course, my lady." There was the slightest of pauses, as if Randall were considering whether she might inquire into what was amiss. Juliana gave her no encouragement. Even had the woman not been a servant, Juliana would never have divulged that she had tossed in her sleep, dreaming of her brother's boot savaging her ribs. Randall read Juliana's silence correctly. "Lady Charles is not feeling well this morning, either, my lady," she said. "Her maid advised me to say her ladyship wishes you will go on to Bond Street without her."

Juliana shook her head slightly. "Not today, Rand. Please inform Haskins I'll not need the carriage either."

When Randall left to fetch her tray, Juliana sank down in a chair to stare out the window at a sky heavy with clouds. She felt heavy as the day, and not only because she'd dreamed of Hugh's beating. When she'd run from him in her dreams, she had run straight into Lord Hampton's arms. Wide awake, her choice of refuge seemed almost a sign of derangement. Dear Lord, but she could even now hear him saying, "I find you trysting in a dark alcove," with as much disgust as if he had found her with her skirts riding up her legs. Or when he had asked, "Who was this acquaintance?" his tone . . . she bit her lip. He thought the worst, whatever that was.

Had Fate decreed that men would doubt her, suspect her of the worst? Sir Arthur had said she had witch's eyes. She shuddered, thinking of the other things her husband had said to her, the accusations so ugly and so horrid and the hand he had inevitably taken to her afterward.

Abruptly, Juliana heaved herself out of the chair. She must compose herself. Men were not all alike. They did not all take one look at her and assume vile things. Mr. Porter had not assumed she was carrying on some sort of illicit tryst the night before. He had been worried for her, and when she had returned, he had said approvingly that her walk in the gardens had returned color to her cheeks. He had also apologized for making a fuss, for he had received her message. The others had eyed her curiously at first, but in the end they had been satisfied by her explanation that something she had eaten had disagreed with her and that hurrying out for some air, she had encountered an old acquaintance. The complaint and remedy were both common enough, and the part about the acquaintance not so great a coincidence. Everyone went to Vauxhall.

Only Hampton had disbelieved her. Mercifully the

evening had ended soon after, or he'd have affected the others. When he had not ignored Juliana completely, he had cast her such narrowed looks he might as well have shouted he thought she was not to be trusted. "Who was this acquaintance?" He'd ask again. Though he hadn't any right to demand to know anything about her, Hampton had not been satisfied, and the earl would not suffer frustration mutely.

Yet . . . yet, she had run to him in her dreams. And would have gone into his arms gladly at Vauxhall had he given her the least encouragement. Surely she had only wanted to go to Hampton, only dreamed of doing it, because he had been the one to find her. She would have wanted to sag against Mr. Porter, or Lord Mannering, or any other man who had come upon her when she was weak and vulnerable from the shock of her confrontation with Hugh. Dear God, she had not thought she would see Hugh for years, and then to have him appear there on the dance floor. . . .

Juliana took a deep breath, calming herself. She had faced Hugh, even held her own with him. She could rely on herself and the power of her purse. Hugh would respect the latter, at least.

As perhaps, given the way he had reacted upon hearing Hampton's name, he had respected the earl's power. Juliana had no way of knowing if Hampton could get Hugh cashiered from the army, but she hoped fervently that Hugh feared he could. If Hugh searched her out, he would discover she stayed with Hampton's sister and surely think her protected by Hampton, for he would have no way to know how poor her relations with the earl were.

As to Hampton himself, though he would demand to know the particulars of her "tryst," she had no obligation to answer him more fully than she had, and she would not. Juliana was determined on that. There was nothing between her and Hampton that required her to disclose her wretched family history. Nothing that demanded she abase herself so. She would not do it, but she recognized that to resist him, she would need all of her stamina, something she sorely lacked at that moment. Until she felt stronger, she meant to avoid him.

At noon, she requested another tray be brought to her. During the years of her marriage, Juliana had often kept to the refuge her rooms offered. That she had to do so now, when she had thought she was embarking on a new life, angered her, then, by turns, lowered her spirits. She picked at the cold meats and pickles and bread Rand brought her but ate little. By two o'clock, she had had enough. She felt ragged, and she was afraid she'd either begin to cry or to snipe at Randall. Anyway, she was relatively certain she would not meet Lord Hampton. He usually went out in the afternoon to his club or his mistress, perhaps.

Still feeling less than sociable, Juliana did not try to intrude upon Fanny. In fact she thought Fanny likely needed a day of uninterrupted rest, given the late hours they had been keeping, and so Juliana took herself to the library. Too busy to explore Lord Charles's library fully before, she found he'd an extensive and interesting collection. Sir Arthur had not been an utter despot. He had showered her with clothes and jewels, and had indulged her with books, having any volume she desired sent from London. Accordingly, she found some old friends on Lord Charles's shelves, as well as some intriguing new titles.

Juliana had spent nearly half an hour skimming through several leather-bound volumes when the door of the library opened. Expecting Haskins, for he had offered to bring her tea, Juliana turned away from the shelves only slowly, her mind on a volume of Lord Byron's poetry that she had not seen before.

An abstracted look on her face, she glanced to the door, thinking to direct Haskins as to where to put the tea tray, only to go stock-still. She might have said something, but she might only have whispered a dismayed "Oh!" to herself.

It did not much matter. The look on her face conveyed

her feelings to Lord Hampton, for it was he who had come into the library.

He leaned back against the door he had closed behind him and crossed his arms over his chest. The look in his eyes was flat and hostile, or in other words, not a whit more charitable than it had been the night before.

"You appear less than delighted to see me, Lady Whitfield."

He even smiled, though Juliana did not think she had ever seen a colder smile. Certainly it did not reach his eyes. "If I appear less than delighted, it is because I am tired, my lord. I was just on my way to my room for a nap."

Juliana was proud of her cool, composed tone. It was exactly what she had wanted, but it availed her naught. Hampton did not politely stand aside to allow her to pass. He did straighten away from the door, but he stood squarely between her and the exit and his expression hardened, though she would not have thought that possible.

For the first time, likely because she had no avenue of escape, Juliana felt a spurt of unease.

"You will not go anywhere, madame, until you have given me a satisfactory explanation for what happened last evening. Why was I put to the trouble of searching the gardens of Vauxhall for you? Why did you disappear? Oh, yes, you left a message with the attendant to our box, but why did you not return with this acquaintance you so fortuitously encountered and present him to the rest of us?"

With each word, his eyes became darker, his voice more scathing. Juliana strove for a steadying breath. "I told you. I . . . I did not feel well. . . ."

"Blast you!" He cut her off, stalking forward, intent on her. Juliana could see a muscle bunch in his cheek. "You are lying! If you felt ill, it was on that man's account. I will know what he wanted, by God!"

"It is none of your affair!"

"You were shaking like a leaf, damn you! Who is he?

What hold has he on you? Was he your lover? Did he demand payment lest he name you an adulteress?"

An adulteress. It would have meant her life had she bedded any man other than her husband. But Hampton could not know that. He would not ask. He would assume, assume betrayal and dishonor were her nature.

"No! You men! You are all alike." All thought of a man like Mr. Porter was lost to Juliana. In that moment, oppressed by Lord Hampton's threatening size, by his anger, by his harshly put questions, Juliana could not think beyond men like her father, her half brother, and then her husband. "There is not one ha'penny's worth of difference among the lot of you! You think you can impose your will upon women because you are larger! Well you cannot!"

Juliana made to charge by Hampton, but he caught her by the arm. He only meant to stay her flight, yet her momentum was such that he jerked her to a halt, facing him. Frustrated, he shook her, too.

Juliana lost all reason. It was as if Sir Arthur had not died, as if she were not free of Hugh, nor ever would be. She lashed out, striking Hampton hard on the chest with her fist. "Let me go!" She struck him again, then again. "You hateful beast! Let me go!" She curled her fingers into claws and swiped at his face. "Let me go! You'll not subdue me!" Twisting wildly, she kicked his shins, feeling nothing of the tough leather of his boot. "Let me go!"

Juliana never knew how long she went on like that, fighting him, lost to everything. Only finally she heard him calling sharply, "Lady Whitfield!" and realized she had heard her name before. Simultaneously, she absorbed that Lord Hampton was not hurting her at all. He was holding her, true, but carefully to prevent her from hurting him, or even herself.

She went still as a doe. Her eyes locked with his. He was staring at her, breathing hard. She realized abruptly that her bosom was heaving. And her hair had come loose from its pins. She felt it hanging heavy and disheveled on her neck, and then, in horror, she saw that she had scratched his cheek.

"Oh, God."

All the fight went out from her, leaving her weak. Carefully, never taking his eyes from her, Hampton released her. She thought he regarded her as if she were some wild creature that could not be trusted. But . . . she had gone mad for a little. She knew it and could not bear that he had seen. Whirling, she fled the room before he could call out more than "No, wait!" She did not. She even flung the door closed behind her to impede him, should he chase her.

Lord Hampton shoved his long fingers through his hair. He was breathing almost as hard as she had been. His hand shook slightly. He had had to hold her that tightly. It occurred to him to wonder if she would have bruises from his grip. Likely, he thought grimly, but what else could he have done? His cheek stung a little. Lifting his finger to it, he vaguely recalled that she had gotten in a swipe at him before he had caught her other arm to contain her. His finger came away with a smear of blood on it. She had scratched him like a cat. Clawed him, really, as if she had been fighting for her life, or herself, perhaps.

He looked blankly around the room, seeing nothing. He could hear her voice still, the frenzy in it born of desperation.

A knock at the door took him by surprise, it sounded so quiet and restrained. Haskins appeared, a maid with a tea tray behind him. Hampton shook his head. "Send the tea up to Lady Whitfield's room, Haskins. I want brandy. A bottle of it."

Great God. The earl half collapsed, half flung himself into a chair. Perhaps she was mad. It would absolve him, if she were. But she was not. When she had come back to him at last, when she had realized she was not so threatened as she had thought . . . he looked out the window, flinching at the memory of the shame he had seen in her eyes.

God. Great God. He had had to let her go. Honor had compelled him not to hold her against her will a moment longer, but it had required every ounce of his will to set her apart from him. He had wanted to take her into his arms so intensely, he had ached with the need, though it was his inability to keep his hands off her that had caused her such panic in the first place.

He tried to breathe deeply to clear his thoughts. He did succeed in banishing her eyes from his mind, but his thoughts went to a stallion his father had bought once. It had been restive, but no more than most stallions. The head groom at Chatsworth had climbed atop the stallion without undo difficulty until a younger groom had innocently flashed a whip in front of the stallion's eyes. At that, the horse had panicked, rearing and lashing out with its sharp hooves. Later his father had learned that the son of the previous owner had whipped the horse bloody more than once.

Had Whitfield beaten her?

Haskins brought the brandy. Alex tossed off a glass while his mind circled the question. Clearly someone had hurt her. Any other woman of his acquaintance would have shaken off his hold with no more than an indignant remark. Or he supposed that was true. He could not say from experience. He had never grabbed another woman like that, angrily dragging her around to answer to him.

Men. You are all alike. She had said it with such loathing. Obviously her husband had accused her of infidelity. And taken a hand to her.

No. Hampton drank off another draft of brandy. She had suffered more than a hand, more than a slap. That would have been bad enough, but not enough to turn her into the kicking, clawing, terrified thing to which he had reduced her.

Flinging himself out of the chair, the earl stalked to the window. He had never in his life laid an angry hand on a woman, could scarcely credit that he had done it that day with a woman who was a near stranger to him.

Near strangers they were, perhaps, but, he admitted, staring sightlessly out the window, there had been something
between them from the first. Or there had been on his side.
She had set him on his heels, when he had opened the door
expecting to see a bleary-eyed footman in Fanny's entry,
but had seen instead a woman who had taken his breath
away, and that though he had just come from Antoinette,
naked and voluptuous in her bed. The last thing on his mind
had been a woman. He had been sated, but God knew he
had wanted Lady Whitfield then. He had wanted to take
down her thick, silky chocolate dark hair, stare into those
oddly tilted eyes the color of the finest, richest amethysts,
and take her full, soft mouth with his.

She affected men that way. He was not alone. He had
watched other men encounter her for the first time, seen the
gleam of masculine interest light in their eyes, seen them
follow her with those same interested eyes afterward. It was
nothing she did deliberately. He had watched her enough to
know that. She was actually reserved in her manner with
men, opening only to a few: George Porter, particularly,
and a little to sober-stick Soames. She'd been at ease with
Houghton, too, but the boy had pushed his luck with the
camellias, or more precisely the note. Whatever Houghton
had written, she had not liked. Yet, Hampton would have
wagered a good deal on the proposition that no matter how
cool she was the next time she met Houghton, she'd not entirely dampen his ardor. Despite her reserve, there was
something about her that drew men, the exotic color and
shape of her eyes, perhaps; or the feminine curves of her
slender figure; or the soft ripeness of her mouth . . . or even
the shadows that did flicker occasionally in the depths of
her fine eyes, just as George Porter had said. Put all those
charms together and it was little wonder he had desired her
at eight o'clock in the morning and sated.

Still . . . he had desired other women. Hampton did not
even smile at the thought. He loved women. He had never
been in love with one in particular, perhaps, but he loved

everything about them and had helped himself to the pleasure of them when he wanted. He had not, however, ever grabbed a woman, whether he desired her or not, with the intent of forcing her to do something, even something so unexceptional as to explain why he had been made to worry over her whereabouts and safety. Dear God. He had no claim on her. None at all.

And frankly he did not want one. He knew precisely what he wanted in a wife: demure, pleasantly attractive, innocent of impeccable lineage, who would be an elegant hostess and a good breeder of children. She would be head over heels for him, too. He did not say that out of arrogance. Women did fall in love with him. Easily. It had happened too often for him not to know very well the effect he had on women. He simply had not been similarly afflicted, had not ever felt out of his depth or lost control. . . .

His eyes narrowed. Was that it? Did he fear her affect on him? That she might render him helpless before her? Did he fear she was some undertow that might pull him in over his head?

Hampton gave an unamused laugh. He was already deep in unchartered territory. He had never constrained a woman physically. But it was understandable that he had lost his control with her. He had never encountered a woman so full of mysteries. The man in that alcove had threatened her somehow. The earl was certain of it. He had only to recall how she had dug her fingers into his arm to pull him off with her, or how pale she had been. It was natural that he should lose patience with her. He only meant to help her.

That he had done the opposite, he must correct. He struck a glancing blow at a chair he passed. He would abase himself if necessary. Almost more than the fear he'd caused her, he could not bear the shame that had dawned in her eyes. She was a proud woman. If he doubted much about her, still, he admired the way she lifted her chin at him. But had she been a craven coward, he'd have apologized. Then, when he had done what he must, he would be careful to maintain the distance they both desired. Certainly he would not press her again about the man at Vauxhall. If he had been her lover, that was her business. It had nothing to do with Hampton, unless she wished to turn to him as a friend. In that case, he would do what he could, mostly as recompense for his treatment of her that day.

Chapter 11

The next morning Juliana went down early to ride, but she did not take Haskins by surprise. Randall had advised Fanny's butler that her mistress would ride an hour earlier than usual. The day had dawned clear, and Juliana, awake to see the sunrise, had wanted nothing more than to escape the confines of her room. She had not left it since she had fled the library the day before.

Haskins bid her good morning and commended her for stirring early. Cook's bones, he said with a twinkle in his eye, were infallible and they predicted that rain would return in the afternoon. Juliana had come to enjoy her brief exchanges with Fanny's butler each morning. Pulling a mock-sad expression, she said she hoped Cook's bones would be proven wrong in this case, as she and Lady Charles were to attend Lady Coke's Venetian breakfast that afternoon and never having attended a breakfast in the afternoon, Juliana told Haskins, she was most curious.

Haskins' reply, that having a breakfast in the afternoon was just the sort of confusion in which, as he understood it, Italians often indulged, made her smile. The spurt of humor, even the lifting of her mouth, felt so unfamiliar that Juliana replayed the exchange in her mind after she had greeted Jared and had mounted Lord Charles's mare. Unfortunately, the power of the thoughts she sought to hold at bay defeated her.

Juliana got only as far as her play on a breakfast in the

afternoon when a fresh, painful wave of remembrance washed over her. She had fought him like a wild thing. She had gone mad. Not enough to be sent off to Bedlam, but for a few minutes there, in front of Hampton, she had had as little control of herself as a Bedlamite.

She flushed painfully and shut her eyes against the memory of what she had done. The memory only came the clearer, and she saw Hampton looking shaken and wary. Both rightly. He could not have known what mad thing she might do next. And of a certainty he would never have witnessed such a loss of control, not on the part of a lady. Ladies were gentle and refined, keeping their emotions in civilized check. They did not scream and hiss and spit and claw like viragos. She had raked his cheek.

Feeling her mouth tremble, Juliana caught her lower lip between her teeth and held tight. Lord Hampton did bear some responsibility. He had no right to touch her. She had never given him leave. The opposite, indeed. And he had not merely touched her, he had restrained her physically, caught her, making her swing around for his inspection. He had behaved badly.

But she had behaved madly. That was worse, much worse. And she need not have fought without restraint to free herself. She need only have given him a frosty, shocked look. He'd have released her. She knew it now that she was calm. He would not have hurt her. He was not the kind of man who dominated women with physical pain. He had regretted precipitating her wild outburst. It had been in his eyes, that regret, along with the dismay and wariness, and at the back of his eyes, beneath all three, the worst, a flicker of pity.

Juliana bit her lip again, stifling an anguished cry. Her father, her brother, and then her husband had trampled her person both literally and figuratively, but she had always had her dignity. She had kept her pride. Hampton had seen her lose both.

Great God, why had she not simply told him that her "acquaintance" at Vauxhall was a kinsman and the business between them private? If only . . . but it was not possible to replay the scene. Hugh's sudden appearance had unsettled her so she had not been able to think clearly, and then in the library anger and fear and bitterness had overwhelmed her completely.

When Juliana rode through the gates of the Park, she kicked the mare lightly. Jared would follow her at a sedate trot, as he did every day, while she tried to outrun all thought of the scene in the library, of Hampton, and even of that queer pain she'd felt when he had accused her so casually of adultery.

It was inexplicable, that pain. Surely the tiny olive branch he'd extended at Almack's—that she'd have found her own way to that esteemed establishment eventually— had affected her beyond understanding. He had meant no more than he had said, and he had not said anything about revising his deepest impression of her: that she was little better than a vulture, marrying a man for the pickings she would enjoy upon his death.

Given what he thought of her, it was natural he would assume she trysted with an illicit lover. Had he found Fanny in a dark alcove with a stranger, he would never have leapt to the assumption that his sister was an adulteress, but the woman he believed Juliana to be would casually betray vows she had made before God.

Now that Juliana had reminded herself what Hampton thought of her, she would not dwell on the fact that she had needed a reminder. She was as human as the next person. She did not want to stand all alone, and she wanted people to think well of her, but Lord Hampton did not, and knowing that, reminded of it, she would not again expect anything of him. Specifically, she would not ever again in the future imagine him enfolding her in his arms and protecting her. She need only recall that it had been Mr. Porter who had sent Lord Hampton in search of her. The earl had resented the duty and had made her feel his displeasure.

Juliana reined in the mare at the end of the row, feeling a little less distraught, a little less unsettled than she had before she set out. She had still to face Lord Hampton. Perhaps every time she encountered him she would recall how she had behaved, and perhaps she would leave London sooner than she expected. But she would not pack her bags that day as she had considered doing. She had been enjoying herself, and, too, she did not care to allow another man to force her into seclusion. Besides, she had not, really, seen much of the earl.

Juliana grimaced in frustration, but had little time in which to despair of a calm that was based upon not seeing Lord Hampton. She heard a horseman galloping up behind her and she never mistook that the rider might be Jared galloping up to hurry back to Grosvenor Square and his chores.

It was Lord Hampton. Yet, though she had guessed his identity, when she turned and saw him, she could not even think to meet his eyes.

"Please do not look like that."

Juliana felt heat rush from her neck up to her hairline. She had no idea how she looked. Likely she looked miserable. God knew, she felt miserable. He looked the perfect Corinthian, every stitch in place, though, to give him his due, he also somehow or other gave the impression he did not care that he was impeccably attired. But the point was he looked like a man who governed his passions, or fed them as it pleased him yet was never governed by them, never turned into . . .

"Stop it!" She blinked. He had not only snapped at her but seemed to have read her mind. "That's better." He nodded sharply, and Juliana realized he approved that she had lifted her chin at him. She kept it elevated only with an effort of will. She wanted to tuck her chin and run, but did not and it helped that Hampton's gaze was level and direct, betraying neither censure nor disgust nor pity, either.

"We must speak, Lady Whitfield." He'd a voice to match

his eyes. Rich and honey gold and compelling. She had not made the comparison before, but then she'd never been quite so desperate to distract herself. "We cannot live in the same residence and have . . . yesterday hanging between us. However, I do not wish to impose myself upon you. I have taken liberty enough as it is." He referred to joining her in the Park, but Juliana thought of the day before and gritted her teeth. He was treating her very carefully, likely fearing she might go mad on him again at the least misspoken word. "Depending upon your preference, we can speak here now, or later at Grosvenor Square, when you return."

Clearly he did not mean to give her the option of skipping the conversation altogether. Shrugging, she said without much humor, "I am not fond of dread, my lord. Now it is. What of Jared?"

She glanced back down the row but saw nothing of the groom.

"I told him that we might take a walk down to the lake," Hampton said, watching her still, "and that he should await us by the gates, but if you wish . . ."

"No, I do not require Jared's presence."

Perhaps she said it a little stiffly, but recognizing that she could not judge her every word, Juliana simply got on with directing her mare onto a smaller path that led to the lake. When she noticed that the earl was dismounting behind her, she slipped her foot out of the shortened stirrup of the sidesaddle and slid to the ground on her own. Hampton's eyebrow lifted, but she did not care what he thought. She meant to avoid his touch, for at least a few of her difficulties, she believed, could be traced to how much she had wanted him to hold her at Vauxhall.

A little further along there was a convenient bush to which to tie the horses. They had grass to occupy them, and the lake was only a few feet away. Juliana could not seem to take her eyes from the light blue waters. Yet she knew when Hampton extended his hand as if he meant to take her arm and assist her. She pretended not to see the gesture and moved away out of his reach toward the lake. Though her back was to him, she sensed when he lowered his arm again.

"Lady Whitfield, I wish you to look at me. I cannot converse with your back."

Juliana made a face at the water and considered saying she did not see why, her ears worked whether she faced him or not. But she was not such a child. She turned, and when she had she acknowledged to herself that a part of her reluctance to face him had to do with nothing more complicated than his good looks. Just the sight of him altered her breathing, devil him, and that made her feel at a disadvantage. And now, on top of that, there was this other business as well.

At least he was not smiling. Juliana did not think she could have stood it, had he sought to smile and cajole her as if she were a child, or some equally unpredictable creature.

Actually he was far from smiling, she realized when she looked full into his handsome face. He looked grave as an undertaker. She had learned the silly pun as a child and unsteady laughter welled in her so she had to take a deep breath to calm herself.

"You wished to speak to me, my lord?" she prodded, clasping her hands together tightly.

"I wish to apologize to you, Lady Whitfield."

She flicked her gaze away from him to the water. But he took a step forward, instantly bringing her eyes to him again, and only then did he say firmly, "I had no right to question you as I did yesterday, nor any right at all to accost you physically."

Juliana whirled away, simply unable to face him, for she was thinking not of what he had done, but of what had happened next, of what she had done. "No, you had no right," she agreed, her voice low. "However, I accept your apology and now consider the matter over and done. You need not think about it again, my lord."

Moments passed. Juliana counted to ten, then to twen
He did not reply but neither did he leave. Why? Why did
not just leave and in the future keep his distance? She h
acquitted him of his part in the encounter. Surely he cou
see she did not want to discuss anything to do with h
past? She wanted him to go.

"Do you think absolution comes so easily, Lady Wh
field?"

Dear God, she wanted him to leave her in peace! Julia
jerked around, but he had walked up much closer than s
had realized. She could see the golden tips of his lash
when she threw up her chin to meet his eyes, and she cou
feel the warmth of his body. The pull of his warmth ma
her almost sway toward him.

Just as it rose to her lips, Juliana caught back a cry
desperation. What was wrong with her? She, who had r
lost her control once in the six wretched years with Wh
field, felt as if she were coming apart at the seams af
only a fortnight in Hampton's vicinity.

Abruptly, she began to walk, thinking she needed som
thing, anything, to do. "I do not know how absoluti
comes." He fell into step beside her, adjusting his stride
hers but making no move to take her arm as he would w
any other lady. "I only know that you apologized for hig
handed behavior, and I excused you. Is it customary
London to belabor apologies, my lord?"

She was proud of her little quip. Hampton was not, r
amused, either. He stopped in midstride, and though it c
occur to Juliana that she could simply walk on, she to
herself she was not such a coward.

The beaver hat he wore made an excellent foil for h
thick, golden brown hair. Juliana could not admire t
sight, however. She had his frown to face. "What occurr
between us, Lady Whitfield, was more than an impertin
question and an objectionable touch. I frightened you out
your wits."

He looked so tall and strong and competent on the o

and, yet so concerned, so bedeviled, and so sorry on the other. "No," Juliana said, but could not speak further for a moment. If she had been tempted by his warmth a moment before, it was nothing to how much she wanted his arms about her then. She could not move for fear of what she might do. He would hold her. She knew it. And he might not ask anything of her afterward.

"No?" He sounded as if he were speaking very carefully. "I did not frighten you out of your wits?"

She shook her head, but she could not stand mute forever and knew it. Clasping her hands together so tightly she made them ache, Juliana took what she hoped was an imperceptible step back away from Hampton, then marginally safer, she sent her gaze over his cheek, noting the thin, fading lines her nails had made before she looked the earl full in the eyes.

"I reacted out of all proportion to what you did, and we both know it, my lord. I am sorry. I am so sorry I scratched you." She felt tears well in her throat and bit her lip. He reached for her, as if he meant to draw her to him, but she shook her head hard. Then, when she could speak, she went on, "I am all right, really, only . . . only ashamed. I acted like a madwoman." There. She had said it. Juliana clenched her jaw and forced her chin up at least a little.

Before she realized what he would do, Hampton reached out and lightly touched his fingers to her taut jaw. When Juliana flinched, startled, he immediately dropped his hand. "I did not mean to startle you. Only . . ." He broke off to gather his energies, or so it appeared to Juliana, for the strength of his gaze seemed to intensify fivefold. "Only you were not mad yesterday. You were frightened and angry, and as I know you are of entirely sound mind, I can deduce easily enough that there was reason for your fear and anger. I will not pry into what caused you to react so to my admittedly insufferable but in all innocent grasping at you. I know you do not want it, but should you ever care to dis-

cuss it, I would take it as true absolution, if you would tu
to me."

He absolved her. And with the most impeccable grac
Juliana felt as if she might fall to her knees and weep. Sl
would not turn to him. She was too uncertain where turnin
to him might lead her, but she was grateful, achingly so.
thank you." His eyes were so rich a golden brown, sl
feared she'd lose herself in them. "I thank you very mu
for so gracefully drawing the sting from my wound."

She could not say more. She was not certain she wou
not burst into tears if she tried, or that she might not beg
to babble mindlessly. She had never imagined that I
would understand so much, or deal so sympathetically wi
her, and she was very much caught off her stride.

All Juliana seemed able to do was to stare up at him. Sl
did not know what was in her eyes, but his searched he
Then, he took her very much by surprise, for he laughe
albeit with little humor.

"I have often cursed women for being chatterboxes. I s
in future I shall have to heed the old saying about takin
care what one wishes for, or in this case, what one curse
You are unusual in many ways, Lady Whitfield."

"I wish you will not enumerate the ways." Despite tl
joke, the smile she managed was more wan than wry.

His expression softened. "To be unusual is not necessa
ily to be outlandish."

He had come so close to the mark of her worst fears, J
liana felt as if she had taken a physical blow. Or perhaps
was the compassion in that near smile of his that caused tl
ache in her chest.

"No," she said, but turning to walk back toward tl
horses, all she could think was that if he knew all there w
to know of her history, from her family to her life with tl
half-crazed old man who'd bought her almost as if she we
a woman of the streets, then Hampton would not call h
merely unusual.

Yet, if he did not know much of her grim history, he h

guessed that she had not been gently treated. And he had not disdained her, nor, after her outburst, had he declared her unfit company for his sister. Indeed, he had named himself the only villain in their play the day before. She would give him all the credit in the world for that. He had roused himself early, too, to make his apologies and soothe her opinion of herself.

She allowed him to lift her onto her mare. Tall and strong, he lifted her easily. She pulled her thoughts from his easy strength. She would not tell him the man at Vauxhall had been her half brother. Hugh's brutishness sickened her too greatly, but she did want him to know one thing. "My lord," she said, "I wish you to know the man at Vauxhall was not ever my lover."

She had taken him by surprise, though whether it was her statement itself or her desire to say it at all that caught him off guard, she could not say. After a moment, though, he nodded. "I apologize for thinking otherwise, but I believe whatever the man's relation to you, he did threaten you somehow, Lady Whitfield. I have no right to demand to know more of the matter, and so I shall not. I have learned my lesson there, but I do wish you to know that because you are a widow does not mean you are alone. Do you understand?"

She could not have smiled had her life depended upon it, but Juliana did manage to nod. "That is very kind of you, Lord Hampton. I thank you, again."

Chapter 12

Cook's bones, as Haskins might have said, misjudged onl[y]
the timing of the rain. The heavens did not open until we[ll]
after midnight, which meant Juliana was able to attend h[er]
first Venetian breakfast. Fanny went, too, though sh[e]
seemed subdued to Juliana. Thinking her friend had n[ot]
rested enough, Juliana said nothing, only made certain the[y]
returned to Grosvenor Square at a reasonable hour. But th[e]
day after Lady Coke's breakfast she felt more concerne[d.]
They were to take Sophie and Harry to Astley's that afte[r-]
noon, an excursion to which Juliana had been looking fo[r-]
ward almost as much as the children, but Fanny sent h[er]
maid to say she was unwell and to ask Juliana to come t[o]
her rooms.

Fanny was not, as Juliana had half expected, sitting up [in]
her bed with stacks of pillows behind her, wearing a pret[ty]
new bed jacket and helping herself to the chocolate candi[es]
she loved. All the curtains in the room were drawn, obli[g-]
ing Juliana to peer through the gloom to see that Fanny l[ay]
flat in her bed, a dowdy sleeping cap sitting askew on h[er]
head and a handkerchief clutched in her fist.

"Fanny! You are ill, indeed. Have you called for a phys[i-]
cian?"

"No, my dear, I've no need of Dr. Hartley. I've nothi[ng]
more momentous than megrims, and Carter knows th[e]
powders I need for headaches."

Fanny did appear to be in pain. Her cheeks lacked col[or]

and her eyes were dull. Juliana frowned down at her, taking her hand. "You have not been well for a few days, I think, Fanny. I wish you had said something yesterday. We need not have gone to Lady Coke's affair."

"But I wanted to go!" Fanny managed a self-amused quirk of her mouth. "I could not miss the countess's lobster patties. They are as renowned as Mr. Porter told you, and truly, I did not feel so low yesterday. The megrim came on me in the night."

Juliana considered her next question a moment. She did not want to pry, but she did want Fanny to know she could confide in her. "Fanny, your low spirits do not have anything to do with Lord Blakely do they?"

"Lord Blakely!" Fanny's cry sounded incredulous to Juliana's ears. "Why ever would you think such a thing, Juliana?"

Feeling foolish, Juliana shrugged negligently. "Mr. Porter thought he might have seen you with Lord Blakely at Vauxhall. I told him it was unlikely, for you had said how little you care for the man, an opinion I share on far less acquaintance, I might add. Then I . . . well, I felt so odd myself that night that I neglected to ask you about it, but thought I should now. Forgive me. I did not mean to upset you."

"You did not." Fanny assured Juliana, clasping her hand tightly. "You meant well, and that could not upset me. I'd only suffer upset if I thought I had spoiled your time in London. Juliana, I wish you to go to Astley's with the children. Will you do it? They will be so disappointed if we must postpone the outing, and heaven knows when we shall have the opportunity to go again. Please? I know you want to go, and I have taken the liberty of asking Alex if he will escort you. The children adore the two of you, you know. They will not miss me, I am certain. They will delight in telling me all they saw. You know how they both love to chatter on about anything and everything."

"They do, indeed," Juliana nodded, adding with a twinkle in her eyes, "I wonder if that is a trait they share with Lord Charles?"

As Fanny was the chatterbox of the family, Juliana expected her to laugh, but to her astonishment and dismay, her friend's pretty blue eyes filled with tears.

"Oh, Juliana, what a ninny I am being!" Fanny dabbed at her eyes with the handkerchief. "I am only tired, and I miss Charley so much! I had not realized quite how much, you see, until yesterday, when I had another letter from him. He may be gone a month longer than he expected. And now I've this megrim attack and feel so weary as well. Please, Juliana? It would make me feel so much better if I knew you and Sophie and Harry were enjoying yourselves."

"You are one of the few people who could say such a thing sincerely, Fanny." Juliana smoothed back a lock of hair that had escaped Fanny's cap. "And because I do believe you, I shall go. However, I wish you will not stir again until you feel well."

"After today I am certain I shall feel much better!"

Fanny's voice sounded oddly high, but Juliana thought that a symptom of the headache she suffered. "If you rest, I am certain, too."

It had been Fanny's plan to leave for Astley's amphitheater at half past one. With that arrangement in mind, Juliana went down to the drawing room to meet Lord Hampton and the children a few minutes late. She wanted the children on hand. She had seen Hampton since their meeting in the Park the morning before, but only in passing, and though he had gracefully excused her outburst in the library, still she felt shy of him, perhaps in part precisely because he had been so understanding.

Despite her planning, Juliana suffered disappointment. Mrs. Jones had not yet brought down the children. Perhaps they were saying good-bye to their mother. Juliana did not spare much thought for the reason they were late. Her eyes had already met Lord Hampton's and all that seemed to matter was that they were alone, and that her heart had executed an odd, almost painful leap when she saw him.

He had risen, when she entered. Dressed in a coat of a deep brown, tan buckskins, and black boots, he looked as handsome as he always did. As his looks could not have taken her by surprise, Juliana could only ascribe the change in her heart's rhythm to uncertainty. To mask it, and to make the meeting as unexceptional as possible—in decided contrast to their last two—Juliana gave the earl a friendly smile and simply ignored the stray, undesired thought that a man as tall and well made as he did not deserve eyes quite so fine and compelling. Nature had given him an unfair advantage, it seemed, but she did not acknowledge even that thought.

Instead, Juliana said what she thought Fanny might have, or a version of it, at any rate. "Good afternoon, my lord. We missed you yesterday at Lady Coke's."

She had not considered that Lord Hampton might feel uncertain about meeting her, but when Juliana saw his shoulders relax slightly, she realized he had been. Perhaps he had feared she might throw herself into his arms in gratitude for his kindness the day before or else burst into grateful tears. At her sisterly greeting, he smiled.

"Come and sit, Lady Whitfield. From my experience, Mrs. Jones is not strict on the subject of time, and we may be obliged to cool our heels for a while. But," he continued smoothly when they were both seated, "I cannot credit that you missed me at Lady Coke's. She is as famous for the entertaining distractions she provides as for her lobster patties."

Juliana chuckled, remembering. "Indeed, one amusement in particular was vastly diverting. Lady Coke staged an archery contest for the young ladies."

"Now that, I might have enjoyed watching," Hampton remarked with such lazy humor that Juliana laughed again.

"I imagine so, and not least because a close acquaintance of yours won."

Lord Hampton cocked his head, studying Juliana. "You are smiling too archly, Lady Whitfield. I know in my bones I will not be glad to hear who she was."

"Oh, my!" Juliana repented immediately. "I vow I should not be smiling so. She seemed a sweet girl, really, if a trifle overexuberant."

"A trifle overexuberant." Hampton pondered a moment, but in truth it was a short moment before his gaze sharpened. "The Bromwells have brought their daughter to town."

"Quite." Juliana regarded him in some astonishment. "How could you have known from so little?"

Hampton grimaced rather wryly. "Did neither Gussie nor Fanny tell you that the Bromwells' small holding marches with my father's? I have known Henry—or I suppose I should call her Miss Bromwell, now she's in town—since she was a child, and you caught the very essence of her. She's had an infatuation for me from the time she was in short clothes and has never been restrained about expressing it."

"You look positively grim, my lord, yet she is a mere girl, half your size and nearly half your age. I am certain you will manage her neatly."

Juliana was trying not to laugh. Hampton saw her struggle and gave her a dark look that nearly defeated all her efforts. "That is what you say, you, who will not be afflicted by her. Do you know that she fell out of a tree upon me . . . a purpose? She was only twelve or thirteen and did not think I had noticed her sufficiently."

It was too much. Laughter bubbled out of Juliana. "Not another word," she cried after a few minutes. "You must be teasing, though I do not doubt she went to some lengths to bring herself to your attention. She clearly does have some interest in you. Even Lady Danley became impatient with her continued questions as to your whereabouts, but I do not think she is quite a hopeless case."

"No?" Lord Hampton gave her the lazily lopsided smile

Juliana had seen only once since their first encounter. Its effect had not diminished in the interim. Like that first time, she felt a kind of softening, as if she had been holding herself tight against him but had had a vital defense breached. "And how might you find Miss Bromwell hopeful, Lady Whitfield?"

"Well," Juliana said, making her tone brisk to counter that languid softening she had no intention of encouraging, "I doubt Miss Bromwell has been in the company of many young men before. I do not mean to imply that she became infatuated with you, my lord, because you were the only gentleman in her vicinity, but . . . I do think she would respond well enough to the attention of other gentlemen. If she can curb her exuberance just a little, and perhaps dress more becomingly, I think she could get on well enough."

"You sound like a general considering a campaign."

"And you sound hopeful," Juliana retorted dryly. Hampton's unabashed laugh confirmed her contention. "Perhaps I shall take up the girl as a challenge," Juliana went on musingly. "She is kind. When one of the other girls missed the target entirely and turned beet red with embarrassment, Miss Bromwell rallied her with some useful instruction. Aside from your niece Sarah, and Miss Desmond, too, on occasion, I have not seen the young girls in town treat one another as friends."

"They are not at school here," Hampton pointed out mildly. "They are rivals on the marriage mart."

Juliana made a face at that. "Well, I prefer Sarah and Miss Bromwell's attitude."

Hampton did not much care, it seemed, why Juliana liked Miss Bromwell, only that she did, and how that might benefit him. "If you should be able to turn Miss Bromwell's attention from me, Lady Whitfield, I should be very grateful. Indeed I would owe you whatever price you may wish to name."

"Really?" Juliana brightened, for she knew what she wanted. "I do have something in mind, actually."

"Oh?" Lord Hampton sounded suddenly wary.

Juliana laughed at him. "Yes. Fanny says you've a sailing ship, and I should like to go for a sail."

He stared a moment, evidently caught off stride. "That is it? That is what you would want for sparing me Henry Bromwell's exuberant, tiresome attentions?"

"Yes. Have we a bargain?"

"You may have two sails, even. And it is a yacht, not a sailing ship. Ships are either in the navy or ply the seas with merchandise."

"I am learning already." Juliana's eyes lit with satisfaction. "I look forward to the actual event."

Hampton could not know that books on sailing had been an antidote for Juliana's misery at Westerleigh. He could only see the light sparkling in her tilted, thickly lashed eyes and wonder what sort of woman she was to be so enthused by a mere day's sail when she could have had something tangible, a necklace of amethysts to match her eyes, for example.

"We've come to our agreement not a moment too soon," he murmured, seeming slow to look from her to the door. "That thumping can only be Harry pounding toward the drawing room."

Astley's Royal Amphitheater boasted the largest stage in England, and overhead, illuminating the wide expanse, hung a chandelier almost as large. The children went into raptures over no more than the setting. Juliana's eyes did not go wide until the first set of six creamy white horses pranced onto the stage. Their manes and tails braided and decorated with flowers, they went up in unison on their hind legs to salute the crowd.

Hampton watched her clap her hands and say something to Sophie and Harry with which they evidently agreed, for both children nodded enthusiastically. He could recall wondering how her eyes would look, were she happy and excited. Now he had seen her violet eyes sparkle with light twice in one day.

Young men in costumes meant to suggest the clothing of the natives of North America came running into the ring. Harry gave an excited shriek and bounced in his seat. Lady Whitfield offered no reprimand. Quite to the contrary, Hampton watched her throw back her head and laugh. He smiled himself. He'd have had to fight not to. She had an infectious laugh.

Perhaps she had driven old Whitfield to his death. It was not difficult to imagine a man straining his capacities just to make her laugh. The earl thought about the sailing excursion she wanted, but he did not dwell on how she would look with her eyes alight and her cheeks turned pink by the breeze. He returned his thoughts to Sir Arthur Whitfield. If the old man had wanted to please her enough to kill himself in the effort, why had he not brought her to London? He'd not have been accepted by society, but they could have visited Astley's, viewed Elgin's marbles, or attended the theater and the Opera.

Whitfield had indulged her. Her stylish wardrobe earned her envious looks aplenty. Clearly she relished fine clothes, though, in truth, as Hampton considered the matter, he could not say she demonstrated great interest in her appearance. He could not ever recall seeing her pause before a looking glass as almost all women did, if only to take a quick peek for reassurance.

So. Perhaps she had wanted her extensive collection of clothes, or perhaps she had not cared one way or the other. But it was indisputable that she enjoyed London. Why had Whitfield not brought her? Had he wanted to keep her to himself? Had he struck her when she'd suggested coming to town? Had he struck her when he had found her bedding another man? She said the fellow at Vauxhall was not her lover, but that did not mean she had not had lovers. Hampton could not believe she hadn't. She was too beautiful . . . too passionate.

But she was not unbridled. Aside from the one outburst in the library and the time he had invaded her very room, she had been as self-contained as Fanny had once described her. Nor when he had made his apologies in the Park had she fallen at his feet. Hampton's mouth quirked wryly. Far from it, she'd kept her own counsel so completely, he still was not certain what had prompted her fear and anger in the library.

Except that he knew she must have been roughly handled. Some man had tried to dominate her physically. Someone who had the power to do it, like Whitfield. Perhaps the old man had been doting, but perhaps he had also been jealous, with or without justification.

It made him ill to think of anyone striking her. He'd have felt so in relation to any woman, he added quickly, but then he glanced at her, took in the pure, fine bones of her profile and the milky smoothness of her skin and his jaw tightened. He'd a fierce desire to hurt the man who had hurt her, and that was unusual.

Acrobats were performing overhead. When one of the men released his bar and went flying through the air, Sophie gave an anguished cry and buried her head against Lady Whitfield's breast. Lord Hampton looked away before she could have seen the envy in his eyes. Watching the flying acrobat complete his maneuver successfully, the earl made no excuse for his thoughts. In fact, he grinned. Wanting to be held to a woman's breast was not an unrecognizable desire. Wanting to take her into his arms in the Park with no desire but to comfort her . . . was less understandable.

The acrobats accepted the crowd's roar of approval. It was time for another performance of the horses, but first a group of clowns trotted onto the huge stage. Sophie giggled, but Harry scrambled onto his uncle's lap. Hampton was on the point of chidingly pointing out that clowns would not hurt him when Lady Whitfield nodded at the boy.

"A very fine vantage point from which to watch clowns, Harry. They can be most unsettling with their false faces."

Harry nodded, relieved, and though he did not leave his uncle's lap he did watch the clowns after that.

Hampton's eyes met hers, and he was conscious of an uncomfortable tightening in his chest. Her violet eyes glowed, but with a softer light than before. She looked wistful. Perhaps she wanted a child of her own, or perhaps she wanted to be held herself. Hampton was conscious of an almost overwhelming desire to stroke her cheek and tell her she could have whatever she wanted. He would see to it.

"Aunt Juliana, why do you not marry Uncle Alex?" The clowns were just trotting off of the stage to roaring applause, and it took Hampton a moment to understand what Sophie had said. The bloom of rose that suddenly colored Lady Whitfield's high, delicate cheekbones served as something of a clue. "He is looking for a wife," Sophie went on, ever so informatively. "Polly told Meg. I heard her. Then you could be our aunt."

Yes. He could marry her. He could give her children, hold her, bring her to town whenever she wanted for however long. He could take her sailing; he could keep her safe.

She did not look at him. She gave Sophie a careful smile. "You call me your aunt now, Sophie, and if Lord Hampton marries another lady, then you will have two aunts in place of merely one."

Sophie considered Juliana's reasoning thoughtfully, but Harry was won over immediately. "Yes!" he cried happily. "Then we may go to Astley's twice as often."

Truth out of the mouth of babes. He had been saved by a child. Always, it was better to have two women rather than one. There was safety in numbers. Hampton did not ask himself to consider why he needed safety. He clapped Harry approvingly on the shoulder. "If I had ever doubted you were my nephew, Harry, I would know you are for certain now. Well said, my boy."

She understood. There was a flash in her violet eyes that was not approving. Hampton gave her a silky grin. She would be demanding, she would want all her husband's attention, if she finally condescended to take one. Well, bully for her. He did not know what he had been thinking before. It had been temporary madness brought on by her softly lit violet eyes. They were potent, those eyes, undoubtedly. But she was no more suitable now to be Countess of Chatsworth than she'd ever been. Perhaps her father had urged her marriage. Likely he had, but he could not have dragged her to her marriage bed. They were not living in the Dark Ages. It was the nineteenth century. A father might have ultimate power over a girl, but she had to say yes at the altar. He could not speak for her.

She had chosen to marry Whitfield. It had not turned out to be such a marvelous decision, but Hampton could not undo the past for her. Mercifully Harry had reminded him how to save himself: only to recall what sort of wife and marriage he wanted. Lady Juliana Whitfield could not be the first nor offer the second. It was time, and more, he decided, to spend a little time away from her. Distance—and Antoinette—would give him the perspective he needed. He would go to Half Moon Street to clear his mind of her and the goblins he'd imagined haunting her.

Chapter 13

"Uncle Alex! Where have you been?"

Lord Hampton did not appear inclined to answer where he had been for the previous five days nor why he had absented himself from Grosvenor Square without warning. His mouth quirking, he bowed lazily to Sophie, who had skipped to him with one arm carefully tucked behind her back. "Good afternoon to you too, sweeting." His gaze lifted and touched upon Fanny and Juliana, both seated near the fire a chilly rain had necessitated. "Fanny, Lady Whitfield."

Before either lady could do more than nod, Sophie thrust up the hand she'd held behind her back hand to show off a bright green-and-yellow parakeet perched on two of her fingers. "Look what Lord Soames brought Aunt Juliana today! Is he not the dearest creature you ever saw, Uncle Alex?"

Despite his niece's excited prompting, Lord Hampton eyed the small, long-tailed bird with little evidence of enthusiasm. "Soames has paid tribute with a bird?" He arched an ironical brow at Sophie. "I had no notion our most estimable lord was susceptible to fashionable crazes."

His remark was clearly audible across the room, though whether he intended for it to be was impossible to say. Lord Hampton might have glanced to Juliana, but if he did, he looked through his absurdly long, gold-tipped lashes, and she could not discern with certainty the direction of his gaze. It was the day of the at-home Fanny held twice monthly on Tuesday afternoons. Juliana wore a merino crepe afternoon dress, decorated with lace at the throat and wrists. The effect of the material, fine wool shot through with silk, was elegant and lovely and feminine all at once, particularly as the light blue color set off her eyes and dark hair. She told herself she was glad she wore it, because the dress was warm. Certainly it could not matter what Lord Hampton thought of her appearance, even if he approved. He was the sort of man to drop in and out of a woman's life at his own pleasure. She lifted her chin a little, just in case he was watching, and schooled her expression to disinterest.

"But, Uncle Alex, do you not like him?" Sophie followed her uncle across the room to the fire and the ladies. "Lord Soames told Aunt Juliana that a lady's beauty is enhanced, when she has a pretty, little creature beside her."

"How very whimsical of Lord Soames, to be sure," Lord Hampton murmured, unable or unwilling to indulge his niece. "The good lord continues to surprise, but for my part, Sophie, I do not find anyone's looks enhanced by a caged animal."

"Alex!" The chiding cry was Fanny's. "Your absence of several days has scarcely improved your humor. Indeed, I should say whatever you have been up to has soured your disposition. You are being quite unfair, and about a gift given in tribute, yet."

Lord Hampton lazed against the mantelpiece lionlike, golden and tall and only seeming lazy as he looked to Juliana. "Were I a bird, I would not like to be captured and caged in order that the so-worthy Soames might more fashionably woo a lady. I apologize if my sentiments offend you, Lady Whitfield."

Despite the way he had of dominating a room merely by being present, Lord Hampton, or his eyes at least, looked tired to Juliana. She did not allow herself to wonder what he might have been doing late into the night for nearly a week. Perhaps it was too easy to guess. She returned him a steady look that was as banked as his own. "You have said nothing offensive to me, my lord."

"Well, I think you are being quite absurd, Alex," Fanny declared roundly. "You have never cared for Lord Soames overmuch. That is the source of your pettishness, for this little bird is, I am certain, quite delighted to be kept in luxury in his cage, protected and cossetted. He does not have to worry about food or water or hawks circling the sky for him."

Juliana glanced to Fanny, caught by the fervency of her friend's tone. Fanny had sounded almost as if she feared hawks searched the sky for her. Lord Hampton, however, appeared to hear nothing unusual in his sister's voice, for he countered without pause.

"Nor can the little fellow go where he will or do what he wishes. What do you think, Lady Whitfield?" He flicked his gaze to Juliana, addressing her without warning. "Given the choice, would you rather chance the wild or live in luxury in a cage?"

Did he know? Had he guessed? She did not allow herself the time to wonder, nor to betray exactly how fierce her views on the subject really were. Answering in the mildest of tones, as if she were a consummate actress, Juliana dodged the question. "I think, my lord," she said, lifting her eyes to his, "that Lord Soames was very kind to have remembered me."

"Oh, pray . . ."

Having heard that tone before, Fanny interrupted. "Alex! Sweeten your mood or depart."

But her brother continued as if she had not spoken, addressing Juliana. ". . . take pity on me and leave off. You know as well as I that Soames is not likely to often forget you, Lady Whitfield."

He really was in a foul mood. He looked as irascible as he sounded. Oddly, Lord Hampton's ill temper seemed to enliven Juliana. The week had been rather flat for one reason or another, she had felt quiet, even subdued. She did not any longer.

"But, Uncle Alex, he is very sweet!" Cooing at the little bird, Sophie stroked his back with her finger. "I have named him Roland."

For a half moment Lord Hampton appeared to weigh the pleasure of further criticizing Lord Soames's gift against the unpleasantness of further disappointing Sophie. In the end, his better nature won out, more or less. "That is an heroic name, Sophie. I approve of it, if I do not approve of caging Roland merely to be fashionable. And as to you, my dear, you are pretty as a picture whether you are holding little Roland or not."

Sophie was not her mother's daughter for naught. She ducked her head and looking through her lashes, beamed prettily. "Thank you, Uncle Alex."

"You are welcome, Sophie. And you, Fanny"—he looked, a smile lingering in his amber eyes, to his sister— "appear to have recovered from your megrims."

In Juliana's opinion, Lord Hampton only just spoke the truth. Fanny had roused herself from her bed the day after the outing to Astley's, but Juliana did not think Fanny's spirits fully restored, though her friend had insisted she was quite recovered. She did the same now, though she also tossed her head, which was more like her usual self.

"I would rather you had said I am pretty," Fanny informed her brother. "But I am feeling better, and have for some days, as you would know, Alex, if you had not left us for so long." She paused, eyeing Lord Hampton significantly, but when he replied with only a slight smile, as if he were amused by her attempt to have him explain his absence, Fanny gave him a darkling look. "You missed my at-home, you scoundrel!"

"Ah," he said, smiling outright. It was a fond smile, and one that would go a good way to making up for his absence. Juliana thought he would use that smile in future with his wife, after he had been with his mistress again too long. It was obvious to her that he had been with his mistress. Would he not have said where he had been otherwise? "But, Fanny," he went on, persuading effortlessly, "you know very well I would not have made a pleasant addition to your at-home. I enjoy sitting about drawing rooms making idle conversation with whatever girl Gussie has brought for my inspection—and the chit's mother—as much as . . . Roland there might."

Juliana watched Fanny succumb to him as surely as the young, starstruck girl he eventually took for a wife would do in her turn. "Roland quite enjoyed Miss Beckford," Fanny returned, but she laughed.

Juliana might have rolled her eyes then, but the very sound of Fanny's laughter sent her thoughts off on a tangent. She realized she had not heard that gurgling laugh in days, and giving Fanny a thoughtful glance, she wondered if her friend's spirits had been depressed, not so much by a lingering touch of megrim as she had thought, as by Lord Hampton's absence. Fanny was accustomed to having a man in the house. Perhaps she had been unduly worried without him. Juliana did not fault Fanny. Their experiences of men in general and husbands in particular were so different, it was natural they would view having a man in residence differently. Juliana was merely glad to have a reasonable explanation for Fanny's lowish spirits.

While Juliana had been following her thoughts, Fanny had served up a cup of tea that Sophie delivered to her uncle. As he sipped, Lord Hampton arched an eyebrow over the rim at his sister. "Miss Beckford, eh? I have met a Colonel Beckford a time or two. Any relation?"

"Yes! She is the colonel's daughter. He is in Russia just now on some mission or other, but Miss Beckford has come to town with her mother. She is very nice and very attractive, too. Alex, I'll not have you look at me that way! I have not given the same report on every girl. You may ask Juliana, if you do not believe me."

Juliana's brow lifted slightly. Time had not made her

fonder of assessing the girls hoping to catch Lord Hampton's eye. She told herself it was because she herself would not have cared to be discussed as if she were a horse the earl was considering buying. "Miss Beckford was quite pleasant."

Though Juliana had deliberately addressed Fanny, it was Hampton who replied, "As pleasant as Miss Bromwell, Lady Whitfield?"

He gave her a smug look, but Fanny responded before Juliana could. "I was afraid you had abandoned town upon hearing that Henrietta had decided to make her come-out after all. But all is not lost for the girl, as. . . ."

"Fanny," Juliana broke in, "I think we should not say any more about Miss Bromwell until Lord Hampton has an opportunity to see her for himself. We wouldn't want to prejudice him."

She turned a limpid gaze upon the earl. He eyed her a little less comfortably. "You have something up your sleeve."

"I protest." Juliana, with the most innocent of looks, made a play of examining each of her sleeves. Sophie giggled. "You see, my lord? Nothing."

"You have something up your sleeve," Lord Hampton repeated. "I know it, whether you have fooled Sophie or not."

"Aunt Juliana has nothing up her sleeves, Uncle Alex!" Sophie entered with enthusiasm into the game, giggling again. "She showed you."

"Good girl," Juliana said, smiling approvingly.

Lord Hampton appeared quite prepared to wrangle further, for he did not take his eyes off Juliana, but Mrs. Jones intervened. Harry having just finished a music lesson, she had come to fetch Sophie to walk with her brother in the small park situated in the middle of Grosvenor Square.

Dutifully, Sophie bid farewell to the adults, and tripping over to Juliana, held out her hand to give Roland over to his mistress. Having been instructed by Lord Soames, Juliana knew to extend her own fingers, whereupon Roland hopped to her, angling his head to examine her with a round little eye. Lord Soames had said parakeets came from the tropics. Roland would not survive if Juliana took him to the window and let him fly free, yet his eye seemed full of reproach, and she walked without relish to the fashionable brass cage Lord Soames had brought for him.

Juliana thought Fanny and Lord Hampton distracted with bidding Sophie adieu, but after she shut Roland in his pretty prison, Juliana found Hampton watching her.

There was too much understanding in his eyes. She wanted to look away from him but somehow could not. "Robin's father has a magnificent aviary an acre wide and two stories high. He's all sorts of birds, parakeets, parrots, toucans, and more, all able to fly relatively free and do whatever birds choose to do."

"You do not mean to give up the bird, do you, Juliana?" Fanny looked quite astonished. "Why, what will Lord Soames say?"

Juliana only wondered what she would say to Lord Soames, but Lord Hampton had a reply for his sister. "Soames be damned, Fanny. No person of spirit wants to look at a dull and lonely bird in a cage. But never mind about poor Roland. His fate has been happily decided. Alert me instead to whatever dangers await me tonight at Derby House.

"You mean to go!" Happily surprised, Fanny was completely diverted.

Not so Juliana. Lord Hampton's understanding of her feelings left her too unnerved to be diverted. While neither Fanny nor Lord Soames had had the least suspicion of her distaste for caged animals, Hampton had guessed it immediately. Perhaps he had divined somehow that Sir Arthur had kept her a virtual prisoner at Westerleigh, but if so, he had divined more about her life than anyone else. Of course he had seen her in a more revealing mood than anyone else had, but her outburst in the library surely could not have revealed so much. Could there be some sympathy between them that allowed him to read her mind? The mere thought made her want to run from the room, and that night at Lady Derby's rout, Juliana found further reason to be unsettled.

After she had made her wager with Lord Hampton, Juliana had taken Henrietta Bromwell under her wing. It had not been difficult. The girl's mother was a country woman at heart, with little experience of London. She had allowed her daughter to persuade her to come to town only because no gentleman in their neighborhood in Suffolk had offered for Henrietta, who at twenty would be considered on the shelf in a year or two. As at sea as she was, and knowing the Chathams as she did, Mrs. Bromwell had appealed to Lady Danley for assistance. Juliana, present because she and Fanny were calling upon Lady Danley themselves, had seized the opportunity to say she would be glad to advise Miss Bromwell upon her dress and her behavior, if Lady Danley and Fanny would assist with the rest of what was necessary for the Bromwells to know. Poor Mrs. Bromwell had nearly swooned with gratitude, for if Juliana was still questioned in some quarters for her marriage, no one questioned either her taste in clothes or her comportment, and Lady Danley, telling her she was a dear, had readily agreed to supervise every other aspect of the Bromwells' lives.

Lord Hampton and Lord Mannering arrived at the rout together and late as usual. Lady Derby, however, was too delighted that they had condescended to join her other hundred guests to quibble. Watching the woman greet the two men as if they were long-lost heroes, Juliana heard a loud voice cry, "Hampton!"

Mr. Porter winced as Miss Bromwell charged by them, muttering "Poor Hampton" under his breath, but Juliana acted.

"Miss Bromwell."

Miss Bromwell gave Juliana a distracted look, as if she had never lain eyes on her, though in truth they had spent three of the previous five mornings together with Hampton's niece Sarah, shopping, and to good effect, if Juliana did say so herself. The dress she'd chosen for Miss Bromwell, of pale pink satin cut on simple lines and decorated with particularly lovely lace, suited the tall, dark-haired girl perfectly. She looked elegant and had attracted the attention of several young men, much to the girl's surprise and considerable pleasure.

Juliana spoke firmly. "Lord Hampton will not be pleased, my dear, if you charge up to him as if he were a fox and you riding to hunt."

Miss Bromwell blinked but her forward momentum had been arrested. "I just want to see him, Lady Whitfield! I have not for a very long while."

"If he is your friend, Lord Hampton will come and speak to you, but you must wait," Juliana told her. "A gentleman does not like to be chased. It makes most of them run to ground. I believe Lord Hampton would be no exception."

"But you are beautiful, Lady Whitfield! Lord Hampton would come to you, I do not think he will come to me."

"He has known you since you were a child, Miss Bromwell. Of course, he will speak to you, if you do not force yourself upon him. But if you do, he will run in the other direction. Which do you want? For Lady Derby's guests to see you chase a man away, or to see you enjoy yourself whether he comes to speak to you or not?"

Miss Bromwell looked around as if she were just realizing that she was, indeed, in a room with at least one hundred other people. A few, watching her, were whispering behind their fans. She flushed painfully, but Juliana was not sorry for the mean-spirited gossips. In seconds, they had managed what Juliana had failed to do in days of talking. Miss Bromwell knew now the importance of curbing her most excessive impulses.

"Now, Henrietta," Juliana continued, "you will come with me. Mr. Porter will lead you out for a dance, and then I do believe that nice lieutenant to whom Lady Danley presented you at Lady Coke's is here tonight."

"Lieutenant Michaels?" Miss Bromwell brightened. "I enjoyed him ever so much. He dances splendidly."

"As do you, Henrietta. With your elegant height, it is a pleasure to watch you dance, something several other young men have noticed. You have danced nearly every dance."

"I have!" Miss Bromwell turned away from the door to smile gratefully at Juliana. "And all due to you, Lady Whitfield. I have had ever so many compliments on my dress and looks. Mama thought it was the thing for a girl to be rigged out in as many bows and flounces as possible, but thanks to you, she has seen the error of her ways."

"I'd have accomplished nothing, had you not had the figure and looks to carry off simplicity, Miss Bromwell. You are a very lucky young lady, you know, having been given the opportunity to come to London and meet all sorts of young men before you are asked to settle into marriage. Make the most of your Season, Henrietta. Do not fix your attention on one man alone and thereby miss another gentleman who may be better suited to you."

They had reached Mr. Porter. Juliana gave him a twinkling, but in all pointed look. "You have met Miss Bromwell, I think, Mr. Porter? She is longing to dance, which I said was quite a coincidence, as you had just asked me to dance, but I could not, my feet having decided to feel their age."

Mr. Porter looked as if he might dispute that Juliana was of an age to have wearied feet, but seeing her brow lift, he bowed to his fate and to Miss Bromwell. "I would be honored, Miss Bromwell."

Juliana wasted little time making her way to Lady Danley. While she could advise Miss Bromwell on her dress, Lady Danley was the one with the aptitude for maneuvering young men in their protégé's direction.

"I saw it all, Juliana!" Lady Danley exclaimed, rising from her seat to take Juliana's hand. "You are a wonder. I do not doubt that Alex would have turned tail the instant he saw Henrietta charge toward him. She is a good girl but impulsive, though I vow I do believe you are making progress even there."

"I am trying, Gussie." Juliana laughed a little. "It is not all smooth sailing, but I think she learned a lesson when she saw the gossips whispering about her. A cruel way to learn, perhaps . . ."

"But not ineffective," Lady Danley finished with a wise nod. "Yes, and now I do not doubt you think it advisable to distract Henry with some energetic young man."

"Lieutenant Michaels, for example," Juliana said, uncertain whether she felt more like a fairy godmother or a general in some campaign.

Lady Danley did not seem to have any doubt. "An excellent thought, my dear. I shall send him after her for the next dance."

In fact, Lady Danley saw to it that Miss Bromwell was kept busy until the orchestra stopped for a brief interval some hour or more later. Having kept watch, Juliana knew that Lord Hampton had not approached the Bromwells even to bid them good evening, and decided, therefore, to interfere. Henrietta had behaved very well and she thought the girl deserved a reward.

She discussed what to do with Fanny. Lady Charles had not danced much that evening. She'd a sore foot, she said, but she was perfectly willing to bring her brother to Juliana for a conference on Miss Bromwell. "I have done nothing whatsoever about the child, and I am relieved to be of some use at last."

He had just danced with Miss Beckford, the "nice" girl Lady Danley had brought to Fanny's at-home, but did not appear annoyed to be called away from her. Indeed, he was half smiling when he greeted Juliana.

"You are in looks this evening, Lady Whitfield, though I hesitate to tell you that you look well. You must hear flattery so often, it seems trite to you."

"Only if the flattery is insincere, my lord, does it seem

trite or insipid." Juliana was aware her reply did not flow as
smoothly as she might have liked, but there was a light in
his golden brown eyes that informed her his flattery was
not at all insincere, and her breath seemed to catch somewhere in her chest. Reflexively, she lifted her chin and too
late saw her error. The gleam in his eyes intensified. Juliana
did not repeat her mistake. She did not grit her teeth, giving
away a second time that he affected her. Controlling herself, she addressed the subject at hand. It would dim that
too-masculine gleam. Indeed, she so feared Lord Hampton
would balk that she'd have liked to have Fanny to support
her, but Lady Charles had been distracted by Mrs. Daviess
and stood talking to her friend a few feet away.

"Have you observed how well behaved Miss Bromwell
has been tonight, Lord Hampton?" Juliana began.

"You had Fanny come after me in order to discuss Henry
Bromwell?"

That lazy, approving gleam had quite disappeared. Juliana half wanted to smile, and she ignored the wants of the
other half. "As you observed yourself, she is Miss Henrietta
Bromwell now she is making her come-out, and yes, I do
want to discuss her. We've a wager on, if you will recall. I
have every reason to desire you to observe how well she is
coming along."

"Where is she?" Hampton sounded grudging, but he did
look about as if searching for Miss Bromwell.

"She is one of a group of young people near Lady Danley and Sarah, my lord, but I with you will not make it appear as if I have instructed you to look for her. Actually,
I . . . oh, Lud, I mean to ask quite a bit," she admitted,
flushing so Lord Hampton's brow lifted. "Actually," Juliana went on quickly, "I wish you will ask her to dance."

A measure of Hampton's response was the very long
time it took him to say, "What?"

"She has restrained herself!" Hearing the defensiveness
in her tone, Juliana made herself take a deep breath and
speak reasonably. "She wanted to run to greet you, but I

persuaded her to compose herself and wait for you to go to her. Now, I wish you would do so. Please? She is young and vulnerable. Ask her to dance. You will establish her credit."

"It is a disease," he said reflectively after a moment. "A disease that is passed from woman to woman." Juliana understood he referred to matchmaking and could not but laugh. Lord Hampton watched her, the lines at the corners of his eyes deepening as if he were amused himself, but when he spoke again, after Juliana had sobered, there was naught but real curiosity in his tone. "Why do you care about Henrietta Bromwell? You do not know her, really, and you could never have been as foolish as she is. At her age, you had been married . . ."

He saw too much too easily. Juliana watched understanding dawn in his eyes. His mouth tightened as well, as if he did not like thinking of her as a young girl married already three years by the time she was twenty. She might have shrugged off his insight, insisted she simply liked Henrietta Bromwell. It was not untrue, but it never occurred to Juliana to do so. She was caught fast by his very understanding, and she could only watch his gaze soften, almost, she thought, despite his wishes.

"Upon consideration, it seems, it would be my pleasure to dance with Miss Bromwell," he said quietly. "I shall establish her credit, as you think I've the power. But I mean to claim payment, Lady Whitfield. I shall return for the waltz."

Juliana gained two insights into herself then: first, she could not always summon speech. She could only nod in reply to his demand for a waltz. And second, she did not find it easy to forgo tenderness. She never broke free of his gaze. It was Lord Hampton who, with a formal bow, broke away from her to do her bidding.

Chapter 14

Fanny's dark green dress blended with the shadows in the Stanleys' garden, and she'd taken care to cover her blond hair with a fashionable satin turban. Still she paused, not breathing, looking fearfully over her shoulder toward the terrace. No one had come out of the ballroom for air. She could hear the sounds of music and gaiety, but they were muted, seeming to belong to another world. Her hand trembled upon the shawl she clutched. She felt so unworthy of that world.

"Ah, here you are at last, little Fanny." Fanny started in near panic, though she had come to meet the man standing in such deep shadow she could scarcely see him even now. "I thought perhaps you had decided to disregard my note."

Fanny ducked behind the thick yews, joining him in the shadows, thinking with despair, she belonged there. "What do you want now, Blakely?" she demanded, her voice trembling. "Why did you demand another meeting? I thought our business over and done. I missed taking my children to Astley's to meet you!"

"Poor darlings." He sounded as sincere as a viper. "How unfortunate for them that their mother is an adulteress, who must pay for her sins."

"I am no adulteress!" Fanny cried, clasping her hand to her throat. She could see his thin mouth twist in a sneer, and though shadows hid his black eyes she knew they would be cold. Cold and conscienceless. Why, oh why, had she not seen what he was in time?

"You may say so, little Fanny, but your letters suggest so strongly otherwise, and I have found another."

"What?" She gaped, her heart seeming to sink like lead to her feet. "But you said you had given them all back to me!"

"Alas, it appears I was wrong." He stood so comfortably, one foot propped against the trunk of a pear tree, swinging a quizzing glass in his hand as he watched her with those cold, conscienceless eyes she could not see. Had she had a gun, Fanny thought she could have killed him without remorse. She did not think God would find a great deal of fault with her, for she doubted she was the Viscount Blakely's only victim. "I happened to be searching my drawers for something else entirely, when I found yet another of those so-torrid missives you wrote to me. I must say, I was flattered all over again, my dear, succulent little Fanny."

"Do not call me that! I am not your anything, Blakely."

"No?" In the dark, she could see a flash of white and knew he smiled. "I do believe, Fanny, my little Fanny, that your husband, and even your brother, should either one read this letter, would call you my mistress."

He enjoyed this, she realized. He liked baiting her, watching her bleed. She had not been his lover, only almost, just after she had married . . . but she'd not think about Charley! No, not now. Not in *his* foul presence.

"What do you want?"

Blakely chuckled, for all the world as if he were truly amused. "You learn quickly, little Fanny. You do, indeed. It is quite a passionate letter, far more than the other three combined. I think . . ."

"Quiet!" she hissed, and they both went still, listening, for Blakely did not want them discovered any more than she. Public knowledge of a relation between them would lower the value of the letter he held.

Two pairs of footsteps crunched slowly over the gravel path leading to the mirror pond in the center of Mr. and Mrs. Gordon Stanley's garden. Fanny held her breath, willing the couple to remain on that more public path. But no! The footsteps turned toward the shadows of the yews and the thick Italian cedars that bordered the garden. A pair of lovers desired privacy.

"I must go!" Fanny whispered, her feet moving, one behind the other, her eyes riveted to the path.

There was no telling whether the pair might not slip into the shadows of the yews. They'd not be seen from the terrace. Evidently, Lord Blakely thought the risk too great to run. Taking Fanny's arm, he half pushed her between their bush and the next. Mercifully, there was just space enough to brush through onto the main path without damaging Fanny's gown. Bending low, he put his mouth to her ear. "Return here in precisely one hour. I'll not wait."

No! She could not come again, skulking like a thief in the night. Fanny shook her head wildly, but already he was gone, disappearing into thin air so that she wondered for a frightful moment if he were not the devil himself.

A woman's giggle brought her back to reality. The couple might reappear at any minute. Walking lightly as she could, Fanny flew toward the house. She felt sick. Blakely had found another letter, and she had used all her pin money to ransom the other three. She would have to sell something. Her mind feverishly searched for some stray bit of jewelry Charley, her good, dear Charley, would never miss. Lud, there were only a few pins and rings given to her years ago. She would have to send to Somerset for them. They meant nothing to her . . . would they be worth enough? Oh God! And to think Blakely had waited all these years to accost her. She had forgotten the letters, had put them from her stupid, stupid mind! How could she have . . . but she was here, at the terrace. She must compose herself. Someone could come out at any moment. She could not appear anguished. What if it was Gussie who saw her?

* * *

Hampton arrived late at the Stanleys' in company with Lord Mannering. They'd supped at White's with Mr. Godolphin and had lingered over their meal and port. Lord Hampton had spent most of his "days away" with his oldest friend. Antoinette's high voice had begun to wear upon him after only a full day of her company, and so he and Robin had hied off to a mill in Kent. It meant nothing that he had tired of his mistress's voice, he assured himself, scanning the crowd on the dance floor and off. Paul Desmond waved heartily, and a second later Lord Hampton saw that the man's daughter Miss Pamela Desmond was sitting out the dance. Great God, but he must settle on a wife. He was sick to death of all this false friendliness. Even now there was Mrs. Beckford straining to catch his eye. A moment or two later, he saw Miss Bromwell. Seeing him, Henrietta smiled radiantly but did not miss a step of the quadrille. He smiled back. Actually, she was not half bad. He felt almost as proud of her as a brother would, though of course he'd had nothing to do with the civilizing of the child. That had been . . . he thought he saw Lady Whitfield. The woman had thick, dark hair and was about the same height, but when she turned, he saw she resembled a horse. Lud, and she even batted her eyes at him. No, she was not Lady Whitfield. Juliana—as he did think of her from time to time— might bat her eyes if she had something to them, but if she found him watching her? She'd have lifted her chin at him and glared pointedly.

"You are smiling to yourself, Alex. Have you seen some tasty morsel? Or perhaps some excellent prospect for your wife?"

"I detest that sweet tone you use, Robin, whenever you make mention of my prospective wife." Hampton eyed his friend lazily. "You are a wretch to derive such amusement from the prospect of my marriage. And as to why I was smiling, I shall thwart you by informing you that I was pleased to have spied Fanny. Lud, but I must say I think she is exceedingly pretty for an old married women of twenty-and-six with two children."

"She is indeed," Lord Mannering agreed in a tone almost as fond as his friend's. "Charley was lucky to get her."

"Shall we pay our respects?" Lord Hampton asked, starting off toward the French windows.

"Yes. Perhaps she'll know where Lady Whitfield is. I do not see her, and I could use a dose of her beauty to counteract the potent memory of Godolphin's visage."

Lord Hampton found he could not respond immediately to the announcement that Lord Mannering was on the hunt for Lady Whitfield. The first words that came to his mind were a sharp reminder that she did not want a husband, nor was the sort to take a lover. But he did not know that last, or even the first, really, with any certainty, and was not sorry to have the obligation of greeting the lords Bute and Derby. When he and Lord Mannering had passed the two older men, he was then able to say with perfect ease, "Godolphin's ugly as a toad, but he's the charm of being an entertaining dinner companion."

"Do you think his information on Lady Whitfield's father was correct?"

Hampton shrugged. "Goldolphin's sister—have you ever stopped to wonder what her looks are—lives in Lancashire. If she says the baron was a dissolute wastrel, he likely was."

Lord Mannering nodded as if he'd come to the same conclusion. "Which would mean he wasted his money, and likely needed it, when Whitfield approached him for his daughter. Or do you suppose the man approached Whitfield? Did you know Whitfield's second wife died under suspicious circumstances?"

"No." Lord Hampton turned sharply, too sharply, but Lord Mannering did not remark his display of interest in Lady Whitfield's husband.

Lord Mannering was frowning at some indistinct point on the floor. "I had it from Badgett, actually. He's my solicitor, you know, and as I learned only this morning when we were going over some business together, he occasionally did business for Whitfield, as well. It seems the old fellow was married an age to some woman of no family. When she obligingly died—of natural causes, Badgett said—Whitfield married higher. The second wife was a girl of the minor nobility, a knight's daughter, but, like the first, failed to bear him a child. He had a doctor in to examine her for the cause. Badgett knew, because Whitfield applied to him for a recommendation on a qualified man, but a year later she was dead, having fallen down a flight of stairs and broken her neck. At her funeral, Badgett heard the disquieting rumor that Whitfield had discovered her in his bed with a lover and that she'd been carrying the lover's child."

And so then the old wretch had taken another, nobler, more beautiful wife, and beaten her when he suspected her of taking an interest in another man. Beaten her and kept her secluded in Lancashire, as far as possible from London. Lord Hampton raked the couples on the dance floor with a hard gaze. He did not see her, however, and they had reached Fanny.

"Fanny?" He frowned, Lady Juliana Whitfield temporarily put aside. On close inspection, his sister appeared excessively pale.

"It is the air in here," she said, understanding his question, evidently. "The ballroom is very close with so many people. I've just been on the terrace a moment, but perhaps I did not get enough air."

"Lady Charles! There you are! Been lookin' for you. On Lady Whitfield's behalf."

Fanny's eyes went wide. "Why what do you mean, Mr. Porter?"

"Evening, Hampton, Mannering." Mr. Porter nodded briefly. "I mean"—he looked back to Fanny, his pleasant, round face creasing with distress—"that she asked me to advise you she has left to return to Grosvenor Square."

"What?"

"When?"

Mr. Porter answered Lord Hampton first, perhaps because his question was the more sharply put. "About half an hour ago, perhaps a little less. She went with Lord Soames."

"Soames?"

Something in Lord Hampton's voice made Mr. Porter blink. "Yes, you see he was with her when it happened."

"What happened, Mr. Porter?"

George Porter shook his head. "I cannot say I understand the whole, really. But the account I got from Sally Jersey and one or two others who happened to be nearby is that as Soames was leadin' Lady Whitfield from the dance floor a lieutenant in the Dragoons approached her. Sally said he was a beefy, coarse-lookin' fellow, though the Thirteenth Dragoons are no poor man's regiment. At any rate he called out, 'Sister,' hailing Lady Whitfield, who went stiff and pale, Sally said. Nor did she greet the fellow, but instead turned to Lord Soames and asked him on the instant to escort her home. I had just come in from the gamin' room when she passed me on her way to the door. She asked me to tell you not to worry, but that she was returning home early. That was all she said."

"Does she have a brother, Fanny?"

He had spoken too intensely, but the others were so caught in the mystery of the little drama Mr. Porter had described that they did not remark Lord Hampton's mood. Fanny's brow wrinkled as she tried to think.

"Yes, I think she may have. But he wasn't her full brother . . ."

"That's it," Mr. Porter said, and Lord Hampton had to restrain himself from shaking his old friend.

"What do you mean, George?" he asked, his voice overly calm.

"Well, the fellow came with Carrington, you see, and Carrington was furious after he heard the incident. You remember that Carrington was in the Thirteenth Dragoons for a bit? Well, he sold out before this man joined, but when the lieutenant asked if he might accompany him to the Stanleys', Carrington obliged him as a fellow officer in his old regiment. Delany—that's the man's name—said he'd a connection to Lady Whitfield, though he did not say what, precisely, and Carrington admitted he's had a desire to become better acquainted with her . . ."

"And thinking she would be pleased to see an old friend, he provided his dear, brother officer an entree to the Stanleys' ball, though he may not have been entirely taken with this Delany's looks," Lord Mannering finished.

Mr. Porter affirmed his friend's summation. "That's it right and tight, Mannering. After Lady Whitfield looked through Delany as if she did not know him and promptly walked out of the room, Carrington knew he'd erred. He did get out of this Delany fellow that he's her half brother, but the lieutenant up and left before Carrington could learn what's between them."

"A commission in the Thirteenth Dragoons would not come cheaply," Lord Mannering mused.

Lord Hampton had already entertained the thought, and several other equally grim ones besides. "Fanny, you must go to her. I would not be surprised if Delany were the man she encountered at Vauxhall, and I do not think it was a happy reunion."

"Oh my!" Fanny turned a distressed gaze up to her brother. "Will you go and look after her, Alex? I . . . I promised Harriet Bromwell I would help her look after Henrietta tonight."

"But . . ."

"Please, Alex? The Bromwells are doing nicely, but they need looking after, and I promised I would take charge of them this evening. Gussie cannot because Sarah and young Arnold Stanley have formed a decided interest in one another, and Gussie believes they need looking after most . . ."

"All right." Fanny could rattle on for hours with excuses,

and Lord Hampton felt as little like listening to excuses as he felt like . . . making meaningless social conversation for hours and hours. She needed someone. He did not question how he knew it. He simply did.

In his carriage, Hampton stared unseeing at the shadowy buildings out the window, his thoughts spinning maddeningly until they landed on something new. He had forgotten Soames, somehow, but it suddenly occurred to him that the viscount might have remained at Fanny's.

The earl shifted restlessly on the seat. She had someone with her. She did not need him. There was no reason for him to have rushed off to her side without thinking.

She had left no message with George for him. She did not want him running after her, and he had no desire to run after her. It was a wife he wanted. A well-bred chit with no louts for brothers. Great God, had the brother taken his hand to her, too? The father? Alex passed a frustrated hand over his face. He was seeing more dragons than George. He was losing his mind. She was robbing him of it. He brooded on her and her mysteries. A great deal. Not incessantly. Nothing so absurd. But a great deal.

When the carriage clattered into Grosvenor Square, Hampton leaned forward to look out the window, half prepared to knock on the box and order the coachman to drive on to Half Moon Street, but he fell back against the seat. The street before Fanny's stood empty. Soames had gone. She was alone.

Chapter 15

In Fanny's garden, Juliana stared into the inky waters of the little ornamental pool. She could see neither the lily pads nor the goldfish. There was no moon that night, but her room had felt too confining, and the library too public.

She winced, thinking of the audience at Mr. and Mrs. Stanley's. Why had Hugh done it? Why had he approached her, given the ultimatum she had issued? She truly had not thought he would. He could only be desperate for money. Gaming debts, of course. She tried to imagine Hugh living on only the sum he'd get for selling his commission. Their father had left him naught but an empty title and a taste for gaming and drink and women. He'd end in the Rookery, London's worst area, stealing and guzzling the gin his ill-gotten gains bought him. If he eluded the gallows, he'd die in rags in an alleyway. And he was her brother.

But what choice did she have? If she did not make good on her threat to revoke the remainder of his allowance, she would never know when Hugh might pop up again to demand more. Or what methods he would use when he did.

At least when he came, she'd not to have to skulk into the shadows to hear his demands. She smiled grimly. No, everyone knew now that he was her brother. And that there were less than affectionate feelings between them. There would be speculation as to the reasons. Her family's dirty linen would be pegged to the line for all to see. She closed her eyes, but saw, nonetheless, the looks of those near her

at the Stanleys': not merely curious, but avid and speculative, too. Perhaps she ought to have at least nodded to
Hugh. But she had warned him what she would do if he approached her, and anyway, she could not pretend warmth
for him, the *ton's* gossip-hungry eyes be damned. She
would leave town before she clasped Hugh to her bosom.
And before she endured a great deal of whispering about
having been sold like a cow. Would they guess? Could
they? It shamed her unbearably, that one thing above all,
that she had been treated by her own father and brother
with less feeling than they accorded their horses.

"Is Lady Whitfield here, Haskins?"

Halfway to the door, it had occurred to Hampton that
Soames might have persuaded Juliana to go to his home for
a restorative glass of brandy, perhaps, or other soothing
pleasures.

However, Haskins informed him gravely that Lord
Soames had not stayed, and further, that Lady Whitfield
was in the gardens. Though it was a trifle cool that night,
Haskins gave no indication he thought her ladyship's behavior odd, and the earl only nodded before he strode pur-
posefully toward the library and the French doors there. He
had come to look in on her, to see she was all right, and he
meant to do it. If she did not want his company, she would
tell him.

She sat on a bench near the pond, staring down, her neck
drooping like a reed, the wealth of her chocolate dark hair
seeming too heavy for it. He started to call out a greeting, a
warning, really, but she heard his step on the gravel, and
started violently, whipping about with a cry.

"Ah!" she gasped, clearly seized with fear. She recovered in the next instant, recognizing him and sagging,
though whether from simple relief or something more it
was impossible to say.

"It is I, Lady Whitfield," Alex said unnecessarily, but
feeling the need to break the silence that seemed to hold her

apart from him in a place of shadow and fear. "Haskins said you were here."

Her hand shook as she dropped it from the vulnerable place at her throat where she had clapped it. But she stiffened her spine at the same moment, straightened her shoulders, and a second later lifted her eyes to his. "As you see, my lord."

There was that tugging sensation again in his chest. He wanted to tell her he thought her brave as anyone he knew, but . . . but the remark seemed the beginning of a slippery slope whose bottom he could not even imagine. Hampton pulled back instinctively and told himself he did not tell her she was brave because he might make her shy of him.

He'd been staring down at her too long. Her brow arched. Hampton's eyes had adjusted to the dark enough that he could see the dark, graceful crescent of her eyebrow lift with question.

"I came to be certain that you are all right," he explained simply. "Fanny would have come, but she thought she'd a responsibility to look after the Bromwells tonight."

"Oh, yes," she said, her voice so distant and colorless she might have been discussing some historical incident. "Fanny did say she would assume Gussie's position as principal shepherdess. As . . . as to me, I am quite all right, Lord Hampton. I thank you for coming, but you need not stay."

She had a history of dismissing him, and regally, too. Hampton was half tempted to go. He felt rather a fool for charging away from the Stanleys' as he'd done, for she did not seem to need him. But then his eye fell to the hands she'd folded in her lap. She wore no gloves. She must have given them into the care of her maid, and he could see that her slender hands were clenched tightly, as if she sought to hold herself together with the clasp.

Lord Hampton walked in front of her to a bench that with hers and two others formed a semicircle before the pond. He would have preferred to remain standing, one foot resting on the bench. But he sat, stretching his legs out before him and folding his arms over his chest.

From the corner of his eye, he could see her hands had not loosened, but Hampton made no effort to ask permission to stay. If she truly did not want his company, she would either tell him outright or go to her room. When after a moment she did neither, he went directly to the point.

"The man at Vauxhall was your brother? This Lieutenant Delany, Lord Blackmore?"

Silence followed, so thick and taut he really doubted she would answer. Then, low but clear enough, she did. "Yes."

The roughness in the low timbre of her voice made Hampton clench his jaw almost as tightly as Juliana clenched her hands. "How did he threaten you?" He was suddenly determined to know. Perhaps she heard that determination, or perhaps she only heard the tension in him, but she turned to look at him.

"What leads you to think Hugh threatened me?" she asked, her guard creeping up again.

Hampton made an impatient sound. "Because you were pale as a ghost when you came out of that alcove with him, and you dug your fingers into my arm to drag me off with you, as if you were afraid of him. I cannot be of assistance to you unless I know. How did he threaten you?"

"How?" she asked softly, looking away again to the pond. "Why, by being larger and stronger. Did you not see Hugh?"

"He was gone by the time I arrived at the Stanleys'. Was he the one who hit you?"

Her head drooped again, abruptly enough that the earl nearly regretted his question, but only nearly. She had nothing of which to be ashamed, and it was high time she knew it. He started to say as much when in an almost inaudible whisper she said, "On one memorable occasion . . . yes."

But that was not all to the story, and Hampton knew it from the heaviness in her voice. "Must I draw out all the particulars? Why did he hit you? To force you to marry

Whitfield? And what of the old man? I have heard rumors about his second wife's death."

With a sob of horror she pivoted on the bench so that she faced the central path that led directly to the library . . . and away from him. Speaking carefully, lest he scare her off, Hampton addressed her slender back. "Their deeds have naught to do with you . . ."

Before he could finish, she shot to her feet. Still, it needed only one quick step for him to reach out and catch her hand, though he made certain he caught her only gently. She went still, though he'd the sense that like a deer in the woods she was poised to flee the instant she thought she could.

He tightened his hold a fraction, and as he did he realized her fingers were cold as ice. It made him furious that she was cold. He did not stop to think why he was furious. He began chafing both her hands vigorously, upbraiding her angrily as he did. "For God's sake, woman, your hands are as cold as ice. Do you mean to make yourself ill because you've a greedy bully for a brother and had, before you were well rid of him, a madman for a husband?"

She yanked her hands free of his. "They knew, damn you!" she all but shouted up at him. "They knew he'd murdered her!"

The words seemed to echo over and over in that quiet garden, unbearable and so infinitely painful Hampton nearly regretted provoking her to say them. They had known, and he knew who "they" were. He could not have controlled himself, even had he thought to. He cupped her jaw with his hand. He felt her muscles tremble. She held herself that tightly, and the pulse at her throat throbbed wildly beneath his fingers. But she did not pull away, she only glared at him, trembling with tension and hurt.

"You have nothing to do with them." His voice was too rough. He had to stop to clear his throat. "Do we think less of the lamb a thief has stolen? No. It is the thief we condemn."

She lifted her jaw away from his hand. For just a moment he had thought she nuzzled into him but apparently not. She stood alone, her eyes great dark pools full of shadows, fringed with lashes thick as a sable's fur.

"Hugh and I are of the same family, my lord. Unlike your lamb and thief, he and I share a father. They are my . . . they are my family, and they sold me to Whitfield. I brought five thousand pounds, with four hundred more to go to my father every quarter. He doled out a portion to Hugh as he saw fit, until he died, when Hugh received the whole allowance."

Hampton thought he could have shot both the elder Lord Blackmore and the younger without a second thought at that moment. "I am so sorry."

She did not appear to hear him, but went on, almost as if she could not stop now she'd started. "They knew he was mad. Ann told me most in Lancashire considered it suspicious that Whitfield's second wife had fallen to her death after he had returned early from a business trip and found the girl in bed with their neighbor. She told him she carried the man's child, or so Ann said. Whitfield never said so, only that he had learned how treacherous young, noble women were by breeding."

Her voice had taken on the quality of a recitation, and perhaps that was why she sounded so young and helpless and bewildered by the betrayal of those who should have protected her. When Hampton cupped her tense jaw again, she leaned into his touch. With the one, unconsidered move, she undid him. He was powerless against the desire to enfold her in his arms.

But she did not let him hold her. She put up her hands, bracing them against his chest. She did not push away but literally held him at half-arm's length, looking up at him with eyes more black than violet. "My father was a drunken wastrel. I rarely saw him as a child. My brother was a brute who beat me so badly, I'd have married anyone . . ."

Lord Hampton shook her then. Holding her by the shoulders, he gave her an impatient shake and said in a fierce voice, "They are not you, damn it! I loathe this Hugh Delany. Make no mistake, I would not regret beating him to a bloody pulp. He deserves that and more. But I do not think the less of you on account of your father or your half brother or the old baronet to whom they married you." Her hands felt warm now on his chest, but he ignored a desire to lift them to his lips. She'd bolt, he thought. "Does anyone judge Prinny the less for having Mad George for his father?" he demanded, his tone no less intense for the heat she aroused in him. "Damn it," he snapped again. "Are you somehow a special case that you must be tainted by the sins of your father, while our own Regent is not? And what of Lady Coke? Yes, she of the renowned breakfasts. No one cares that her mother was an opera dancer, precisely because she does not. Ah, I see I've taken you by surprise, but then you do not thrive on gossip. You've too much generosity in your heart to gossip, too much integrity and honor."

"Oh, stop!"

But Hampton only shook her lightly again. "I will say it. You've not a mean-spirited bone in your body, giving the lie to your heritage, and . . ." Tears spilled from her eyes. They glistened on her cheeks and cut him as surely as if they were crystal shards. "Oh God, no. Do not cry. I did not want to make you cry." When he pulled her to him then, she went, unresisting, though she kept her chin lifted, as if she were so unaccustomed to being held that she did not know to bury her face against his shoulder.

Holding her tight against him, he freed one hand to wipe the tears from her cheeks, then bent to lay a single kiss like a whisper on her lips. Her mouth tasted as sweet as he'd known it would, and her lips went soft beneath his. Hampton kissed her again longer. Then, when he lifted his head, he heard her give a little, protesting sigh. At the sound, a rush of heat flared through him. He had wanted her for a long time, and she was receptive. But he never kissed her again. As he bent toward her, one of the French doors in the library opened, and Fanny called out. "Juliana! Alex!"

Juliana whirled out of his arms with a cry, as if she had been awakened from a dream and without a backward glance half ran to the terrace.

Chapter 16

Juliana awoke late the next morning, groggy from a restless sleep. She had dreamed the night long, mostly of her father and brother and husband. Drifting into awareness, however, and feeling an odd heaviness in her heart, she did not think of them at all. As vividly as if Hampton were kissing her there and then, she recalled the feel of his lips just brushing hers. And the longing even that light touch of his lips had roused in her, the aching for more, and then, the getting of it. But only for a little. She remembered how he'd lifted his mouth from hers too soon, and how she had moaned with disappointment, moaned out loud. He could not have missed it.

Juliana threw back her bedcovers with enough force to send the blankets half onto the floor so that Randall, entering the room, looked at her mistress in surprise. "I shall want a walking dress, Rand," Juliana said forcefully after only the briefest of greetings. "I am going to call upon my solicitor Mr. Mumford this morning. But perhaps I should send a note by one of Fanny's footmen to notify him of my intent? Yes, yes, I am certain that would be advisable. Fetch me a note and paper, would you?"

"You will not be riding this morning then, my lady?"

"Riding?" Juliana sounded as if the idea were foreign to her. "No, no, Rand. It is too late, I am certain, and anyway, I must see Mr. Mumford as soon as possible."

"Yes, my lady. I shall fetch what you need, only allow

me to advise you that Lady Charles wishes to see you, whenever you are able this morning."

Juliana hesitated a half second, but could not bring herself to ask if Lord Hampton were taking chocolate with his sister, as he did on the rarest of occasions do. It was not even that she did not wish Rand to know she was interested in Lord Hampton's whereabouts. Juliana did not ask, because she'd have had to admit to herself just how shy she was of meeting the earl on the day after she'd not merely allowed him to brush her lips reassuringly, but warm and secure in his arms, had moaned aloud for more.

When she had dressed and sent off her note to Mr. Mumford, Juliana went along to Fanny's rooms, holding her spine very straight. She understood what had happened to her in the garden the night before. She had felt lost and vulnerable, estranged from every well-bred person in London as if she were tainted. Hampton had come along to give her understanding and comfort. Of course, she had felt a softening toward him. And he had given her those soft, brushing kisses, perhaps taking advantage of her, perhaps only wanting to give her a tangible reassurance that she was not beyond the pale. She would give him the benefit of the doubt and say the latter. At any rate, it could be no surprise that having felt somehow unworthy and then having been reassured that she was no different from many . . . well, that she would want even more tangible reassurance. She had not often been kissed.

Juliana bit her lip hard. The truth was no man but Whitfield had kissed her before, and Sir Arthur had never wasted his time with soft, brushing, teasing kisses that could not produce heirs. Oh, yes, it was little wonder she had been susceptible. But with the day had come clarity. Marching along to Fanny's rooms, Juliana told herself that she need not think of herself as alone and helpless. She had a solicitor who could assist her. He was a capable man. Mr. Mumford had come to Westerleigh several times since Sir Arthur's death, and she had found his advise excellent. She would have him see that Hugh signed a document renouncing any claims on her but the two hundred pounds in quarterly allowance she was willing to give him and swearing at the same time never to approach her again. The legal document would force Hugh to recognize the extent of her determination. If he did not, the results would be on his head.

She could take care of herself and would. Not that she feared men. It would have been impossible not to acknowledge that there were enormous differences among them. Mr. Porter, Lord Soames, Lord Houghton, Lord Mannering were all different one from the other and . . . to give him his due, Lord Hampton could not have been more different from Sir Arthur. The earl might not claim to be a model of perfection, but he had offered her understanding and sensitivity when she had needed them. She was grateful.

Juliana's step slowed briefly. She really was grateful to him. Twice he had come to her when she had been in the deepest distress, doubting herself and her worth, and both times he had restored her self-respect. Lud, yes, she was grateful. And she could not be entirely sorry she had kissed him. The kiss had seemed right at the time. Only now, in the light of day, she owed it to herself to remember that it was he who would never marry her. Not that her own views on marriage had changed entirely. She was not looking for a husband, but if she was at least fractionally more receptive to the notion of marrying—at least to the extent that she recognized that not all men would use the rights allowed them by law to dominate her unmercifully—she did understand that the Earl of Hampton would never choose her. He would want a girl of spotless background . . . and of malleable spirit.

Juliana looked rather bleakly at Fanny's door, then quickly made herself knock on it. If he was with Fanny, then he was. She would treat him in a friendly, but no more, manner.

Fanny had her children with her, but Hampton was nowhere to be seen. Juliana did acknowledge the breath she released, but seeing Fanny, she was reminded of the end of the last evening and half forgot Lord Hampton.

They had wound up in the library, after Juliana had half run from Hampton to his sister. Leaving out the more miserable details, she had then explained to Fanny a little of why she was estranged from her half brother, saying he and her father had profited by her marriage and had forced her into it. She did not describe her marriage, except to say it had not been easy and had ended with the half sheepish remark, "I fear I have been distressed that society might think the less of me for coming from a family that would treat me with so little honor and respect. Call me an oversensitive fool, and rightly, I suppose."

At that, Fanny had burst into tears. Juliana had been so astonished she had looked to Lord Hampton, whom she had been studiously trying to ignore. He had looked somewhat surprised, but more accustomed to his sister, he had offered his handkerchief and had chided her teasingly for being a softhearted ninny. Fanny's head had bobbed up and down at that, but she'd protested between sniffles that she thought Juliana unbearably brave. Embarrassed, Juliana had declared it was time for bed. The whole, she had said, and of course she referred to more than Fanny could know, would seem vastly different in the morning.

And Fanny did, indeed, look calmer that morning. Her eyes were dry, but she did not appear to have slept well. At Juliana's look of inquiry, however, she smiled.

"I have just been reading to Harry and Sophie. Up now, loves. Say good morning to Lady Whitfield and then be off. I shall finish your story later."

Juliana thought them so obviously reluctant to leave that she opened her mouth to bid them stay, but Fanny shook her head, and they trotted off as planned. "Never you mind about them. I wish so much to speak to you, Juliana!" Fanny caught her friend's hand and drew Juliana down onto a small chintz-covered couch beside her. "I'll not have you fear that society will think the less of you for the abominable way your family behaved toward you!" Her brow knit in earnestness. "What if it should become common knowledge that your father married you off to Whitfield in order to pay gaming debts? Or even if people should realize that he knew Whitfield to be half mad? The sins are his, not yours, my dear. Your must believe that!"

"I do, Fanny, I do. Lud, you look as if you've lost sleep on my account, and I do regret that, for I am in a much better frame of mind today. Lord Hampton helped me to see how unfounded my fears were. He did, truly."

"But you are dressed for traveling, Juliana!" Fanny waved her hand over Juliana's walking dress. "I thought you meant to leave town."

Juliana shook her head quickly. "No, not at all, Fanny. I am dressed for a visit to my solicitor. This morning, I realized I could send Mr. Mumford to Hugh. He can draw up a legal agreement for Hugh to sign about his allowance. If Hugh refuses, then his difficulties will be on his head. I will have done what my conscience requires."

"It is more than I would do!" Fanny exclaimed, though Juliana had confided nothing of the beating Hugh had given her. "But I can see that you do not want me to dwell on your merits. You look as if you mean to bolt. Please do not. I'll not say how brave I think you and how . . . truly noble . . . oh, I am crying again! Forgive me, Juliana. I have become the veriest watering pot, I know!"

"Fanny, my dear!" Juliana exclaimed half despairingly. "You've the softest heart imaginable. Lord Hampton is quite right. Here, I shall pour you some tea. The pot is still warm."

Fanny drank the cup Juliana poured rather like a dutiful child. "I am better," she said after a few sips. "I'll not say another word about last night. I vow it. Rather, I shall address today."

She looked so grimly determined that Juliana smiled. "Is today so very bad, then?"

"Not now that you've said you do not mean to return to

Lancashire. But, Juliana, why do you not have Alex see to your brother for you? I am certain he would do it, and that he would be effective in handling the odious man."

Juliana reacted all the more stiffly for having ever-so-briefly thought of just that course. "I am certain that Lord Hampton would attend to Hugh. He has been . . . very kind. But . . . I want to manage my affairs myself. Does that sound odd to you, Fanny?"

"Odd?" Fanny seemed to look inward, considering. "Perhaps. I . . . I am not half so brave and strong as you, but I think I understand a little. You were so outrageously denied any control of your affairs, first by your father and then by Sir Arthur that yes, given your strength of character, Juliana, I can understand, though I must add, I do not think Alex will understand so easily. You did not see his face when you told me what you did of your history with your half brother. He looked quite fierce."

"I must learn to stand on my own, Fanny," Juliana replied, meaning it. "It is to Lord Hampton's credit that he cannot abide injustice, but he has his own affairs to attend to."

Fanny appeared about to argue further, but even as she opened her mouth she shrugged. "Very well, Juliana. You must decide for yourself about your brother, I suppose, but I hope I may advise you in another area? I do hope you wish still to attend the Opera with Gussie and Sarah and Danley, as we planned. Gussie intended to say something to Alex last night. Perhaps she still means to do so. I left so shortly after the Bromwells that I did not see her. But it does not signify about Alex. The important thing is that you are seen holding your head high, for the way to scotch gossip is simply to behave as if there is no reason on earth for it."

Juliana had not known that Hampton might be one of the party attending the Opera. Still, she managed a smile for Fanny's worldly wisdom and professed herself quite prepared to face whatever awaited her that evening.

*   *   *

Juliana did encounter speculative looks, as well as simply curious ones, but in all, Fanny's remarks proved true. Because she appeared in public for all the world as if nothing were amiss, the gossips began to doubt that anything was. It did help, she knew, that Lady Danley and Fanny both gave out the simple truth when asked: that Juliana's half brother had long resented her for being better born than he. It was a resentment those in society could understand very well, having been educated from the cradle to consider the fine nuances of who was above whom—and who was below—on the social hierarchy. The gossips nodded sagely, and if they guessed the brother might have had something to do with Juliana's lucrative but lowly marriage, they only turned a more sympathetic eye Lady Whitfield's way.

In all, Juliana found the evening better than bearable. The soprano made a marvelous leading lady, and Lord Hampton failed to make an appearance at all. He had not been expected. Evidently he had seen Fanny while Juliana was out consulting Mr. Mumford, her solicitor. To Fanny's surprise, he had taken that news with little evidence of emotion. Specifically she reported that his eyebrow had lifted sharply, and that he had asked Juliana's solicitor's name, but upon hearing he was the well-respected Mr. Mumford, Hampton had said no more except to advise his sister, upon being asked, that he could not attend the Opera that night as he had made other plans. Juliana did not ask what those other plans might be, but even had she had the inclination, she'd not have had the opportunity. Lady Danley inquired into them before she could and frowned in frustration when Fanny replied that their brother had not chosen to enlighten her.

Juliana learned the reason for his absence the next day. She and Fanny went riding in the Park with Mrs. Daviess in her open cabriolet. Juliana had half an eye out for Hampton. She still had not seen him since he had kissed her, and

the more time that went by, the more uncertain she became.
Had the kiss meant nothing at all to him, she asked herself,
only to answer that of course it had not. But the answer did
not satisfy her as it should have. On the one hand she felt
angry that he would have kissed her when he did not care a
fig for her, while on the other, she felt unmercifully frustrated that she cared at all. In short, she felt like a green
schoolgirl and resented feeling so uncertain.

To Fanny's surprise, they met Lady Bedford, Lord
Charles's mother in the Park. The duchess had only just arrived in town, and had driven out just to see Fanny to inquire about her grandchildren. While the two women were
occupied, Mrs. Daviess took the opportunity to assure Juliana that no one thought the less of her for her father's unfortunate first marriage or because he had pushed her into
marriage with Whitfield.

"You ought not to regret the talk, Juliana," Mrs. Daviess
remarked in her airy way. "You come out quite the heroine,
you know, and as to your family, well, everyone has skele-
tons, my dear. La, I could tell you of a few infinitely more
scandalous . . . but lo! Here's an *on-dit,* now, if not a skele-
ton!"

Mrs. Daviess's eyes had taken on such a delighted, avid
sparkle that Juliana turned to look. Seated in a smart open
conveyance much like theirs, talking to two gentlemen on
horseback, sat a magnificent beauty with gleaming red hair
exposed to the sun by the dashing tilt of her elaborate, exceedingly fashionable and expensive bonnet. Juliana could
see that the woman wore an equally costly pelisse and that
she was voluptuous.

"She's Hampton's mistress, Antoinette Duvenay," Mrs.
Daviess whispered excitedly in Juliana's ear. "La, is it any
wonder he is reluctant to wed? Is she not stunning? Mr.
Daviess told me this morning that Hampton celebrated her
birthday last night in quite a riotous fashion at the house in
which he keeps her in Half Moon Street. Evidently he
hosted a dinner party, if an entertainment with dozens of

demireps can be called anything so ordinary. She must be quite pleased with herself. Normally Hampton does not keep a mistress overlong, but La Duvenay has been in his keeping at least half a year, and he is still indulging her, it seems. I shall deny it, if you quote me, but I vow, Juliana, that I half envy the woman. Hampton is a too, too attractive rogue."

Thanks to Mrs. Daviess and her whispered remarks, Juliana returned to Grosvenor Square in a considerably more decided frame of mind than she had enjoyed when she left. Hampton was a rogue. He not only kept a spectacular mistress while he considered which young lady he would deign to wed, he actually flaunted the beautiful demirep, giving birthday parties, of all things, for her. Wild ones, too, that were certain to be talked about. Obviously he liked women for the pleasure they brought, and if he had extended himself to listen to Juliana's tale of woe the night before, he had done it only as a favor to Fanny. The kiss could not have meant anything to him. He might very well have bid her and Fanny good night in order, his dreary duty done, to go to the lush Duvenay creature.

Juliana's mouth tightened. Now she very much wanted to see Hampton. She wanted him to know that their kiss had meant not a deuced thing to her, that she had no intention of repeating it, and that she thought of him, when she thought of him at all, as a friend, a very unimportant friend.

However, her rather furious desire to treat Lord Hampton to an airy, disinterested greeting was to go frustratingly unfulfilled. When they arrived home, Haskins informed Fanny that Lord Hampton had been called to Suffolk and gave her a note in which Lord Hampton informed his sister that he had some business, he did not specify what, that he wished to discuss with their father. Perhaps it was the truth. Or perhaps he had fabricated an excuse to escape Grosvenor Square, because he feared Juliana had read more into his embrace in the garden than he had meant by it. Perhaps her overeager response had given him a fright.

Juliana could not see what to do, but to stay where she was. If she left town, it would surely appear to him that his departure had hurt her. And above all things, she would not have him believe her affected by him. For she was not, after all.

To prove it, Juliana persuaded Fanny to help her plan an entertainment. The weather had turned warmer with the coming of May, and so they decided on an outing to Richmond. As it was an informal affair, they included the children along with the Daviesses, the Bromwells, Lord and Lady Danley, Sarah, and several of her friends, Mr. Stanley and his friends, Mr. Porter, and finally, Lord Soames. The day was a beautiful one, the children wildly excited, the young people amusing to watch, and the refreshments Fanny's staff prepared excellent.

Juliana enjoyed herself. She would allow no other possibility. Determined to make the day as lively as possible, she even allowed Lord Soames to drive her back to Grosvenor Square, with the result that she arrived some quarter of an hour after Fanny, her cheeks rosy from her exertions and her eyes sparkling with humor because Soames had taken care to tell her one funny story after another about his girls.

In return for his escort, she invited Soames to take tea with her and Fanny and the children. Having spent most of the day with him, she did not expect him to accept, but when they neared the drawing room Juliana discovered she had reason to be delighted that he had. Through the open door of the drawing room, she caught sight of an unmistakable, tall, broad-shouldered figure.

Lord Hampton had returned. Her heart skipped a beat, then as if to make up for the miss, began to race so she felt almost dizzy. The children bounded up from the chairs at the sight of her, and alerted, Lord Hampton looked over their heads directly into her eyes.

Juliana forgot even Lord Soames, upon whose arm her fingers rested. It seemed to her as if she had never seen Hampton before, his good looks struck her so. His eyes really were the same golden brown as his hair; his face really was so handsome in its masculine way. She thought she forgot to breathe, but in truth it was only a second before the children forced her to look away from the earl to acknowledge them. When Juliana looked up again, she was in time to see Hampton lift his gaze from the hand she held still on Lord Soames's arm.

Juliana kept her hand where it was as she brought Lord Soames into the room with her. "Good afternoon, Lord Hampton." She had had a long, long time to rehearse how entirely affable and entirely unaffected she would sound. To Juliana's immense satisfaction, she sounded just as she'd planned. "I hope your journey into Suffolk was pleasant?"

Then and only then did she remove her fingers from Lord Soames and make her way to a seat near Fanny. She chose a couch, where Lord Soames, not surprisingly, joined her.

"Soames." Hampton made the viscount a brief, dry greeting before answering Juliana. "My journey was quite pleasant, yes, thank you, Lady Whitfield. As I understand your outing to Richmond was pleasant."

"Oh, yes, it was," Juliana returned, and smiling brilliantly, recounted a few of the pleasures of the day.

He listened, but he did not look wildly pleased to be wasting his time in Grosvenor Square hearing about an outing he'd likely have found dull. At one time, Juliana might have thought the earl's expression unreadable, but wiser about him now, she thought that rather flat, expressionless look hid simple impatience. He yearned for the lush Duvenay, for even he would stop to assure Fanny of their father's health before he went to his mistress.

With rather grim amusement, Juliana watched him as the children took up her story, telling of their walk through the famous maze, including the to-them-grand news that Juliana and Lord Soames had become separated from the party.

"We thought them lost!" Sophie said.

"Have you never been through the maze before, Soames?" asked Lord Hampton in an ironic tone that only intensified when Lord Soames allowed that he had. "Then, you cannot have been too distressed by the separation from your party."

Hampton flicked his gaze to Juliana as Lord Soames answered that he had not been concerned for himself, though he had been worried that the others might wander about all the longer. Juliana, looking Hampton directly in his tawny gold eyes, added, "For my part, I was delighted to be in Lord Soames's company. He is not only an amusing companion but has an excellent sense of direction, and I never feared we were tramping about aimlessly."

"No," murmured Lord Hampton, "I should think Soames would always know his way, not to mention his purpose."

Even Fanny glanced at her brother then, but there was nothing in his expression to indicate he had meant insult to Lord Soames. His eyes seemed to have grown heavy-lidded in the last several moments, making it impossible to read them, but the rest of his expression appeared bland enough. Still, his sister seemed to think it time to change the subject, and subduing the children, commended her brother for returning in time to attend Almack's the following night. "Gussie and I had a wager on it, and I am delighted to say that I won."

Stirring the cup of tea Sophie had brought him, Lord Soames addressed the earl then. "I believe you will enjoy yourself tomorrow at Almack's, Hampton. My cousins have come to town since you left. You've met Hardwicke and his wife, I am sure, but this year they've brought their daughter Lady Elizabeth."

Lord Hampton's eyebrow lifted. "Never say you, too, have caught the matchmaking disease, Soames? I did not think men susceptible."

Lord Soames did not take offense, though Juliana thought a pricklier man might not have liked Hampton's tone. "I am not scheming to throw you together with Lady Elizabeth, Hampton. Hardwicke is amusing, that is all. I regret that I shall not see him, but I shall have to wait for the pleasure of his company. Lady Whitfield has graciously consented to accompany my sister and me to the theater tomorrow night. We shall see Keen in *The Tempest*. Lady Whitfield says it is one of her favorite plays."

Fanny had not known that Lord Soames's sister was in town. Juliana explained Mrs. Fitzpatrick had arrived only that morning, while she herself had only accepted Lord Soames's "very thoughtful" invitation to the theater earlier that afternoon. She did not say she had forgotten all about Almack's, nor that she was glad to avoid Lord Hampton. He listened a little to Fanny go on about missing Juliana's company, then, evidently bored to tears, the earl made his excuses and bolted, Juliana guessed, to the Duvenay's charms.

Chapter 17

At eleven o'clock on Tuesday morning, Hookham's bookshop hummed with the quiet murmurings of its customers. Juliana greeted several people she knew, including Mrs. Bromwell and Henrietta, before she found a quiet corner in which to scan the book she had selected. The volume weighed heavily in her hand, and Juliana grimaced wryly. No pleasure book this. Mr. Blair's book of sermons and lectures would literally be heavy-going.

The improving book had been recommended to her by Lord Soames's sister. Older than the viscount, her children grown and gone, Mrs. Fitzpatrick seemed to have taken on her brother as a project. The comparison to Lady Danley did not escape Juliana. Both were managing ladies very certain of their direction. However, where Lady Danley thoroughly enjoyed London's social life, Mrs. Fitzpatrick disapproved most such frivolity. She said a ball or two for the "marrying off of young gels" was acceptable, but the continual round of entertainment she decried as only just short of wicked. Fanny called her priggish and overweening. Juliana could not really disagree, though she had found reason in the past week to respect the woman. Mrs. Fitzpatrick successfully managed the considerable estate her husband had left her, and Juliana, from the year and more she'd been in charge at Westerleigh, knew just how difficult that was. When Mrs. Fitzpatrick expounded on the methods that had brought her success, Juliana listened receptively.

It was as well that Juliana wanted to hear about the positive results of crop rotation, for she had been much in the woman's company in the last week, having attended the theater with her and Lord Soames on Wednesday, taken dinner with the pair on Friday, attended church on Sunday, and gone to the Argyll Rooms to enjoy the music of the Philharmonic Society on Tuesday.

Fanny had come down with a cold, which had left Juliana free to accept the invitations Lord Soames had taken care to couch as pleas for assistance with his sister. Juliana suspected the viscount was more interested in her than in the entertainment of Mrs. Fitzpatrick, but he knew her views on marriage. She had deliberately repeated them to Mrs. Fitzpatrick in his hearing. She had done so from guilt, for she was unabashedly using the viscount and his sister. True, there was much she could learn from Mrs. Fitzpatrick, but Juliana had accompanied Lord Soames and his sister on one improving outing after another for quite another reason.

She was a coward. Juliana stared blindly down at the first of Mr. Blair's ponderous lectures. There had been time and more for her to consider her response to the sight of Lord Hampton, unexpectedly arrived from the country and standing in his sister's drawing room. She could see him even now, leaning negligently back against the mantelpiece, his light brown hair appealingly disarranged from his ride. The memory of her response frightened her. Her heart had leapt, then had raced dizzyingly. She had been glad, more than glad, to see him. Juliana had only to think of his striking mistress and the party he had given for her the very evening after he had kissed Juliana to know how foolishly dangerous that gladness at the mere sight of him was. If she were to give him her heart, the Earl of Hampton would hurt her far more than Sir Arthur ever had.

"Lady Whitfield, how nicely you enhance Hookham's."

Juliana started. She had almost forgotten she was in Hookham's and had allowed Lord Kettering to take her unawares. The unpleasant man bowed, his eyes gleaming as they roved her in a presumptuous way she did not like.

"Good day to you, Lord Kettering. I am beholden to you for rousing me." Juliana rose, gathering her books while taking care to keep a distance between her and Kettering. "I had become so lost in my book that I quite forgot the time. You will excuse me, I hope? I am to meet Lady Charles at the linen draper's and am behind time. Until later, my lord."

Juliana was out of the booklender's with her three books before Lord Kettering had quite shut his drooling mouth. She had no maid with her or footman, as Fanny was to return from the linen draper's to collect her at Hookham's, but Juliana calculated that being a widow she would be granted a little license, and besides she intended to hurry to Fanny before anyone could remark that she walked down Bond Street alone.

There were only a few people to be seen on the normally crowded shopping street that morning, and Juliana was smugly congratulating herself on how smoothly her escape from Lord Kettering had gone when she heard thunder. Glancing at the darkening sky, she felt a smattering of rain on her nose and increased her pace, uncertain how far the linen draper's shop was but hopeful she would find it soon. There were several carriages standing in the street, but Juliana could not see Fanny's. When she heard thunder again and a gust of wind brought a harder shower, she was grateful that the high brim of her bonnet protected her face, as she dared not take cover in the nearest shop for fear she would miss Fanny.

Juliana's determination did her credit, but it also got her soaked through to the skin. Only a few seconds after the second clap of thunder there was a third and with it, the skies seemed to open. In seconds, she felt rivulets of cold water run down her neck and under the high collar of her walking dress. Peering to little avail through the sheets of rain, feeling like nothing so much as a wet rat, she cursed Lord Kettering and had just decided to dash into a jeweler's for a respite when a carriage pulled up beside her.

Assuming Fanny had come for her, keeping her head bent against the downpour, Juliana veered in its direction. It was not Fanny at all, but Juliana did not realize it until the door was thrown open and a man leapt out. Then she did not have to look beyond his long, booted legs to know him. She knew the way he moved even.

The thought alarmed her, but Lord Hampton had his hand under her arm almost before his footman had the steps down, and he had handed her into his carriage, dripping wet before they had exchanged a word of greeting, much less held any discussion of Juliana's wishes. She knew she could have shrieked a protest at the first touch of his hand, but she was relieved to be in out of the rain, and she consoled herself with the thought that she need be with him for only the few minutes it would take to reach the linen draper's Fanny favored.

Lord Hampton closed the carriage door with a bang sharp enough to bring up Juliana's head. "Devil it," he growled scathingly, "I suppose I should not be astounded that a woman who would keep company with Mary Fitzpatrick does not have the sense to get in out of the rain, but there you are, I am astonished. Is it that you wish to catch your death of cold, Lady Whitfield?"

They had not exchanged more than a few words since he had returned to town, or since he had kissed her and she had moaned for more. Juliana had hoped against hope that if she could not avoid conversation with Hampton for the rest of her life they might speak of anything but that interlude in his sister's gardens. She had not, however, hoped that in place of remarking upon her response to his kiss, the earl would take her to task quite as if she were Sophie's age over something as petty as a getting wet.

She'd have liked to ignore him and his absurd question

completely. It was not possible, however. He had flung himself onto the seat across from her, and looking unfairly large in the small confines of the carriage, his knee touching hers, he held her in the unfriendly glare of his amber eyes.

Coolly Juliana advised him, "I was looking for the linen draper's Fanny frequents. She was to collect me at Hookham's, but I found my books early."

"And so decided to stroll with them through a downpour?" He seemed so set on finding fault with her, Juliana gave him naught but a sharply lifted chin for answer. He flicked his eyes to her stubborn chin but otherwise ignored her gesture. "I wonder what it is you have that you thought worth ruining completely?"

He moved quickly, plucking a book from her arms before she had the least idea he meant to do anything of the kind. "Well, well. Mr. Blair. How positively fascinating." His looked at her, his eyes glinting unpleasantly. "Tell me, Lady Whitfield, do you read Mr. Blair because you feel the need for moral improvement after kissing me so wantonly in Fanny's gardens?" Juliana went rigid at the unexpected attack, but Hampton allowed her no response. Looking directly into her flashing eyes, he shook his head. "Careful now, Lady Whitfield. I am certain neither Mrs. Fitzpatrick nor Soames would want you to reply in passion. Does Soames know you are passionate, by the by? Have you allowed him a taste of your charms, too?"

Juliana flushed painfully. She had kissed him . . . had wanted more of him than she'd gotten even. She had behaved badly. She admitted it, but she had thought him in sympathy with her. Even if he had no deep feeling for her, she had thought that he had some small care for her. Clearly she had misjudged him entirely.

"Stop the carriage this instant! I will not sit and listen to insults."

"I am afraid you shall have to, Lady Whitfield," Hampton replied with a carelessness that galled her almost as much as his words. "Were I to put you out looking as you do now, I would be responsible for whatever the first man who saw you did to you, and I daresay the sight of you in that clinging dress would move even Soames to something more dangerous than pious prattle."

Hampton's sudden appearance and his impossible mood had caused Juliana to forget her dress. It was made of zephyrine, a new light silk especially designed for walking in town. But not for walking in the rain. When he deliberately raked his eyes over her, she looked down to see that she might as well have been dressed in a wet shift, given the way her dress clung to her, to her thighs, to her breasts even.

She felt unbearably exposed, but overriding even that, Juliana felt furiously angry. "Lord Soames would lend me his coat!" she snapped, then added frostily, "but then he is a gentleman!"

"Oh, no doubt," Lord Hampton agreed too pleasantly. "So thorough a gentleman is Soames, he's a prig and possessed of as much feeling as a log. What a grand change he will be from your doddering first husband. But then, quite unlike Whitfield, Soames would keep you on a pedestal, would he not, my Lady Whitfield? He would adore you in his so-restrained way, giving you caged birds to enhance your beauty and taking you to uplifting Sunday sermons on the virtues of moderate living. How delightful."

"You insult me," Juliana said through clenched teeth, "not to mention Lord Soames, who has been nothing but honorable and kind to me. Let me down this instant."

"You may not be concerned for your health, or your virtue, but I am, Lady Whitfield. You must either change out of that dress posthaste, or, I fear, lose both."

As he spoke, Hampton again sent his eyes traveling over Juliana. She meant to hold herself stiff as a board, entirely unaffected, but despite her best intentions, his slow appraisal stoked some sort of unholy fire in her. Feeling it, feeling her skin heat, feeling her breasts tighten in an unexpected way, Juliana shrank back in the seat and crossed her arms over her bosom.

Their eyes met and held. She hoped more than anything in the world that she glared angrily at him. But Lud, she could not be sure, for there at the back of his golden brown eyes gleamed a heat related, and she knew it, to the warmth licking even then through her veins.

Breathless, feeling as if time itself were slowing strangely, Juliana shifted in alarm, sending the other books she'd found at Hookham's tumbling to the floor, where Hampton reached them before she could.

Again he read the titles, taking his time. "Lord Byron," he said, lifting his gaze to hers. His mood had changed. He did not smile outright, but almost and lopsidedly. If Juliana had not fully understood before, she realized then just how much she had to fear, for even after all he'd said, so little as a suggestion of his crooked smile could make her heart ache. "Two volumes of George's much-condemned poetry. Soames would not approve, you know. His tastes run to Blair, instead. Don't tie yourself to him. He and that horse-faced sister of his will turn you into a dry, sanctimonious stick before a year is out. Marry me, instead."

Marry him? For one endless moment, Juliana's answer hung in the balance. She could not even breathe, and she knew why. She felt the same wild recklessness she would have felt had she been about to gallop hell for leather down a highway under a full moon. Marriage to him might be the thrill of her life, but she would end with a broken heart. He did not love her. He either mocked her with his suggestion, or he had grown tired of the marriage mart, and thinking her besotted after that kiss, had decided she would make as accommodating a wife as any.

Of course that last was the answer, and acknowledging it, she felt as if her heart had fractured already. He would never know, though. "Of all the absurd starts you may have had in your life, Lord Hampton, surely this is the prize!" Juliana said coldly. "Marry you? I would as soon marry a monkey. They've more constancy. When would I see you? Before or after you went to your mistress of the moment? And do not bother to deny that you have a mistress! Everyone knows of her."

His eyes narrowed so Juliana could only catch a glimpse of the dark glint playing in them, and a number of seconds passed with no sound at all but that of the rain pounding against the roof of the carriage.

She held his gaze, determined to do it. "I would not dream of denying I keep a mistress," he said at last. "Unlike a monkey, I am a free man, and I like my freedom. No wife will change me so that I do not recognize myself, I promise you. Well then, you may keep Soames in your pocket, Lady Whitfield. I see he will suit you very well after all. Ah, it does seem we've settled the matter just in time. For here we are in Grosvenor Square. You will forgive me if I do not escort you to the door? I have an appointment with my mistress for which I am frustratingly late. Here is a carriage rug, however." Dragging it out from under the seat, the earl all but heaved the thing at Juliana. "I apologize for quite forgetting its existence. You could have been warm, but then I'd have been deprived of the opportunity to so thoroughly inventory your charms. Luckily, I find my mistress better suits my tastes."

He smiled even, but so coldly Juliana wrapped the carriage rug around her like a shield, and when the postillion let down the steps, she scrambled from the carriage without a backward look.

Chapter 18

Juliana dashed up the stairs to her room, the carriage rug wrapped tightly around her shoulders. She could not remain at Fanny's, not with Hampton there. She could not live under the same roof with him.

Marry me. No need to ask why he had proposed the idea! Doing the polite night after night bored him. He chafed at the bit, impatient with the time deciding upon a wife took from his mistress. Therefore, on purest impulse, he had asked Juliana to marry him. Had she agreed, he'd have acquired both a fresh source of wealth and a convenient wife he planned to ignore beyond the stray effort when he could pull himself from his mistress to get an heir by her.

A child. Juliana bit her lip, fighting the weakening. She did want a child. It was true, but not a marriage with him! *I find my mistress better suits my tastes.* Well, he was welcome to her!

In her room, Juliana jerked the bellpull as sharply as if it were Lord Hampton's well-clad neck. She would have Rand pack at once. First, though, she must get out of her wet clothes. Devil take him and the way he had looked at her! She peeled off the ruined walking dress, and wadding it up, flung the wet ball hard across the room. Lud, but she'd have liked the wall to be his handsome, mocking, infuriating face. *You may not be concerned for your health, or your virtue, but I am, Lady Whitfield. You must change out of that dress or lose both.*

Only Randall's knock at the door kept Juliana from crying out in fury. The maid's eyes flared wide, though whether she was more astonished by Juliana's sodden state or the hot anger smoldering clearly in her mistress's violet eyes, it would have been impossible to say. She was too well trained to stare when her mistress shivered.

While Randall wrapped her in a warm robe and toweled her hair dry, Juliana calculated which clothes she must take with her, and which she might leave to be sent after her. It was a bit deflating to realize how little she would need in Lancashire. Westerleigh was situated some ten miles from her nearest neighbor, a country squire she scarcely knew, but she would not dwell on her impending isolation. There was no help for it.

She had already begun directing Randall about the packing when Fanny burst into the room without knocking.

"Alex found me at the linen draper's, Juliana! He gave me this note for you!" Fanny waved a note in the air, looking distraught. "He told me of the wetting you got! He told me he took you up in his carriage, and he told me he was unforgivably rude to you! Oh, Juliana! I do not know what to think. Alex is famous for his address with women. I am sure he has never been rude to any other woman. It must be this business of looking for a wife! I had not realized how deeply he chafes at the duty. He did not say so, you understand, he only told me he'd exercised his temper on you and that he could not excuse himself enough to you. He will not return here. He has already given orders to have his things sent to Lord Mannering's town house. He will stay with Robin, he says, to spare you his company. Oh, my dear! He must leave, if he has been so horrible to you. He must. But say you do not mean to leave as well. Alex said he feared you might go! That you might leave me all alone. Oh, Juliana! Please! I beg you do not leave me alone. I . . . I could not bear it. Not just yet!"

Juliana did spare a thought for the earl, who would not come himself to apologize for his inexcusable remarks to her. She detested him, and she decided she would not read his note. Fanny waved it still in the air, but no matter the intensity of her feelings in regard to Hampton, Juliana would have had to be made of stone had she not been diverted by Fanny. Lady Charles looked as frantic as her spate of words had been.

"Fanny!" Pocketing the note, Juliana put her arm around her friend. She thought Fanny's distress was out of all proportion. If Lady Charles did not want to rattle about alone in a large town house, she could invite any number of people to come to stay with her. She could even bring back her brother. Yet it did not seem the time to point out anything so reasonable, nor certainly to announce that Juliana was indeed leaving. Fanny seemed unsettlingly fragile at that moment. "Please do not take on so," Juliana coaxed. "I would not cause you distress for anything in the world."

"And you will not leave?" Fanny cried on a high, thin, desperate note.

Juliana scarcely hesitated. "No, Fanny. I'll stay for as long as I am welcome. There now, is that not better?"

But to her dismay, Fanny did not brighten. Not at all. She burst into tears, and covering her face with her hands, sank down onto the foot of Juliana's bed.

Juliana could not think what to do but to sit down by her. "Fanny. Dearest Fanny, what is it? What has overset you?"

"I am a stupid, silly creature!" Fanny cried between sobs. "I miss Charley! He is so good to me, Juliana!"

In some ways Juliana could understand why her husband's absence would upset Fanny so deeply. Fanny had been cosseted all her life, cared for by indulgent parents and an equally indulgent husband. Now, for the first time, she was the head of her household, and though she'd servants aplenty, not to mention a brother and sister nearby, responsibility for their house, for their estate in the country, and their children rested, ultimately, with her. Still . . . Juliana frowned in perplexity. Fanny's bouts of tears, her pale cheeks, the frantic expression in her eyes, even the way she clutched at Juliana all seemed more than the weight of temporary responsibility warranted. Nor had Fanny been so troubled when Juliana had first arrived in town, and Lord Charles had been absent at least a fortnight then. Yet, if there was more to Fanny's distress, her friend had never given the least hint of it. It seemed at least for the time that Juliana must take her at her word and hope that standing by her would help.

They did not go out much that week. Fanny complained of having megrims again, and Juliana was too concerned about her to feel the least like enjoying herself at balls and routs and dinner parties. Instead, she and Fanny, when Fanny felt up to it, spent a good deal of the time with Sophie and Harry, drawing with them, reading stories and walking in the small park in the center of Grosvenor Square. Juliana considered consulting Lady Danley about Fanny, though not Lord Hampton. She had burned his note unread, and that was the last she meant to think of him, but she did not in the end go to Lady Danley, either. She suspected Fanny would not forgive her for dragging in her elder sister, as if Fanny could not manage her own affairs. However, Juliana promised herself she would reconsider her decision if Fanny's mood deteriorated further. In the meantime, she did what she could to sustain her friend and confined her few outings to a drive with Mr. Porter and a trip to church with Lord Soames and Mrs. Fitzpatrick, during which she prayed for guidance about Fanny but found little.

Fanny's retreat from the gaiety of the Season could not last forever, though. Nor could Juliana hope to remain in London and never see Lord Hampton. Specifically, they'd an obligation to attend Sarah's come-out ball at Shelbourne House.

To Juliana's considerable surprise and some amusement, Lady Danley did not take the grand event in her normal stride. Quite to the contrary, she demanded assurance almost daily on every minor detail down to and including the number of items to be served at the supper interval. Indeed, on the very day of the ball, Lady Danley suffered such an attack of nerves, she sent her carriage to Grosvenor Square to collect Juliana for a last-minute, desperate consultation on the flowers.

"Do the yellow roses seem too insipid, Juliana?" she demanded to know, having hurried Juliana into the ballroom. "Tell me the truth, now! I trust your judgment. You've excellent taste."

Juliana assured her the yellow roses were perfect, while Sarah, rolling her eyes at her mother, proclaimed that the roses did not matter, only her dress, and it was so lovely she was certain it would enthrall Mr. Stanley. Her father, calmer even than she, interjected that he believed the world should be enthralled with her ball gown, given the cost of it, whereupon Lady Danley stamped her foot and waved them both out of the room for the distraction they caused her.

"Dear me, I do hope everything proceeds smoothly tonight!" She fretted, adjusting the gold of one of the linen tablecloths. "It is not only the Stanleys' I must satisfy, you see. Alex appears to have taken an interest in Lady Elizabeth Verney. Her father is the Earl of Hardwicke, you know. It is an excellent old family, though I had thought . . . well, but who knows with Alex, and the child does possess quite pleasing manners. She's not the least forward, and of course she is a pleasure to look at. But what of this table, Juliana? Shall I place these candlesticks in the center of the table or one on each end?"

Juliana advised Lady Danley to have the crystal girandoles placed in the center of the table, lest they be knocked to the floor by a careless guest or servant, and then she took herself home. She did not care that Hampton had found an earl's daughter of impeccable lineage and pleasing looks. She was glad Fanny's father could rest easy in his old age, assured of his succession, and she only took pains with her appearance that evening because she wished to do Sarah honor.

Even Fanny was roused sufficiently to exclaim in approval when Juliana entered the drawing room, where Mr. Porter waited to escort them to Shelbourne House. She had chosen a dress of a lustrous silk called glacé that shimmered when she moved. Of a silvery rose, it set off her dark hair, her fine-grained skin, and the mysterious deep violet of her eyes. The décolletage was low, allowing a glimpse of the soft swell of her breasts, and at her throat she wore a diamond necklace that matched the diamond earrings sparkling in her ears.

Poor Mr. Porter had to clear his throat before he could tell her in a solemn voice that she was the most lovely lady to ever go out in London, except, of course, for Lady Charles. At that, Fanny actually laughed for the first time in days, and the three left Grosvenor Square in good spirits.

Juliana simply forbade herself to think about Lord Hampton. When she saw him, she had determined that she would behave as if nothing had happened. Not that she would linger in his company. Of course she would not, but she would be polite for Fanny's sake, Lady Danley's, and Sarah's.

Good intentions are only intentions, however. Fanny had promised Lady Danley they would be on hand early to lend her support, but Juliana had never considered that Lady Danley might have extracted a similar promise from her brother. Juliana expected she would be able to accustom herself by degrees to the earl's presence, seeing him first from across a crowded ballroom, perhaps, or dancing by in the opening minuet, before she was obliged to speak to him.

When Juliana walked into Lady Danley's drawing room, however, he was there. Fanny entered ahead of her, greeting her sister. There were maids scurrying about attending to last-minute tasks, and Lord Danley was called out by their butler to consult on some matter, but Juliana missed all the hubbub the moment she caught the gleam of his tawny brown hair. As if he were a magnet, her gaze shot to his tall, elegantly powerful figure, lounging as per usual against the mantelpiece.

Their eyes locked. *Marry me.* She could hear him say it as clearly as if she were in his carriage again. And quite unexpectedly a longing so fierce she almost cried out overcame Juliana. He was, she realized in that moment, the only man in the world for her, all tawny and strong and compelling.

"Ah, Lady Hardwicke and Lord Hardwicke, come in! Come in, Lady Elizabeth."

Lady Danley's greeting snapped Juliana out of what felt like a trance. She had been lost, staring at the earl. No one else appeared to have noticed, but she knew she had forgotten herself. And forgotten his insults. *I find my mistress better suits my tastes.*

Juliana would have liked simply to disappear at that moment. How could she conduct herself with any composure when she felt as if she had taken a blow to her stomach? How could she not have realized what he meant to her? How could she have allowed him to come to mean so much? How could she turn about and pleasantly greet the girl he would take for a wife?

But she had no escape. No fairy godmother appeared to whisk Juliana away from the ball. And so she did turn about, only to have her chest tighten suddenly.

Lady Elizabeth Verney was the perfect match for Hampton. Blond, with soft, lovely blue eyes that were alight with excitement for the evening, she held herself with an assurance that was rare for a young girl. Yet she was not so assured when it came to the earl. When he strolled across the room to greet her and her parents, Lady Elizabeth kept her eyes downcast, though Juliana saw the girl glance at him sidelong, and saw as well, the corners of her perfect Cupid's bow mouth lift. Lady Elizabeth liked Lord Hampton. And would have him.

Juliana would have made some excuse to leave had it not been Sarah's ball. She felt as cold and lifeless as old ashes. Just then Lord Danley, returned from his errand, came to greet her. She smiled and replied appropriately, though she had no notion what she said or how convincingly she smiled. She was telling herself that she could not have married a man who thought it his right to betray her with an openly installed mistress. Her mother had lived that unhappy life. Yet even as she knew the truth of what she told herself, Juliana could not keep from rubbing salt in her wounds. Covertly she watched Hampton bow over Lady Elizabeth's hand, watched him greet her as if he knew her well, and watched him bring the girl to a fetching blush with his smile.

The Desmonds came, and the Bromwells, and Mrs. Daviess with her niece, Miss Petersham. Lord Hampton behaved charmingly with them all, but when the first dance of the ball came, after Sarah had finally descended and all the guests had passed through the receiving line, it was Lady Elizabeth Verney he led out.

Juliana decided she would return home early, pleading weariness, for in truth she felt as weary as if she were weighted down by lead. She knew Hampton must feel the greatest relief that she had not accepted his impulsive offer of marriage. Lady Elizabeth was the very essence of the accepted standard of English beauty. She had guileless blue eyes with long curling lashes, not violet ones which more than one man had warily called "witch's eyes." She had short, gently curling blond hair, not a dark, dark unruly fall. And there was her family. "Excellent," Lady Danby had described it, and of a certainty the Earl of Hardwicke was as different as could be from a wastrel who would sell his daughter for cards and dice and loose women.

Juliana gritted her teeth and tried to ignore her dismal thoughts, but they would not let her be. He had not even made her a greeting, nothing beyond the one look when she had first entered the drawing room. It had been intense, that one look, catching her fast and making the rest of the world disappear, yet for all its intensity it had been shuttered. Perhaps he had been trying hard not to betray his relief at escaping her. Certainly there had not been the least hint of apology in his eyes. No, he'd given her a look piercing enough to penetrate to her soul and then passed her by to kiss Lady Elizabeth Verney's pretty white hand.

Of course, Juliana did dance that evening. Indeed, she made certain she carried on as if she hadn't a care in the world, pinning a vivid smile on her face and dancing almost every dance. Lord Houghton said the sight of her robbed him of breath, while Lord Mannering smilingly told her every entertainment for the past week had been insupportably dull without her. Lord Soames, on the other hand, told her he resented sharing her company with Lady Danley's guests. Juliana found the remark, spoken with unusual earnestness, only further lowered her spirits, and after receiving it coolly, she made it a point to avoid Lord Soames for the remainder of the evening. If she had led him to expect more than she meant to give, it was time she ceased.

By the end of the evening, Juliana felt as if her head had been clamped in a vise, and she sought refuge with Mr. Porter and Mrs. Daviess, who had found chairs near an open window. The blessed breeze stirred the hot air of the ballroom, and Juliana was just relaxing when Lord Blakely approached her.

Juliana found she liked the man less with every meeting. When he bowed elaborately over her hand and smiled, she thought of a wolf baring its teeth and resolved, when he asked, that there was no reason she must dance with him. "I am sorry, my lord, you do me honor, but I have accepted Mr. Porter's suggestion that we sit out this dance in favor of enjoying the fresh air here."

It was not a rude dismissal, but it was a contrived one. Had she wanted to dance with Lord Blakely, Mr. Porter would have been content to be left with Mrs. Daviess. Lord Blakely shrewdly saw the truth and his wolfish smile altered subtly, becoming more than ever a mere baring of teeth. "I am so sorry you are not free, Lady Whitfield," he replied with little grace. "I believe you will regret your choice in time."

Mrs. Daviess sniffed derisively as the viscount walked away. "Lud, but Blakely becomes more unpleasant with every day. Perhaps it is because he's not a feather to fly with, or so they say."

"Indeed, he's not a feather to fly with," Mr. Porter affirmed. "The tradesmen are even refusing him service, he's not paid his bills in so long. Still, that don't give him leave to speak like that to Lady Whitfield. Why, his words sounded like a threat to me!"

"They did," Mrs. Daviess agreed, but she waved her hand dismissively. "Yet, Blakely is given to the dramatic. It is another point about him I have never cared for. Of course he meant nothing, Juliana, only wanted to put a pall on your evening."

With dark humor, Juliana thought Blakely had failed there as surely as he did at paying his bills. Lord Hampton had put the pall on her evening. But even as she had the thought, she shook herself. She was absurd to grant the earl such power over her. She could not, would not, regret refusing him. He'd have made her a miserable husband.

Chapter 19

The next day Juliana went riding in the Park. She had forgotten she had accepted Lord Soames' invitation until he had reminded her toward the end of Sarah's ball, and by then Juliana was too weary to exert the energy to cry off. She tried to persuade Fanny to go, saying she needed amusing company, as Mrs. Fitzpatrick had at last begun to wear on her, but Fanny, though she laughed at the criticism of the woman she liked to say was "prudish as a prune," could not go. She had promised to walk with Sophie and Harry in Grosvenor Square, she said.

Oddly, Juliana thought she saw Fanny's carriage as she was returning to Grosvenor Square with Lord Soames and Mrs. Fitzpatrick, but knowing she must have been mistaken, she dismissed the notion. Besides, she had other thoughts to occupy her. She had seen Lord Hampton in the Park. She had recognized him from a distance by no more than the easy way he sat his horse, for he gave the impression, in all, that he'd ridden before he had walked. As she watched, he stopped to speak with a party in an open curricle. Juliana recognized the Earl of Hardwicke seated facing her, and deduced the girl in the pretty blue bonnet must be Lady Elizabeth.

Lord Soames did not see the earl. He and Mrs. Fitzpatrick were diverted by a close acquaintance. Thomas Dibdin, the parson who lectured with rather grim and demanding zeal in the chapel they attended in South Audley

Street on Sundays, was walking that afternoon with his wife. Juliana nodded to the couple, but to speak to them she would have had to sit forward. Mrs. Fitzpatrick sat on their side of the carriage, and by sitting back, Juliana disappeared both from view and conversational obligation. Free to do what she wished, she glanced back toward Lord Hampton and the Verneys. Their meeting was just ending. The earl turned his mount as the curricle of his bride-to-be rolled away. Juliana expected him to go off as well, but he did not. He looked suddenly in her direction, as if he had known she were there all along. Their eyes met only glancingly before he flicked his gaze to Lord Soames and Mrs. Fitzpatrick. When he looked back at Juliana, the earl's mouth was set in a derisive slant. He did incline his head, a fraction, but she thought the salute mocking, and stiffening, she deliberately looked away without returning his unsatisfactory nod. She waited a few minutes, but when she looked his way from the corner of her eye, he was gone.

So. He was not even to be her friend. She, who had so few, could not but feel the loss, and when Lord Soames begged Juliana to take dinner with him and Mrs. Fitzpatrick, she declined the invitation. Instead, she took a tray in her room and went to bed early, too low in spirits even to keep Fanny company.

Yet, for all that, Juliana slept more deeply than she had feared she might, so deeply in fact that when the knock came on her door, she did not waken at first, and when she did, finally, she could not think what had awakened her.

"My lady?" It was someone speaking softly but urgently.

"Rand? Is that you?"

"Yes, my lady. I am sorry to disturb you, but I thought you would wish it. A footman of Mr. Porter's is below. He asked for Lady Charles on urgent business, but when her maid was sent for her, it was discovered she is not in her room or anywhere in the house. The footman then asked for you."

Juliana pushed a stray tendril of hair out of her eyes and tried to sort out the essentials. "What is the time, Rand?"

"It is two o'clock in the morning, my lady."

"Two o'clock," Juliana repeated, then, still hazily, "and you say Mr. Porter sent a footman to ask for Lady Charles at two o'clock in the morning?"

"Yes, my lady. I do not know the reason. Perhaps he told Mr. Haskins, but I have only been told that Lady Charles is not here and that the footman would speak with you."

The reminder that Fanny was not in her rooms and seemingly not in the house finally penetrated Juliana's sleepy fuzziness. She assured herself there was a perfectly logical explanation, but she could not help recalling Fanny's tears and megrims. Leaving her hair in the braid Rand plaited every night, Juliana dressed herself to go downstairs with all haste.

Haskins had put Mr. Porter's footman in the library. Young, he was shifting from one foot to the other either from nerves or excitement. "Good evening, m'lady." He executed a smart bow beneath Haskins' watchful eye. "Beggin' yer pardon for rousin' ye so late, but 'twas my master that sent me."

"Yes, of course. I do understand. You came for Lady Charles, I believe?" Juliana prompted.

He nodded energetically. " 'Twas like this, m'lady," he said, and Juliana saw from the way his eyes sparkled that he was more excited than nervous. "Mr. Porter was on the box of his carriage. Happens he takes the reins from time to time, y'see, and when he pulled into the mews, he saw another carriage up ahead. At the first, he thought nothing of it, but the carriage did not pull up into one of the stables in the mews. It started off suddenlike. Well, Mr. Porter looked hard then, and when the carriage turned out of the mews, my master saw a lady was in the carriage. He saw her for just that long"—the boy snapped his fingers—"then it was like someone pulled her down out of sight. Starin' as he was, and with the gaslight there at the corner, he recognized the carriage as belongin' to Lord Blakely. That worried him a good deal. He feared Lord Blakely might have taken you, my lady, and so he followed after the carriage and sent me to rouse Lady Charles. He wished her to see if you was here, and if you wasn't, he wanted me to ask her to send for Lord Hampton. But the deuce of it is now, m'lady, that you are here and 'tis Lady Charles that's missing."

The boy looked as bemused as Juliana felt. The whole thing seemed so impossible, she turned to Haskins. "Lady Charles is nowhere in the house, Haskins? Perhaps the nursery?"

But the butler grimly shook his head. "I have sent servants to every room, my lady."

"And her maid, Haskins? Has she any light to shed on this?"

"Nothing but that Lady Charles went out this afternoon, taking her along, to sell a piece of jewelry. Otherwise Lady Charles passed an uneventful day, retiring at eleven. However, if I may add one thing, Lady Whitfield?"

"Yes, please, Haskins. What is it?"

"It is my duty to see that all the doors in the house are locked before I go to bed. As always, I tried these doors that lead to the gardens. They were locked at eleven o'clock, yet one is unlocked now." To prove his point, Haskins stepped across the room and opened the door.

In the distance, Juliana could see the small door cut into the stone wall surrounding the garden. "And what of the garden door that leads to the mews, Haskins. Is it kept locked?"

He regarded her with keen approval. "It is always locked, my lady, and seldom used, but it is not locked now. I tested it myself."

"Good Lord." Juliana stared in dismay at the butler. "This all seems like a very bad dream, but I suppose we should send for Lord Hampton. And what of Mr. Porter?" she asked, thinking aloud. "How will we know where he is?"

The young footman spoke up importantly. "My master took his coachman and another footman with him, my lady. He said he would send one of 'em back with word, if there is need."

"As to Lord Hampton," Haskins said, returning to Juliana's first point, "I took the liberty of sending for him when we discovered Lady Charles was missing."

"That is excellent, Haskins!" Juliana commended on a sigh of relief, but the butler shook his head. "Neither Lord Hampton nor Lord Mannering are at Lord Mannering's residence, my lady, and the staff there could not say where to find them. In the hope that Lord Hampton is at his club, I sent a footman there."

As if the statement were a cue, they heard someone approaching the library, and Fanny's footman appeared in the doorway, breathing hard. His eyes sliding to Juliana, he shook his head. " 'Is lordship weren't there, m'lady."

"Did anyone at his club have an idea where we might send for him?" Juliana asked.

The young man hesitated uncomfortably, but only a moment, for Haskins made an impatient sound that evidently decided him. "There was some talk that 'is lordship might be in 'alf Moon Street, m'lady."

Half Moon Street. Juliana had heard it mentioned before, and after a moment recalled the reference. Mrs. Daviess had said that Hampton kept a house there for his mistress. Juliana's mouth tightened in an involuntary response, but she did not allow herself to dwell on the corresponding tightening in her chest. There were more important things to worry her than Hampton's fondness for his mistress.

"Go there, then," she said, "to Half Moon Street and seek him. And perhaps . . ." She had intended to instruct Mr. Porter's footman to go as well as he'd the original story, but the sound of voices in the hallway interrupted her. Realizing the latest arrival must be the messenger from Mr. Porter, Juliana and her band of assistants hastened from the library.

"My lady!" She recognized Mr. Porter's coachman, and as he was clearly surprised to see her, Juliana hurriedly explained that Mr. Porter had evidently mistaken Lady Charles for her.

"But what has happened?" she demanded. "Where is Mr. Porter?"

"At a old buildin' down near St. Catherine's docks, m'lady. 'Tis empty by the looks of it, but Lord Blakely went inside with his coachman, who was carryin' the lady. We couldn't see her goodlike. She'd a cape with a hood, and she looked to be asleep. Mr. Porter told me to bring Lord Hampton there as quick as I can."

Juliana calculated swiftly. To bring Lord Hampton to Grosvenor Square to tell him the story would only waste time. Yet, if she sent the servants to him in Half Moon Street with the incredible news that Lord Blakely had seemingly abducted Fanny, Juliana feared he either would not believe them or would take so long to be convinced that, again, they would lose precious time.

She would go with the servants, she decided, and if he were not at his mistress's house, she herself would to go to Mr. Porter, and the two of them would decide what to do. There did not seem much other choice.

Juliana considered appearances to the extent that she took Randall along with her, but in the carriage when her braid fell heavily over shoulder, she realized she had not thought to pin up her hair and that she'd forgotten her gloves as well. Leaning back, trying to calm herself, she sought for humor, assuring herself neither tidied hair nor gloves were *de rigueur* at abductions. The joke went flat, however, for she could not even smile. Lord Blakely had abducted Fanny. It simply seemed too outlandish to be true.

When the coachman pulled up before the small but pleasant-looking house in Half Moon Street, Juliana judged that the earl was already abed with his mistress, as there were no lights to be seen. She could not know where that bed was, however. Perhaps they had made do with a couch in the parlor. She had had almost half an hour to prepare herself for what she might encounter, but she had not prepared well enough, evidently. The thought of him in his mistress's arms made her sit stiffly against the seat and look out the other window while Fanny's footman raced up the steps to pound on the door.

In the end, however, Juliana's pain did not prove so great as her anxiety for Fanny. Not only did it seem to take hours for someone to hear the footman knocking, but then the old retainer who answered the door appeared inclined to close it in the footman's cherubic face. Minutes, precious minutes, during which Blakely could be doing anything to Fanny passed, while the footman pleaded and pleaded his case.

Finally, Juliana thrust open the door of the carriage and scrambled to the ground, Randall following close behind her. "We must see Lord Hampton!" she ordered, charging up the steps, and at the authoritative note in her voice the butler or whoever he was, stepped back almost involuntarily. Juliana took advantage of this and brushed by him into the house. All was dark within, and the house had an oddly deserted feel to it. "Is Lord Hampton here?" she demanded, nearly despairing.

"As to that, I, ah, I cannot say, ma'am."

"He is here or he is not," Juliana snapped, losing all patience. "This is a matter of life . . ."

"What is going on here?"

At the familiar voice, Juliana spun around. Hampton and his mistress had, indeed, been cavorting in one of the ground floor rooms! The earl was not descending the steps to the second floor, but approaching down a hallway behind the entryway. Juliana clasped her hands together tightly. It did not matter. She would not think of it. Fanny's life was at stake.

A soft light spilled from the door he had left open. Either by that light, or the light from the single candle the old doorman held in his doddering hand, the earl identified Juliana. She saw his brow lift. "What a surprise you are, my Lady Whitfield. You do not respond to my notes, nor do you see the least need to acknowledge me when we meet in public, and yet you have come here in the middle of the night, giving yourself up for the plucking all unbidden."

"I am no hen, sir!" Juliana retorted angrily, and when he actually laughed she longed to slap him. "I am not here for anything of that sort."

"Indeed?" he drawled, cocking his head, studying her. "I am that sorry to hear it."

"Oh! Listen to me! This is serious!"

Perhaps he heard the desperation in her voice, or perhaps he only felt chilly in the entryway, but Hampton inclined his head and gestured toward the open doorway from which he'd emerged. "Come along then, and tell me what is so serious that you would beard me in my den in the darkest hours of the night."

Juliana went before him, assuring herself that even Hampton would not show her into a room where his mistress lay in dishabille or worse, and indeed, when she entered the room, she saw no sign of Miss Antoinette Duvenay. Instead, on a low table near the fire, Juliana saw an empty decanter and beside it a glass with only a swallow or so of port left in it. She swung about, alarmed. "You are not foxed are you?"

He closed the door behind him, and leaning back against it, considered Juliana from beneath half-closed lids. "Only trying to be, Lady Whitfield. Now tell me why you are here."

Juliana did not reply at once. He was half undressed. She had not realized it in the hallway, but in the better light of the room she saw he had not only shed his coat and cravat, but had unbuttoned half his shirt as well. Springy, golden brown hair gleamed softly in the candlelight. It covered the top of his chest, while the bare skin below it looked sleek and taut. Juliana could not deny that her mouth went a little dry, or even that just for a half second she could almost feel her fingers trailing through that soft golden hair and down over the smooth, bare skin below. But she felt a surge of anger, too. Obviously, she had interrupted him with his mistress, and as obviously, for he had made no move to right his appearance, he meant to flaunt what he'd been about before she came.

Taking a breath, she met his eyes and saw an odd gleam there. She did not need to read it. She knew he was mocking her. At once, she forced her chin up. She'd not have him know just how much the sight of nothing more momentous than his bare chest unsettled her. Besides, she had reason to be there. Serious reason. "It is Fanny."

"Fanny?" Hampton's brow drew down sharply, and suddenly Juliana felt the enormity of what she would say.

Warning the earl first that what she was about to tell him would seem unbelievable, Juliana related what she knew. "I cannot say whether Fanny went into the gardens of her own volition and opened the gate for Blakely, or whether he slipped into the house with the help of an accomplice." Juliana shook her head, frowning. "It is a mystery. Fanny has expressed a dislike for Lord Blakely, though once, the evening we went to Vauxhall, Mr. Porter thought he saw Fanny leaving the rotunda with the man. Fanny said he was mistaken, but since that time her mood has been exceedingly fragile. She has kept to her bed a good deal, complaining of megrims, and she has cried easily."

Lord Hampton nodded, considering. "Yes, I recall how she cried when you explained your estrangement from your brother." That had been the night he had kissed her, but the earl did not seem interested in their interlude in the garden. He was thinking of Fanny, adding, "I did think she seemed overset at the time. But Blakely? Did you say that George thought Blakely had abducted you?"

"Yes. You see, last night at Sarah's ball, when I refused Blakely's request to dance, he advised me that I would regret doing so. Mr. Porter overheard him and fretted over his intentions, then when he saw a woman seemingly being pulled down out of sight in Lord Blakely's carriage there in the mews . . ." Juliana shrugged, the rest obvious.

Lord Hampton's response was enigmatic. "St. George," he murmured, but before Juliana could question him, he straightened away from the door. "I've preparations to see to. Make yourself comfortable, if you would."

Hampton returned after only a very few minutes, shrugging into a coat as he entered the room. His shirt, Juliana saw, was now fastened and stuffed into his breeches.

"Do you think Fanny and Mr. Porter are all right?" she asked. "I am so worried for them both, but particularly Fanny. Blakely must be mad."

She was thinking of Sir Arthur, and how he had hurt her when she had angered him. Lord Hampton seemed to understand, for his expression softened, and when a knock sounded at the door, he ignored it, crossing the room to Juliana, instead. She thought she saw something more than concern in his amber eyes, but it was impossible for her to be certain. The room was full of shadows with only two candles lit and the fire burned low.

"I would not have you worry," he said, holding her anxious gaze. "Everything will be all right in the end. Blakely knows I would suspect him, should any harm come to Fanny. Whatever his game, it cannot involve anything monstrous. Trust me. On this at least. Now, do you wish to await us here? It is closer to the river."

"Here?"

Juliana did not say, "with your mistress," but Hampton understood, and his mouth slanted in a smile that seemed somehow more self-mocking than anything. "There is no woman in this house, but you, Lady Whitfield, and your maid. It has been virtually empty for some little time now, actually." He watched her, though he revealed nothing of his own thoughts beyond that faint, almost grim smile. "Tell me . . . why did you not respond to my note?"

Unprepared for either the revelation he had made or the

question he asked. Juliana stared at him. Finally, she said half defiantly, "I burned it."

A muscle in his jaw tightened. She did not know what he might do and expected anything, though in the end, strangely, she was not prepared for what he did do. With a low, muttered curse Hampton leaned down to kiss her hard and swift on the mouth. Juliana would have liked to think she would strike him for using her so, but the kiss lasted only a second, and during that tiny moment she did not once think of slapping him.

"Stay here," he commanded, releasing her and turning for the door in one motion. "Though I do not think Blakely will have hurt Fanny, he may have frightened her enough that she will want time to calm herself here before she returns to Grosvenor Square. I will have Daimes bring you tea. Ask him for anything else you may want."

Without looking back at her, Hampton threw open the door and strode off down the hall, giving orders as old Daimes followed. From the sitting room, Juliana caught the gleam of gunmetal in the old man's hand, and her first thought was that Hampton had lied to her. He must think the situation more dangerous than he had admitted to take a pistol with him. Unthinking, she hurried out of the room to the front door. Hampton was already halfway down the steps.

"My lord," she called. He turned, his brow lifted in surprise. And suddenly Juliana felt foolish for running after him. Yet she could not think of anything to say but what she had intended. "Take care."

Even in the near dark, she could see the white flash of his smile. "You may be certain I shall, my lady. And do not worry. Overmuch anyway," he added before leaping lightly down the steps and up into Fanny's carriage.

questioned her since. Inhuman, uncaring, unjust. Finally, she was half defiantly, I deserved it.

A muscle in her jaw tightened. She did not know whether

...

The August moon in his rising figure gave...
...her head...
...figure...

Chapter 20

In the sitting room again, Juliana looked about half reluctantly. The furniture was unexceptional mahogany for the most part with only one distinctive feature. The chairs and couch were covered in green-and-gold-striped damask. She did not have to ask who had chosen the colors. They'd have set off Miss Duvenay's flaming red hair perfectly, and Juliana found it did not much amuse her to think of the woman decorating the room to emphasize her considerable charms. Walking restlessly to the fire old Daimes had stoked to a crackling blaze, she called herself a fool. How could she detest his mistress's parlor? Be even reluctant to sit in his mistress's chairs?

Particularly when Fanny's life might be in danger. And Mr. Porter's.

But was Miss Duvenay his mistress still? *There is no woman in this house, but you. It has been virtually empty for some little time now.*

Had he dismissed the woman, given her her congé, as they said? Had he grown tired of her? Surely his decision had had nothing to do with her, with Juliana?

Juliana whirled about to stalk to the window. The dark night revealed nothing but her own reflection in the windowpane. She grimaced at herself. Clearly she was not a simple fool, but the greatest of fools, if she must remind herself that he had told her bluntly how he preferred his mistress's charms to hers. And then had not spoken to her even to bid her good evening since he'd made the unfavorable comparison!

Randall entered the room, mercifully disturbing Juliana's thoughts. She brought tea on a tray. Almost grudgingly, Juliana nodded toward the one chair covered in dark gold. The largest chair in the room, it was close to the fire and was the one before which Hampton's port glass and decanter had been placed. It felt warm when she sat down, which she knew only confirmed her conclusions about her foolishness. The chair surely could not have retained his warmth so long. Still . . . it was a wing chair and soft in its depths. She felt some comfort seated in it and did not fight the feeling, for she was anxious about what might be occurring. It was Juliana's belief that Fanny had gone to the gardens to meet Lord Blakely, for had he stolen into the house and abducted her, Juliana thought someone would surely have heard him. But why would Fanny meet him in the dead of night? It could not have been a lover's tryst. Her professions of dislike had been too sincere.

Juliana sipped her tea, considering one possibility after another, though to little avail. She could speculate all she wanted, but she would not know the truth with any certainty until Fanny revealed it. Sighing, she shed her shoes and drawing her feet up under her, rested her head against the wing of the chair. She did not mean even to doze, but the house was quiet as a tomb, and when the door opened hours later, Juliana did not hear it.

Hampton paused, seeing her. He had half doubted she would stay. But she had, and had even fallen asleep. Had she trusted him when he had said all would end well? Was that why she could sleep? She looked like a trusting wife, awaiting a husband away on a journey, with the thick, rich, dark plait of her hair hanging over her shoulder onto her breast and her legs tucked under her. Perhaps she felt the weight of his gaze, for her thick lashes parted suddenly and she stared at him, obviously sleepy and uncertain of where she was or why. Then as obviously, she remembered, for she sat up with a jerk, her violet eyes flaring wide with question. Where her head had rested against the chair, her hair was mussed, the dark chocolate tendrils playing over the smooth, creamy skin of her temple. She looked very young to him then, and almost too beautiful.

"My lord?"

Lord Hampton shook himself out of his reverie. If she was almost too beautiful, she was also worried. "Fanny and George await us in the carriage. They are unharmed. That is, Blakely did give Fanny some filthy concoction to make her sleep so she'd not escape, and George did hit his head on a door in the dark and has a swollen eye as a result, but otherwise, they are both well. We'll go on to Grosvenor Square as soon as you come."

"And Blakely?" Juliana asked, sensing something had gone amiss.

The earl looked from her to the fire, and in profile the set of his mouth was grim. "We came to blows. I struck him hard, and he went down seemingly senseless. As we'd not found Fanny, I left him in the charge of two of the footmen, but unfortunately he was not so incapacitated as I had thought. When a scurrying rat distracted the footmen, Blakely seized the opportunity to scramble out of the room. He ran for some old steps built onto the outside of the building at the back. They led to a wharf that's long since rotted away. The inlet is full of silt and has not seen a boat in decades, and I imagine the steps had not been used in all that time. At any rate, they gave with his weight and sent him to his death on the old wharf."

Little wonder Hampton looked so grim. He had seen death that night, and held himself, at least a little, to blame for it. Quietly but firmly she said, "Had he not abducted Fanny, Blakely would neither have been in that building nor trying to escape it. He brought his untimely death on himself." She waited until he looked to her, his expression at least a little softer, to add solemnly, "I am sorry for his soul, however."

Hampton nodded at that, more of the tension easing from him. "Yes. I feel the same. Not many will mourn his passing. He was quite as rotten as those steps, yet it is not easy to see a man die so. But come, my lady. We shall send up a prayer for Blakely at the proper time. For now, you must be ready for your own bed."

Juliana swung her legs out from under her and slipped her feet into her shoes, aware all the while that Hampton watched her. She moved as quickly as she could, but still afforded him a glimpse of her ankles and her bare feet, and when she was done, she rose to give him a somewhat rankling look. He responded with a half smile, as if he were more amused than not to have discomforted her, but he took her arm before she could say anything and led her out to the entryway, where Randall awaited with her wrap.

In the carriage, Juliana found Fanny sleeping soundly with her head on Mr. Porter's shoulder, while Mr. Porter rested his head on the seat and held a wet cloth to his eye.

He lifted it to greet her, and Juliana gave him a sympathetic look. "I am so sorry you suffered an injury, Mr. Porter! You've my greatest admiration for acting as alertly as you did."

"It is nothing, Lady Whitfield," Mr. Porter said, looking rueful. "I merely hit myself with a door."

"You injured yourself while acting on Lady Charles's behalf," Juliana corrected him in very firm tones. "We'd not have had her back half so quickly had you not acted as cleverly as you did."

"Lady Whitfield is quite right, George." After some last instructions to Daimes and Randall, Hampton had followed Juliana into the carriage. The closing of the carriage door acted as a signal to the driver, and they rolled smoothly forward as Hampton fixed Mr. Porter with a level look. "Without you we would not have known Fanny's whereabouts, and she'd have been in Blakely's power that much longer. The debt Fanny and I owe you is unmistakable, George."

As sunrise was nearly upon them, Juliana could see that

Mr. Porter flushed deeply. " 'Tis nothing of the sort," he insisted gruffly. "You'd have done, would do, the same for me, Hampton. Indeed you did."

"Intervening in a schoolboy's quarrel was nothing to what you did tonight," Hampton retorted.

Juliana did not know the story, but she could guess easily enough that boys at school would find Mr. Porter an easy target. And recalling who had taught Mr. Porter to drive a gig in order that he could best his cousin, she was not wildly surprised that Hampton had intervened on Mr. Porter's behalf. As the two men continued to debate the issue of relative debt, she smiled a little.

"I do believe the two of you sound like schoolboys, wrangling in this way over who owes whom the greater debt. I think that instead you ought to be giving thanks you've each other to rely upon. I know I am exceedingly grateful I had the both of you this evening."

She meant it and looked from Mr. Porter, who colored fiercely again, to Lord Hampton. However, it was impossible in the thin, gray, early light to read the earl's thoughts. That was difficult enough in the full light of day, and anyway, Mr. Porter was saying how he would always be at her service, and Juliana had to answer him. She did learn that the two men had found the ransom note Blakely had intended to send to Hampton that morning, but they pulled into Grosvenor Square before Juliana could discover anything else.

Hampton carried Fanny to her room while Juliana directed Haskins to send for her physician. Mr. Hartley came within the hour, and after he assured them that Fanny would waken groggy in an hour or two but otherwise unharmed, Juliana took herself off for a rest.

She did not sleep well. The day had dawned, and there were unanswered questions that plagued her still. Though she understood that Blakely had meant to hold Fanny for ransom because he was deeply in debt and because he'd a grudge against Lord Hampton, Juliana still did not under-

stand how he had lured Fanny into the garden in the middle
of the night, nor why Fanny had been so emotional the last
few weeks.

Restless as she was, Juliana had risen and taken a cup of
chocolate before the young maid came to inquire if she
would go to see Lady Charles. Dressing quickly, she went
along to Fanny's rooms and found her friend sitting up in
bed but looking pale as the sheets and so uncertain, Juliana's heart went out to her.

"Oh, Lud, Fanny, what a terrible time for you!" She
crossed the room to sit down on the bed, and when Fanny
caught her hands with a little moan, Juliana squeezed them
tightly. "I cannot imagine how frightened you must have
been."

"I brought the whole on myself, Juliana!" Fanny said,
her face crumpling.

But Juliana only squeezed her hands the more tightly.
"You did not abduct yourself, Fanny, and you need not
make any explanation to me, you know."

"But I want to! I must. I was wrong to keep it all secret.
If I had not . . ."

Juliana knew she was thinking of Blakely's death and
would not allow it. "Lord Blakely fell to his death because
he had committed a heinous act and wanted to escape punishment. You will not blame yourself for that, Fanny.
Whatever you did, you did not send him fleeing down those
steps."

Her staunch tone had a good effect. Fanny smiled, albeit
tremulously. "You do make me feel better, Juliana, but you
must hear the whole, before you judge me so blameless."

"You need not tell me anything," Juliana repeated, but
Fanny shook her head.

"I want to tell you. When I tried to hide my sins, I created disaster, and I have decided to have done with se-
crecy." She looked so very solemn there did not seem
anything for Juliana to do but nod. "Just at the first of my
marriage, scarcely a month after we wed," Fanny began,

swallowing nervously, "Charles was asked to go to Moscow. It was some delicate thing to do with Bonaparte and the French, and he felt he could not refuse. I scarcely knew him, really. Our parents had arranged the match between us, and though I had not resisted it, was happy with it even, I had not spent a great deal of time in Charley's company. And so there I was, young, new to marriage, and quite alone in London, for it was summer. Alex had gone up to Scotland to visit friends, and Gussie was in the country, awaiting the arrival of Andrew, her youngest boy. None of that is any excuse, but I would not have done what I did had I not been alone and so uncertain of Charles. I began to doubt that he even felt affection for me, much less love, and then . . . then, Lord Blakely began paying me attention. He was elegant, older, sophisticated, and so very attentive. I . . . oh, Juliana, I accepted his attentions!" Fanny clung to Juliana, her eyes filled with dismay and bitter self-reproach. "I was infatuated with Blakely and wrote him several passionate letters, expressing my affections and how much I wanted him. I might even have betrayed Charley fully, I cannot say, for Gussie had a difficult time with Andrew's birth and called me down to the country to her side. Away from Blakely, free of the spell he'd created, I saw how wrongly I had behaved, and when I returned to town, I broke off with him. He was ugly and spiteful, Juliana. Lud, he opened my eyes! I realized how dreadfully I had misjudged him, but he did not make me pay then. After the one horrid scene, he left me alone for years, allowing me to pretend I scarcely knew him. Then, that night at Vauxhall, he approached me. He had kept my letters. I was shocked, for I had put them out of my mind! I did not even recall how many I had written, but he said there were three and that he wanted money for them. I met him the day you and Alex took the children to Astley's."

When Juliana started in surprise, Fanny nodded miserably. "I have lied so often I scarcely know myself, Juliana! I never suffered megrims or weariness. I was sick with

shame and fear! Then, after I had given him all my pin
money for the three letters, he said there was yet another.
He had me meet him at the Stanleys' ball in the gardens.
He was the reason I could not come to you, for I had to stay
to hear his terms, and he wanted a great deal for the last letter. He could not game, you see, for he had lost so much to
Alex in play one night at White's that no gentlemen would
game with him, for fear he'd never be able to honor his
vowels. I imagine Alex thought it fitting justice, as there
are rumors that Blakely cheated, but the catastrophic loss
he suffered made Blakely all the more determined to force
me to pay one way or another. When I met him last night
with only half of the money he had demanded, he abducted
me to hold me for ransom. Perhaps he'd have abducted me
anyway, however, for he had come prepared with that horrid potion, and he laughed when he forced it down my
throat, saying he thought it too appropriate that Alex would
be the one to enrich him in the end. Oh, Juliana! The last
two weeks have been so wretched! Lud, I had only to think
of how you never betrayed your vows to a man like Whitfield, while I could not remain entirely faithful . . ."

"That is quite enough of that line of reasoning," Juliana
interrupted so flatly that Fanny blinked, taken aback. "I was
never put to the test, Fanny. The only company Sir Arthur
allowed me at Westerleigh was that of older people. His solicitor came twice a year, and the vicar of the parish
brought his wife for dinner every month or so. I liked Mr.
and Mrs. Tenneby. They were kind and enjoyable, but they
were older than Sir Arthur, and the solicitor only a very little younger. In the six years I was married to him, Whitfield never once allowed me to go to a ball or dinner party.
On occasion he would take me to Blackburn to shop, but he
accompanied me even to the dressmaker's, and when I rode
at Westerleigh, he sent two older grooms with me. I was
kept in a luxurious prison, Fanny. I cannot say what I might
have done, given the opportunity. Sir Arthur was half mad

and sometimes brutal, and in all honesty, I admit I was not sorry when he died."

"Dear God, of course not! Heavens above, Juliana, I had no idea how awful your life was."

"Do not waste your time crying for me, Fanny," Juliana advised stoutly. "There are many worse fates than mine, and I have no wish to dwell on the past, anyway. I find I prefer the far more appealing present. I advise you to do the same, my dear. You erred once, but you saw the error of your ways, and you repented before any real harm was done."

Fanny nodded lugubriously. "I did repent! Over and over, I regretted what I had done, but I did not confess to Charley. Now I mean to do it when he returns. I swore I would when Blakely abducted me, and I saw what dreadful harm keeping secrets from Charley could do. Lud, and I never want him to learn about the business from someone else. I think . . . I hope he will forgive me!"

Juliana's experience half made her want to argue against Fanny's decision, but to do so was, she recognized, to live in the past. Fanny had lived her married life under a cloud of secret self-recrimination. Perhaps it was time to dispel that cloud. From all Juliana knew of Lord Charles, he was a good, generous man, who would likely forgive his wife her one transgression.

Chapter 21

Juliana left Fanny asleep some half hour later. They'd both been rueful about how much they had tried to hide from each other and a bit astonished, too, at how little reason there had been for their reticence. Knowing the other's secrets had only seemed to deepen the regard they felt for one another. For Juliana, who had come to London with no friends at all but one whom she'd not seen in years, it meant a very great deal to have found a friend as true as Fanny.

She was half smiling, feeling a deep gladness at how matters had turned out, when Randall approached her to say that Lord Hampton wished to see her in the library, if Lady Whitfield was not too tired.

She was not. Juliana's heart leapt at so little as the sound of the earl's name. Exasperated, she told herself that he only wanted to ask after Fanny, for though he had seen his sister before Juliana had, he would want to know how she fared now after her second confessional interview. The kiss he'd given Juliana at the house in Half Moon Street had meant . . . in truth, she feared to think what it might have meant. Sometime that morning after she'd awakened and before she had gone to Fanny, Juliana had remembered Lady Elizabeth Verney. The girl was too perfect a match for him, too well bred and well reared. It had occurred to her that Hampton could not but want Lady Elizabeth to preside over Shelbourne House, which left the house in Half

Moon Street for Juliana. Were he to offer her the position of his mistress, he'd crush her.

Still, though she feared she was putting herself in the way of pain, she was powerless not to go down to him.

Lord Hampton stood at the windows when she entered, looking out, hands on his hips. From the garden, Juliana heard the cries and giggles of Sophie and Harry at play, but the earl turned away from his niece and nephew readily enough when he heard the door open.

Juliana swallowed uncomfortably. With the light from the windows behind him, she could not see his face well, but she knew for herself that she'd been thinking only minutes before that he might ask her to be his mistress.

"Fanny has fallen asleep," she said quickly, before he could speak. "But I should say that all in all she is doing very well."

Feeling at a disadvantage because he could see her clearly, Juliana drifted across the room, passing the large reading table in the middle and a smaller writing desk in the corner. When she reached the windows, she kept some ten feet between her and Hampton, but she could see him a great deal better, and what she saw gave her a pang for thinking so much of herself. The sleep he'd missed and perhaps Fanny's revelations had taken a toll on him. He looked tired. Yet his tiredness did nothing to lessen his appeal for her. She felt an overwhelming desire to cup his cheek with her hand and smooth his tousled hair back from his brow.

He was studying her, half frowning. "You really think she'll be all right after she has rested? He did not hurt her in some way she would not divulge to me?"

"No, set your mind at rest there," Juliana said forcefully, realizing at least some of what was wearing upon Hampton. "Blakely did nothing but make Fanny feel ashamed and foolish. She is teary, of course, but she's stronger than most realize."

"And more foolish," Hampton said, raking his hand through his hair. He did not sound angry, only wry.

Juliana shrugged a little. "She was very young. And all alone . . ." Her voice trailed off as she flicked her gaze out the window. Sophie and Harry were chasing Sophie's puppy about the garden. Juliana watched their innocent play, thinking of their mother. "Fanny is determined to confess to Lord Charles, for she does not wish to have this secret between them any longer. I am sure she is right."

But of course Juliana was not at all sure, and Hampton understood. He crossed to her and took her hand. She looked up at him, startled, to find his eyes very gentle on her. "Charley adores Fanny and would not hurt her for all the world. And as to this particular business, he will be astonished that she allowed Blakely to threaten her at all, for Charley will think her transgression precisely what it is: exceedingly small."

His hand felt very warm and large and strong upon hers. Juliana could not be certain if it was his touch or his assurance about Lord Charles, but she felt almost giddy suddenly.

"I am glad to hear that about Lord Charles," she said, leaving her hand where it was. "Fanny reacted as she did only because she loves Lord Charles very much and did not want him to suffer any hurt on her account, though as you say, what she did was very little. Indeed, I can almost hear Mrs. Daviess exclaiming that if a few old letters were the best *on-dit* of the day, then it was not a very good day for *on-dits*."

Lord Hampton laughed aloud, his fatigue and concern seeming to fall away in a moment. "That is precisely what Adrienne Daviess would say, and exactly how she would sound saying it. You captured her exactly, and having seen you do the same with Mrs. Drummond-Burrell, I can only say you've a talent for capturing the essence of others. I hope . . . you've an equal talent for forgiveness."

She had been thinking to say something about how he'd

watched her ape Mrs. Drummond-Burrell without her knowing, and so his last remark caught her completely off guard. She stared up at him, going still, at least on the outside. Inside, her heart had begun to race. "What do you mean?" she asked as unsteadily as she felt.

He did not smile at her breathlessness. Far from it, he'd sobered and looked almost grim. "I mean that I tried to think the worst of you, and I beg your forgiveness now."

"Tried?"

"Hmm." He began rubbing his thumb in slow circles over her palm. The sensation was so delicious, Juliana found her eyes slipping to his mouth. "Do you realize that you do not seem even half aware of your beauty?" Juliana did not think it was what he had meant to say, but she could not quite concentrate enough to recall what they'd been discussing. "That incredible oblivion," he went on lazily, "is one of your most potent charms, along with your . . . mouth."

His gaze fell to her mouth, whereupon her lips seemed to take on a life of their own, tingling and swelling even. Perhaps Juliana swayed toward him. It was impossible to say, for Hampton lowered his head and kissed her. She had wanted to taste him, feel his mouth on hers since he'd kissed her in the garden. Juliana lifted her hands to his shoulders. He groaned then. The sound set off a dizzying, heated reaction in her. Her knees seemed to buckle, and he gathered her in his arms, holding her close as she twined her arms around his neck.

He was breathless and so was she, when after a long time, he pulled back an inch or so. "Marry me," he said. His eyes were heavy-lidded, and he might have been discussing a matter of life and death, he looked so intense. "We'll sail to France. I owe you a sail, remember, and then we can take our wedding trip to Paris."

Juliana wondered if she could go to Paris in his arms. She did not want to move out of them, now he held her and she knew he wanted her for more than his mistress.

"That sounds like bribery," she said. She could smell that hint of bay rum again and feel his warmth all around her.

"It is," he said, still not smiling. "You refused me the last time I asked, and so I thought to sweeten the offer. Did I succeed?"

He had insulted her then, comparing her charms unfavorably to his mistress's. Juliana exacted retribution, making him wait. "Why did you want to think the worst of me?" she asked.

"Because I had never reacted so strongly to anyone before," he admitted after only a half moment's hesitation. "I had thought to remain independent even when I married, you see, and I was frightened out of my wits by your power over me."

He had been frightened? She went up on tiptoe and kissed him quickly full and soft on the mouth. "We've that in common, then, my lord, for the mere thought of marriage terrified me. Yet I did not seem to have any control of my heart. I loved you before I knew it."

She sounded almost afraid, and Hampton's arms tightened about her. "I want to keep you safe, Juliana. Never would I hurt you."

She shook her head slightly. "I know you would never lift a hand to me. But you've my heart, you see, my lord, and holding it, you have the power to hurt me as Whitfield never could."

"And you think you haven't the same precise power over me?" His voice was husky, and he dropped his forehead to hers. "Dear God, I have not said a civil word to or about Soames in two months, yet, despite Fanny's notions to the contrary, I have always thought the damned man a worthy fellow. Lud, I've even been jealous of George. And Robin. Ye gods, when you did not even read my note—I not only apologized, you know, but told you that love had made me not so much a fool as a prickly boor . . ."

At his grim expression, Juliana giggled softly, cutting him off. "Forgive me for not giving you a hearing. I was unbearably hurt, not only because you said—plainly—that you preferred your mistress to me, but because I thought you offered to marry for no better reason that the convenience a wife would be to you."

"I was afraid; you were afraid," he whispered, his lips almost on hers. "I would not say what was in my heart, only write it. And you would not read what I wrote."

"What a pair we are," she whispered, rubbing her nose against his.

"Well," he said, rubbing her nose back, "there are, actually, some saving graces to our pair." And he kissed her again.

She gave a muffled laugh, but only until the kiss deepened. Then Juliana forgot all but the feel of the earl.

"You'll marry me?" he asked again, some very long minutes later. Her cheeks were flushed, and his eyes heavy-lidded and gleaming.

She nodded, though hesitantly. "But . . . you must realize, I will never share you."

It had taken some courage to voice the one stipulation. She did not know if she could let him go, now that he'd held her.

He met her gaze, looking grave again. "I have not been interested in another woman since I first saw you in Fanny's entryway. Why do you think I was so terrified of your power? I've even put the house in Half Moon Street up for sale."

"You gave a birthday party for your mistress the day after you kissed me."

It was his turn to stare. "Jove, I had no idea the gossip mill was that effective. Did you know of the party when I asked you to marry me in the carriage?" When Juliana nodded her head solemnly, he ungallantly grinned. "You were jealous! Devil it, but I am glad to know you suffered as I did. Now, now, you may not bustle off." He tightened his hold when Juliana made a rather poor attempt to break free of him. "You were jealous for little reason, for I told you the truth. No one, not even Antoinette, interested me. Having promised her the party weeks before, I felt an obligation to have it, but it was a farewell party, not a birthday party. I did not even stay the night."

A slow but deep smile lit Juliana's eyes. "You went to Suffolk that night?"

Hampton hesitated too long. When her brow lifted, he shook his head slowly. "I met your brother, Juliana."

"Hugh?" Juliana regarded Hampton in astonishment. "But . . ."

"But he beat you and got off scot-free," Hampton said, sounding as hard as his expression had suddenly become. "Nay, more than that, he prospered. He deserved a comeuppance, and he got it."

"But I thought Fanny told you that I sent my solicitor to Hugh."

"She did, but bullies do not respect solicitors and contracts. They respect only force. Lieutenant Hugh Delany, Lord Blackmore, will never bother you again."

So. Hampton had punished Hugh physically. Juliana knew it was wrong to feel glad, but she could not help herself. "Why did you not tell me?"

Lord Hampton's eyes narrowed distinctly. "The next time I saw you, you were waltzing into Fanny's drawing room on Soames's arm, looking wonderfully happy after having been all alone with him in the maze and for the entire journey back from Richmond. Had I spoken privately with you, I very much feared I would throttle you."

It was an odd speech to produce a wide smile, but it did. She knew very well he'd not have throttled her.

He flicked her nose with his finger. "You like me positively green with jealousy, I see."

Juliana's smile faded, but not the light in her violet eyes. "I, my lord, like you anyway at all."

He groaned and kissed her but only for a moment. Then he pulled back, looking very serious. "I love you, Juliana. I want to care for you, to make a life with you, to have children with you, to wrangle with you likely, too. Will you marry me?"

"Yes," she said, beginning to smile. "I will marry you, Alex, as soon as may be."